By the Same Author

Blue Lonesome
A Wasteland of Strangers
Nothing but the Night
In an Evil Time
Step to the Graveyard Easy
The Alias Man

The Nameless Detective series

THE CRIMES OF
JORDAN WISE

THE CRIMES OF
JORDAN WISE

A NOVEL

BILL PRONZINI

Walker & Company
New York

First published in the United States of America in 2006 by
Walker & Company
Distributed to the trade by Holtzbrinck Publishers

For information about permission to reproduce selections from
this book, write to Permissions, Walker & Company,
104 Fifth Avenue, New York, New York 10011.

All papers used by Walker & Company are natural, recyclable products made from
wood grown in well-managed forests. The manufacturing processes conform to the
environmental regulations of the country of origin.

Library of Congress Cataloging-in-Publication Data has been applied for.

ISBN 0-8027-1493-5
ISBN-13 978-0-8027-1493-0

Visit Walker & Company's Web site at www.walkerbooks.com

Typeset by Westchester Book Group
Printed in the United States of America by Quebecor World Fairfield

2 4 6 8 10 9 7 5 3

For Marcia,
for all the good years

and

for Barry Malzberg,
because of all the wasted years

ST. JOHN, VIRGIN ISLANDS

THE PRESENT

A S ON MOST DAYS, I sit at my usual place in Jocko's Café, in front of the open-air window facing Long Bay.

Jocko's isn't much. Just your standard back-island roadside bar and grill, mostly frequented by locals black and white and a few slumming tourists; on the southeastern tip of St. John, the smallest of the U.S. Virgins. The road that loops around from Coral Bay ends fifty yards from Jocko's dirt parking lot. End of the line.

The building is two-storied, made of pink stucco, flanked by palmettos and elephant ears; bar and food service downstairs, Jocko's quarters upstairs. Pocked plaster walls hung with nautical paintings, none of them very good. Dozens of color snapshots of customers with and without Jocko. Old, mismatched furniture. A couple of ceiling fans, a bleached steer head mounted above the bar, a dartboard, and a blackboard with the daily menu chalked on it. Today's specials are every day's specials—conch chowder and callaloo, a pair of West Indian dishes.

This is because Jocko is West Indian, a native of St. Croix. Plump, hairless, skin as sleek and shiny as a seal's. In one ear he wears a big gold hoop that gives him a lopsided, faintly piratical appearance. He smiles a lot, laughs often. Jocko is a happy man.

3

The open-air window frames a view of the narrow inlet, where a handful of fishing boats and catamarans bob at anchor, and the broad expanse of Long Bay and Round Bay beyond. If you sit at the table in the exact center of the window, you can also see much of the far shore—the villa-spotted hills above Coral Bay and the jungly slopes of Bordeaux Mountain, the highest point on St. John at 1,277 feet. That table and chair are mine by tacit agreement. On the rare occasions when I'm not in the café, Jocko refuses to let anybody else sit there. My seat, my window, my view.

In front of me on the scarred tabletop is a double shot of Arundel Cane Rum. I won't drink anything else. Jocko imports it for me from Tortola in the neighboring British Virgins, once the largest pirate community in the Caribbean. He does it because he likes me. And he likes me for the same reason he reserves my table: I'm his best customer.

We are the only two people there when the big, belly-fat man in the yachting cap comes in. About time. I've been waiting for him. He has been in twice before this week, once to eat lunch and once to drink a beer and cast curious looks in my direction. I know that look. It was only a matter of time until he came back again.

This visit, he doesn't sit at the bar. Thirty seconds after he walks in, he is standing between me and the window, smiling in a tentative way. His rough-textured face is like something sculpted out of wet sand. The yachting cap has no significance; he isn't off any of the pleasure craft anchored in the inlet or up at Coral Bay.

I say, "You're blocking my view."

"Oh, sorry." He gestures at one of the empty chairs. "Mind if I join you?"

"Why?"

"No particular reason. I've seen you here three times now—always alone. I thought you might like some company."

"As long as you don't block the view."

4

He positions the chair carefully to my left, sits down, and fans himself with his hand. "Hot."

"Not so bad today. You should be here during hurricane season."

"I'd rather not, thanks. My name's Talley, John Talley."

I already know this, but I don't admit it. I say, "Richard Laidlaw. No. Jordan Wise."

"Which is it?"

"Take your pick."

"How about the one you were born with?"

"Then it's Jordan Wise."

He gives me a penetrating look. "Buy you a drink, Jordan?"

"I wouldn't say no. Arundel Cane Rum, a double, neat."

"I'll just have a cold beer. Too early and too hot for rum." He calls out the order to Jocko. "I'm a writer," he says to me.

I know this, too, but I say, "Is that right?"

"Books, stories, magazine articles. *The Man in the Glass Coffin* was a modest best-seller a few years ago, maybe you heard of it?"

"I don't read much."

"You're not alone there," Talley says ruefully. "I'm between projects now. Down here on vacation and to soak up a little local color."

"And you think I might qualify in the color department. Rumpled, unshaven, rumsoaked—an old character."

"Well, I'll admit you interest me. My sixth sense says you might have a story to tell."

"Everybody's got a story to tell."

"But only a few are worth listening to."

Jocko brings the drinks and I taste some of mine. Out of the corner of my eye I see a sleek blue-and-white ketch tack in from the sea, her Dacron sails fat with wind. Forty-footer with a clipper bow and enough beam to handle weather in blue water. She reminds me of *Windrunner*. A little larger, and *Windrunner* was a yawl, but the two types are similarly rigged. It'd be cool out there on her foredeck. The trades are blowing today.

"I'm staying up at Coral Bay," Talley says. "I like St. John better than St. Thomas and this side of the island better than Cruz Bay. Fewer people, none of the conventional tourist atmosphere."

"So do I. For the same reasons."

"Been in the Virgins a long time, have you?"

"Twenty-seven years."

"Practically a native. You live out here on the tip?"

"That's right. A saltbox not far away."

"What's a saltbox?"

"Small square house. Cheap rent."

"Mind if I ask what you do for a living?"

"I don't do anything," I say.

"You mean you're out of work?"

"No. I mean I don't do anything. Except come here to Jocko's most days."

"Retired?"

"No."

"Independent means?"

"No."

"Then how do you make ends meet?"

I empty my glass. The blue-and-white ketch glides up toward Hurricane Hole, passing a big motor sailer flying the British flag. Her sails and brightwork gleam in the hard glare of the sun.

After a time I say, "You want to know about me? All right, I'll tell you. Here's the short version: I moved down here after committing a crime, a perfect crime. Later on, I committed two more. Three perfect crimes over a period of about six years."

Talley sits still, his beer bottle poised halfway between us. His eyes reflect sharp interest for a few seconds. Then his mouth quirks and he lowers the bottle to the table.

"You're putting me on," he says.

"Am I?"

"Three perfect crimes?"

"That's right."

"One would be a hell of a trick. But *three*?"

I smile. "Damn few people can make that claim."

"If it's the truth. What kind of crimes?"

"Oh, they were all major felonies."

"And you got away with them?"

"I wouldn't be sitting here if I hadn't. That's what 'perfect crime' means, doesn't it?"

"You must've been born lucky, then," Talley says.

"Lucky? Well, luck had something to do with it. Other factors, too. But mainly it was ingenuity. All three, in one way or another, were creative as hell. If I do say so myself."

"You made money from these crimes?"

"Just the first one. A small fortune."

"But the money ran out, is that it? Or you squandered it."

"Wrong on both counts. I still have a fair amount left. That's how I make ends meet."

He frowns. "Then what're you doing living way out here on the cheap, spending your days drinking in a place like this?"

"That's the long version of the story."

"And I suppose you wouldn't care to provide details."

"I didn't say that."

"So you are willing? Why?"

"Why not?"

"Oh, I get it," Talley says. "After more than twenty years, the statutes of limitation on your crimes have run out."

I don't answer. The motor sailer has caught my eye again. I watch it move down the bay, cleaving the water smoothly, her wake a long smear of cream on the dark blue surface. I have always preferred sailing vessels—ketches, yawls, schooners—to those big power yachts, but there is something majestic about any boat taking the sun on her way out to sea. For a few seconds, I feel a stir of the old yearning. But it doesn't last long. It never does.

"Wise? Did you hear me?"

I look at Talley again. He taps a small device he has taken from the pocket of his shirt. "Voice-activated tape recorder," he says. "Of course I won't use anything you say without your permission. I'll give you a signed statement to that effect—"

I wave that away. "Go ahead and turn it on. But it'll take a while to tell it the way it needs to be told."

"I've got plenty of time. And a spare cassette."

"Talking's thirsty work."

Talley says, "So's listening," and signals to Jocko for another round.

When I have a full glass in front of me, I say, "From the beginning, then. The summer of 1977, when I met Annalise . . ."

SAN FRANCISCO

1977

NONE OF IT would have happened if I hadn't met Annalise.
Sure, I know—that's the way a lot of stories start. Mister, I met a man once. Mister, I met a woman once. You go along living a normal life, more or less on the moral high road, and then you meet the wrong person and suddenly everything changes and you find yourself losing control, running against the wind. It's almost a cliché. Hell, it *is* a cliché.

But it wasn't like that with me. Annalise was no Circe-like temptress luring me to ruin. The reverse was true, in fact. I was the one in the helmsman's seat all along. The tempter on the first crime, the prime mover on all three. She was the catalyst. If it hadn't been for her, I wouldn't have and couldn't have done any of them.

Yet I didn't corrupt her, any more than she corrupted me. I don't believe one person can corrupt another by intent alone. I think you have to be born with the capacity to commit acts of what some might term moral anarchy; to possess a dark side that you might not even be aware of until the right set of circumstances reveals it. If you meet another person who has the same sort of dark side, as Annalise and I did, fusing the two spreads the darkness through both, until they're consumed by it. Like when you mix chemical agents that individually are harmless but that together produce a volatile reaction.

I was thirty-four when I met her, the summer of 1977. But before I get to that, I should give you a little background on those first thirty-four years of my life, so you'll understand the man I was then.

Born and raised in Los Alegres, a small town north of San Francisco. Father a cabinetmaker, mother a clerk in an arts and crafts store. I was their only child, a surprise change-of-life baby—they were both forty-two when I was born and had long since given up any hope of having a family. You might think, given my sudden arrival, that they'd have lavished a great deal of love and affection on me, but you'd be wrong. It wasn't that they resented me, or that they didn't care; it was that I was a new and difficult complication at a point in their lives when they could least afford another one. They were hardworking, gray little people who'd spent the years of their marriage in a constant struggle to maintain a comfortable lower middle-class existence. Before I was born my father developed a lung disease that ate up most of their savings and kept him from working more than two or three days a week. My mother had to quit her job to take care of me. There was no family member on either side to help out, and no money to hire someone to do it.

So I grew up in a shabby rented house with no frills—a radio instead of a TV, few toys, no books because my parents had no interest in reading. Just enough food to keep from going hungry, just enough clothing to keep me warm and dry, just enough of everything to get by. I grew up listening to long silences broken now and then by mild complaints and heavy sighs and my old man's dry, consumptive coughs. I grew up pretty much alone.

School wasn't much better. I didn't make friends easily—too quiet, too shy. Average student, except for mathematics, the one subject I excelled in. All types of math, anything to do with numbers and calculations. That's the kind of mind I have. Logical, deliberate, precise. Give me an equation in algebra or trigonometry or calculus, and sooner or later I'll work out the answer. Present me with a nonarithmetical problem to which I can apply the principles of mathematics, and the same is true. There has never been any conundrum, no matter how difficult, that I haven't been able to solve. That gift is the central reason my three crimes remain perfect to this day.

My father died when I was a senior in high school. My mother was so tightly bound to him that she went into an immediate decline and died four days after my graduation. Both of them had small life insurance policies that they'd managed to keep up the premiums on. I was my mother's beneficiary, and there was a little left from my father's policy as well—a total of about five thousand dollars. I took this money, and another few hundred from the sale of my parents' meager possessions, and moved to San Francisco.

The only career option that seemed both worthwhile and affordable was accountancy, so I enrolled at Golden Gate University to pursue a BA; they offered a very good accounting program and had a reputation for placing their top graduates in well-paid positions. I found a studio apartment on the fringe of the Tenderloin, I took a part-time job to help with expenses, and I spent most of my free time studying. The hard work paid off. When I graduated I was second in my class and highly regarded by my professors.

I was hired at the first place I applied to, as a clerk in the accounting department of Amthor Associates. You may have heard of Amthor—a large San Francisco–based engineering firm along the lines of Bechtel Corporation, with the same sort of worldwide activity. I applied myself there as determinedly as I had at Golden Gate University and received my first promotion, to junior accountant, in less than three years. Over the next ten years I worked my way up to assistant chief in charge of accounts payable, at an annual salary of $37,000 with health benefits and stock options.

By then I had moved into a comfortable one-bedroom apartment on the lower slope of Russian Hill. I owned a three-year-old Ford, a small portfolio of conservative stocks, a twenty-one-inch TV, a stereo system to satisfy my taste for classical music, a closet filled with Arrow shirts and Roos Atkins suits, and a shelf of books about sailing and seafaring adventure, subjects that had interested me since my teens. I ate dinner fairly often in medium-priced restaurants. I went to an occasional movie or play or symphony performance, alone or sometimes with a date. Sports bored me; I left the only baseball game I attended before it was half over. I paid no attention to politics, or to what was going on in remote places like Vietnam. (I'd avoided the draft out of high school because my vision is less than perfect and I had an inner-ear problem that made me prone to mild dizzy spells.) I was sympathetic to human rights and environmental causes, but never to the point of activism. I lived in a tight little world of my own choosing. I was neither happy nor unhappy. I had few experiences and no expectations, and so there was little to judge happiness by.

Most of the time I was accepting of my life, if not completely content with it. It was what it was; I was what I was. But there was a restlessness in me, a vague, persistent yearning for something else, something more. I thought I'd like to learn how to sail, but I never got around to doing anything more than daydreaming about it. I had other daydreams, too, usually triggered by a book or magazine article or TV show: faraway places, islands in the sun, tropical breezes and sunset voyages on dark blue water, a life of luxury and ease. I made tentative plans for trips to Tahiti and the Caribbean, but I didn't follow through on those either; faraway places seemed too expensive and too far away. The only vacation I took outside California was six days on Maui. It wasn't what I'd expected and I had a lousy time.

This life I was leading, by conservative standards, was exemplary. By other standards it was pedestrian, dull, empty. I broke no laws of any consequence, I paid my bills and taxes on time, I was a model citizen by every measure. The only difference between me and millions of other model citizens was that I had never been married and I lived alone, not so much by choice as because I'd never met anyone I cared to share my life with. That, and inertia.

Not that I led a monkish existence. There were women before Annalise, a few casual relationships. Some women seem to like quiet men of average height, average weight, average looks; men who wear glasses that give them a studious appearance. We come across as nonthreatening, I suppose. Blue eyes had something to do with it, too. My best feature, Annalise said, and she wasn't the first. Now and then one of the women would consent to go to bed with me, and this happened often enough to satisfy my normal carnal instincts if not theirs. I considered my instincts normal at the time, anyway, but I see myself now a lot more clearly than I did then.

None of the affairs lasted beyond a month, and I suspect one of the reasons is that I wasn't much of a lover. I'd never felt completely comfortable with my sexuality, had a fairly low sex drive as a result. I didn't get laid for the first time until I was nineteen, and it wasn't much of a confidence builder. I don't remember the girl's name or what she looked like. All I remember is her saying, "Not so fast, not so fast," and "Oh God, couldn't you wait," and thinking there must be something wrong with me because I wasn't able to do it right.

But for all of that, I was ripe for someone like Annalise. Not just someone to fall in love with, to fill the void in my life. A kindred spirit, a kind of female alter ego, even though I didn't realize it until months afterward. Alone I was nothing, would always have been nothing. With Annalise, because of Annalise, I was capable of anything, any possibility.

I met her at a wedding reception in Sausalito at the beginning of June. The groom was a young guy named Jim Sanderson who also worked for Amthor Associates, in the research and development division. I knew him casually—we'd had lunch together a few times, more by accident than design—so I was surprised when he included me among the dozen or so coworkers he invited to the reception. When the day came, I almost didn't go. I'd never felt comfortable in large crowds, among strangers; never been much good at small talk. At any sort of social gathering I tended to hide in corners or to wander around aimlessly, avoiding contact as much as possible. Sanderson and his bride both had large families and a broad circle of friends and acquaintances, very few of whom I knew.

But the day turned out bright and clear, balmy, and I didn't feel like holing up in the apartment and I didn't want to hurt Sanderson's feelings by not showing up—not that he'd have noticed. So I went. The reception was held at the Alta Mira Hotel, on the hill overlooking the waterfront and the bay. Tables groaning with food, an open bar, waiters circulating with glasses of champagne, a five-piece orchestra. The swarm of guests was as thick as bees in a hive, setting up the same kind of constant, pulsing buzz.

I located Sanderson and his bride and congratulated them. Then I filled a plate and snagged a glass of champagne and tried to find a corner to hide in. There wasn't any inside, so I wandered out to the far end of the terrace. I'd finished the food and champagne and was looking out over the harbor, about ready to make my escape, when a voice behind me said, "You look a little lost, standing there." I turned, and there she was.

The effect she had on me was cumulative, not immediate. The first two things I noticed were her size and how much hair she had. A couple of inches over five feet tall, so that I had to look down into her face; hair the color of dark honey and worn in a thick feathery wave the way Farrah Fawcett wore hers in *Charlie's Angels,* the top-rated TV show that year. Then: Nice smile. Lightly tanned and freckled skin. Brown eyes, heart-shaped face, a bump of a nose with a slight upward tilt. Slender body, small breasts, slim legs. White dress with a red flower pinned to it, and a string of pearls at her throat. It was minutes before I realized just how well her features blended into a harmonious whole, that she was close to being beautiful.

Usually I was at a loss for any kind of clever repartee; I don't think well on my feet. But that day I managed to summon a reasonably bright response.

"I was lost," I said, "but now I'm found."

"What? Oh," she said, and laughed. Nice laugh. Rich and deep, not one of those tinkly giggles that some small women have. Then her eyebrows pulled together and she said in serious tones, "Did you mean that literally?"

"Literally?"

"What you said about being found. The way it's meant in 'Amazing Grace.'"

"You mean am I religious?"

"If you're a born-again . . ."

"I'm not. Being born once was enough."

"Good. I have a problem with Holy Rollers."

"I'm sorry to hear that."

"As long as you aren't one." She smiled again. "You know, this is a pretty odd conversation."

"I guess it is."

"Not that I mind. I find odd appealing—up to a point."

"Is that why you came over to talk to me?"

"No. Because you looked like a lost stray."

"I don't deal well with crowds," I said.

"Shy?"

"You could say that."

"I'm just the opposite. Outgoing. I love parties, the bigger the better." She sipped from the glass she was holding. "Champagne, too. But I think I've about had my limit. What's your limit?"

"One or two glasses. I'm not much of a drinker."

"Mine's five or six. This is number six."

She was a little drunk, I realized then. There was a flush across her cheekbones, and the brown eyes had a glaze.

I asked her if she was a friend of the bride or groom, and she said, "Neither. Friend of a friend who went to school with the bride. You?"

"I work for the same company as the groom."

"Which company would that be?"

"Amthor Associates. In the city."

"That's an engineering firm, isn't it?"

"Yes." I didn't tell her what I did at Amthor and I was glad she didn't ask. Some people equate being an accountant with being dull, uninteresting, and the fact that I fit the stereotype embarrassed me in situations like this. "What do you do?"

"I'm a buyer for Kleinfelt's. The department store. Well, assistant buyer. Women's lingerie."

"That sounds interesting."

"Actually," she said, "it's a pretty shitty job."

I didn't know what to say to that.

"Bad Annalise," she said. "Six glasses of champagne makes me say and do things I shouldn't."

"Annalise. That's an unusual name. Euphonious."

"What's that, euphonious?"

"It means pleasing to the ear. What goes with Annalise?"

"Bonner. Is your name euphonious?"

"I doubt it. Jordan Wise."

"You're right, it's not. Are you a wise Wise?"

"Not as often as I'd like to be," I said.

"Me, either. Who is? Well, Bert is. Thinks he is, anyway."

"Who would Bert be?"

"The fellow I came with. But he seems to have disappeared."

"Boyfriend?"

"Jury's still out on that. Why? Are *you* interested?"

"Yes," I said. Bold. And I'd never been bold before. She brought that out in me right from the first. "I'd like to see you again."

"Are you asking me for a date?"

"Lunch, dinner, a movie, whatever you like."

She thought about it, her head tipped to one side. "Well, maybe," she said. "Jury's still out on that, too."

"When will there be a verdict?"

"After due deliberation. Which just began, so it might take a while. You never know with juries."

"How do I find out?"

That was as far as it went. She didn't have a chance to respond, because another voice said loudly, "Annalise, there you are," and a blue-eyed blond guy, half a head taller and a yard wider than me, came barreling up. He didn't even glance at me; as far as he was concerned, I wasn't even there. "I've been looking all over for you. Come on, there's somebody I want you to meet." He took hold of her arm and started tugging on it.

It caught me flatfooted. I didn't have a chance to say anything more. She smiled at me and shrugged as if to say "What can you do?" and let him drag her off into the crowd.

I felt a rush of anger at the blond guy. Asshole! Yanking on her like that, taking her away! But the anger didn't last long. The dull acceptance that had characterized so much of my life replaced it. So what's the big deal? I thought. She'd probably have said no anyway. Forget it. Forget her.

But I hung around the reception for another half hour, working my way through the crowd. Annalise was gone, or at least I didn't see her anywhere. Finally I left and drove home, feeling flat, putting the flatness down to the crush of strangers even though she was still on my mind. She stayed on my mind the rest of the day, and I dreamed about her that night.

Forget her? Even then, at some level, I knew I never would.

★ ★ ★

It took me nearly a week to work up the nerve to call her. I would've done it sooner if she'd had a listed phone number, but she didn't and nobody I knew who'd been at the reception knew her. I was reluctant to call her at her job. Amthor Associates frowned on personal calls on company time, and I thought Kleinfelt's Department Store would probably feel the same. But it was either that or give up without trying, so I rode the elevator to the lobby on my morning coffee break and called Kleinfelt's on one of the public phones.

She answered with her last name and a Miss in front of it. I identified myself and said that we'd met at the Sanderson reception on Saturday—"Lost and found, if you remember."

"I remember," she said. Not as if she were glad to hear from me, but friendly enough. "I didn't have that much champagne."

"I was wondering," I said, "if the jury has come in yet."

"Jury?" Then she got it and it made her laugh. "Oh, the jury. Right. Well, let's see. Which case were you interested in?"

"Mainly the one involving me."

"Mmm. Just now, as a matter of fact."

"What's the verdict?"

"In favor of the plaintiff, I think. Why don't you call me again tonight to confirm it?"

She gave me her home number. And when I called her that night, she confirmed the favorable verdict. She was busy Friday and Saturday, but Sunday would be all right for dinner as long as it wasn't a late evening.

She lived in an eight-unit apartment building near Golden Gate Park and the University of California Medical Center. I picked her up there and we went to Castagnola's on Fisherman's Wharf for dinner and then to the Top of the Mark for drinks. Annalise wore white again—a white flared skirt and a pale-blue-and-white blouse under a white jacket. If white is a color, it was her favorite, with pale blue a close second. She drew a lot of male eyes. Being with her made me feel proud and privileged and a little possessive, feelings I'd never had with any other woman.

It wasn't like most first dates: there was no awkwardness between us. She was as easy to talk to as she had been at the wedding reception— naturally gregarious, so comfortable in her own skin she put you at ease right away. She talked freely about herself, but without the constant ego focus of a lot of attractive women. She was twenty-six. She'd grown up in Visalia, in the Central Valley. Her father, a career soldier, had been killed in Korea when she was a baby; her mother died two years later, she wouldn't say from what. She and her younger sister, Ariane, had been raised by their mother's sister—"one of those religious fanatics who quote the Bible fifty times a day and think all men are sex fiends and girls shouldn't be allowed to wear makeup or date before the age of twenty." That was the source of her dislike of Holy Rollers. The aunt had dominated her husband, treated her nieces like "a couple of heathen slaves." Annalise's sister had been brainwashed into following the same path—she ran a Christian day care center in Visalia—but Annalise had moved out and away as soon as she was of age. She'd gotten a sales clerk's job at Kleinfelt's in Fresno, showed initiative, was promoted, applied for and was given the assistant buyer's job at the store's main branch in San Francisco, and moved to the city three years ago.

She didn't like the job; she used the word "shitty" again. It was demanding, time-consuming, barely paid enough for her to afford her apartment. She was on the lookout for something better, more challenging, in the fashion industry. Not as a buyer; as a designer of women's clothing. Her ambition was to move into the world of high fashion. She'd designed dozens of outfits in her spare time, a few of which she felt were quality work, but so far she hadn't had any luck in interesting a potential buyer. Not even Kleinfelt's, she said with some bitterness.

Eventually we got around to me. My background sounded pretty mundane when I related it. When she asked what I did at Amthor, as I was afraid she would, I told her the truth. She took it well enough, but I could tell she was disappointed, that she'd hoped I was a design engineer or even a junior executive. I couldn't lie to her, either, about whether I had ambitions to be anything other than an accountant. I had none at that time, beyond a promotion to chief accountant someday, and I said as much.

I didn't try to kiss her good-night when I took her home. I felt I was on shaky ground as it was and I didn't want to do anything that might make her like me less. When I asked if I could see her again, I half expected her to say no. But all she said was "Call me."

I waited two days. It was a big relief when she agreed to another date. Saturday night, this time—a step up on her social calendar. My self-esteem was low enough for me to wonder why a woman as attractive and desirable as Annalise would bother with somebody like me. Pity, maybe? Or maybe a quiet, average-looking numbers cruncher was a respite from the usual macho type she dated. It didn't really matter. All I cared about was seeing her again.

That night we ate at a French restaurant on the bay side of Powell Street. Drinks and dancing afterward in the Tonga Room at the Fairmont. She liked to dance close and the feel of her in my arms was as intoxicating as the mai tais we drank. The evening went well enough so that I risked a brief good-night kiss. She didn't object. "Call me," she said again before I left.

It went on like that for three months. I'd call her early in the week, and she'd tell me whether she was free and on which weekend night. Three weekends she was booked up, or said she was. I knew she dated other men; she'd been open about that. One of them was Bert, the big blond guy she'd been with at the reception. Was she sleeping with him, with any of the other men she saw? The one thing she didn't talk about was her love life, but it seemed certain she had one. She wasn't the virginal type. It made me jealous, but all I could do was bide my time and hope to be favored someday. Her game, her rules.

Usually we went out to dinner, then a nightclub or a movie or a show of some kind. Once we drove down to Half Moon Bay; the rest of the time we stayed in the city. After each date I kissed her good-night, a couple of times lingeringly, but that was all. She didn't invite me into her apartment. I wanted desperately to make love to her, but I was afraid to suggest it or to make any aggressive moves that might lead to rejection. Twice, in the car afterward, the memory of her body pressed close and the taste of her mouth gave me a hard-on. I'd only masturbated three times in my life before then, in my teens, but on both those nights I gave in to the frustration and the need for release as soon as I got home. My attitude and my behavior seems ridiculous now, looking back. But that was the kind of man I was then. The kind of half-man I was then.

Things changed on the last in our string of dates. Annalise drank a fair amount of wine, and when I took her home, she returned my kiss with more passion than ever before and invited me in. We sat on the couch, began making out. Her hunger was as great as mine at first; her tongue worked into my mouth, she ran her fingers through my hair and moaned a little when I slid a fumbling hand over one breast. I was certain we would end up in her bedroom.

But it didn't happen. Without warning she put a stop to it. Pulled away, breathing hard, and said, "No, we can't do this, it's all wrong."

I said, "Why?" in a choked voice.

"It just is. Wrong for me, wrong for you."

"Annalise—"

"No. You'd better go, Jordan. Right now."

I went. What else could I do? I went with my heart racing and my pants bulging and my head full of confusion. Drove home, jerked off, lay in bed trying to understand. She wasn't a tease and she hadn't been faking her passion; she'd wanted me as much as I wanted her. Then why the sudden turn from hot to cold? Why was having sex wrong for us?

I found out the following week. I called her on Tuesday, as usual, and at first she said she was busy that weekend. Then she said, "No, that's not fair to you," and said she'd see me Friday night. Not for dinner; for a drink, at Perry's on Union Street, where we'd gone a couple of times before. After work, say six o'clock. No, she didn't want me to pick her up, she'd meet me there. I tried to get her to tell me what was wrong, but all she'd say was "We'll talk about it on Friday."

Bad week. I sensed what was coming. I tried to tell myself I was over-reacting, but by the time I met her at Perry's I'd given up the pretense. She was already there, sitting in one of the booths with a glass of wine. As soon as I saw her, I knew what she was going to say—I knew it was over.

She waited until I'd ordered a drink for myself. Then she sighed and said, "There's no point in prolonging this. You've probably already guessed anyway. Jordan, I'm sorry, but I don't think we should see each other anymore."

"Why not?" I had myself under tight control, but the words still came out sounding weak and plaintive. "Somebody else? Bert?"

"No. I haven't seen him in more than a month. It's not that."

"Then why?"

"I'm a bitch, that's why."

"That isn't an answer."

"All right. Can you stand brutally honest?"

"Yes."

"I'm fond of you, I really am. More so than any other guy I've been out with in a long time. I can talk to you, you're gentle, you don't make demands. But that's not enough for me."

"Why isn't it enough?"

"You want an intimate, long-term relationship. So do I. But I don't see any way we can have one together. That's why I didn't go to bed with you last week. I wanted to, I wanted to give you that much, but I couldn't go through with it and then hurt you like I'm doing right now. I'm not that much of a bitch."

"I don't understand," I said. "Why can't we keep on seeing each other?"

24

She said, "We're a bad mix, that's why. You can't give me what I need out of life. And I can't give you what you need."

"That isn't true . . ."

"Oh yes it is. In the long run you're looking for a wife, kids maybe, a nice little house in the suburbs. Stability, security. Respectability. None of that suits me. I grew up in a household like that and I'd go crazy, do God knows what, if I tried to live that kind of life again. Even without the Bible-thumping. No, don't say it wouldn't have to be that way with you. It would. It's already heading in that direction and that's why I have to end it now. We go out, we do the same kinds of things, all our time together is nice and orderly and predictable. Sex would spice it up for a while, but then that would become nice and orderly and predictable too. It almost always does in a long-running relationship."

The words stung, even though she was speaking in a low, matter-of-fact voice. I could feel myself wincing under the lash of them.

"What *do* you want, Annalise?"

"I told you I was ambitious, didn't I? I want to be a fashion designer, live in New York or Paris. If I can't have that, I'll settle for enough money to live well and dress well and travel, and I don't much care what I have to do to get it."

"You don't mean that—"

"I do mean it. I've already done things that would shock you if I told you about them. You see? I know you, but you don't know me at all."

"You've never let me know you, never even hinted at any of this before."

"I should have. I came close more than once."

"Why didn't you?"

"I don't know. It doesn't matter. The point is, now you know what a greedy bitch I am. And you might as well know what else I want that you can't give me: thrills, excitement. You may not believe this, Jordan, but a lot of the time I don't really feel alive. I feel like I'm on hold, or caged, or worst of all, as if I'm running in a wheel like a goddamn hamster. I ache to go places, do things that are exciting and dangerous—live on the edge so I can feel alive *all* the time. Can you understand that?"

"Yes."

"I mean really understand. I don't see how you can."

"I may be dull, but I'm not insensitive."

"No, you're not," Annalise said. "And you're not stupid or self-deluded, either. You're as aware as I am of what you are—a nice, quiet, unexciting accountant who'll never be anything else. That's your future, and I don't want any part of it. Now, is that enough for you or should I say more?"

I hated her in that moment. The hate flared hot, a white stabbing brilliance like a matchhead struck in a dark room. It burned bright for three or four seconds, flickered, went out and crumbled away into ashes. Left me feeling numb.

She finished her glass of wine. I heard her say, "We'd better leave now." I got up when she did and followed her outside, two paces behind like a dog at heel.

On the cold, windy sidewalk she said, "My car's just down the block. We might as well say good-bye right here."

I said, "Annalise, I love you."

"Oh, God. I don't want to hear that. You're only making it more difficult."

"I can't help how I feel. Please, won't you just—"

"I won't because I can't. We can't. There's nothing more for us, can't you just accept that?"

"I don't know, I can't think right now."

"Well, you'd better accept it, because that's the way it is." She took my face between her hands and leaned up and kissed me on the mouth, a cold dry kiss that left no taste of her at all. "Good-bye, Jordan. Have a good life."

I watched her walk away, thinking it might be the last time I would ever see her.

The thought was unbearable.

You hear a lot about love. All the psychological and physiological interpretations, the mystique manufactured and built up by Hollywood, fiction writers, ad agencies, greeting card companies. It's sexual attraction and raging hormones and the mating urge and the need to perpetuate the race. It's God's will. It's Cupid's arrow and hearts and flowers and Valentine's Day and sweet-sad songs and sappy movies. It's daydreams and night sweats and long-range plans and lavish weddings and paradise honeymoons. It's feeling as though you'd been hammered and walking around in a daze, or waking up some morning and grinning at yourself in the mirror and saying out loud, "Jesus Christ, I'm in love." It's being unable to eat or sleep or work. It's thinking you'll die or go crazy if what you're feeling isn't returned by the other person. It's this and that and a hundred other things.

And most of it is crap.

The simple truth is, you can't define love or put labels on it. It's an individual experience. You really have no idea of what it'll be until it happens to you, and even then you might not recognize it for what it is for a long time. I didn't. Neither the word nor the concept entered my head until "Annalise, I love you" popped out of my mouth on that cold sidewalk outside Perry's. Before then, she was just a woman who'd gotten under my skin a little deeper than most, a woman I yearned to sleep with and who would eventually pass out of my life whether I got into her or not. I thought about her a lot, I liked being with her and wanted to be with her more often, but that was as far as it went. I didn't walk around in a daze. My appetite was the same, I slept my usual seven hours almost every night, I crunched numbers at my desk with the same precision as always. Love? No way. I wasn't in love with Annalise Bonner.

Except that I was.

And that night I said it, and that night I admitted it to myself.

I'll tell you some of the things love was and is for me. The voice of my experience, the gospel according to Jordan Wise.

Love is that intolerable feeling of loss.

Love is as much suffering as it is joy.

Love is forced self-analysis, having to peel away the outer layers of self so you can see who you really are.

Love is dying and being reborn as something more and something less than you were before.

My rebirth didn't come immediately. I moped around all that weekend, still numb and hurting, and when I went in to work on Monday I must have looked pretty bad because two coworkers asked whether I was ill. I hid from them and the others in the office in columns of numbers and mathematical computations. I'd always been able to do that; mathematics is an orderly world, clean and simple, one in which I functioned supremely well. My retreat, my safe haven.

The fact that Amthor Associates' annual internal audit was scheduled for the next week made it even easier. The firm's fiscal year ran from September to September, the thirtieth of that month, and preparations for it and then the audit itself made for an extra busy time. The audit was mostly a routine procedure, conducted exclusively for tax purposes. The accounting department ran at a high level of efficiency, so there was never any problem aside from a few minor errors and discrepancies. No errors or discrepancies had ever been discovered in my records. My reputation as a skilled and completely trustworthy employee was the primary reason I had been promoted at a relatively young age to assistant chief and why I would be in line one day for the chief's position.

The idea came to me while I was preparing for the audit.

Every day in the office, I was responsible for the disbursement of thousands of dollars to subcontractors and suppliers, yet I'd never thought of stealing any of it. Never thought seriously, I should say.

Once in a while a vagrant thought had crossed my mind. You know the kind I mean. Everyone has them, even people born without a dark side. Momentary impulses, little imps of the perverse that appear and disappear so quickly you hardly realize they're there. All that money going out and I'm the one controlling it. Good thing I'm an honest man, because it would be easy enough to turn dishonest. That sort of thing.

This time it wasn't just a stray thought. The idea came suddenly and clearly, not as idle speculation but like a revelation.

I could take some of the firm's money . . . a lot of the firm's money. A staggering amount, in fact, if it were done slowly and with great care. And it wouldn't be all that difficult to accomplish, given my position.

Enough money to do all the things I'd yearned to do.

Enough money to give Annalise everything she wanted.

I could still have Annalise.

It was a mad notion—I told myself that a dozen times. Siphon off thousands of dollars, embezzle it, steal it? I'd never stolen anything in my life. I was honest, I was loyal, I was too damn timid, I'd never be able to go through with it.

You're a nice, quiet, unexciting accountant who'll never be anything else.

Annalise had been right. No matter how much I rebelled against it, that was who I was and that was my future. I didn't blame her for pointing it out, or resent her for cutting me out of her life. How could I? If our positions had been reversed, I would probably have done the same thing.

But I couldn't get rid of the idea; it had already put down roots. The enormity of it and its potential consequences terrified me, yet at the same time it was fascinating, energizing. It gave me something to focus on, a way to lift myself out of the mire of depression and self-pity. All right, I thought, so I wasn't capable of actually doing it. I could still treat it as if I were. Determine whether or not it *could* be done. An intellectual exercise, like solving sophisticated puzzles and cryptograms.

For the next two weeks I worked on the problem every weeknight and all day Saturday and Sunday. I approached it mathematically, as a complex algebraic equation. Only in this case it was a problem I had to design myself, in its entirety, in order to arrive at a viable solution. I broke it down into two main linked equations: how to appropriate the money, and how to disappear with it without getting caught. The first was the easier to construct, with fewer corollary difficulties; the second was the harder, with more corollaries. I worked on the equations one at a time, shaping and building each with care and noting the corollaries on separate sheets of paper. Once I had the basics in place, I addressed the secondary problems individually, working on each in turn until I had its solution and then plugging it into the main equation.

By the end of the first week, it was no longer an intellectual exercise but a solid possibility. By the end of the second week, it had become a probability.

I knew something else by then, too: it not only could be done, I *was* capable of doing it.

Annalise hadn't been right, after all. I was not just an accountant who would always be an accountant; I was not a nice, unexciting guy who was too timid to take risks. Not any more. The enormity of the plan and its potential consequences no longer frightened me. If by some chance I was caught and sent to prison, life behind bars couldn't be much worse than the restrictive life I'd been leading behind invisible bars of my own construction.

I saw myself as I really was. And discovered my dark side.

I went over the equations half a dozen times, factor by factor, backchecking, refining. There was room for further refinement, but in the main they were flawless except for two factors. One was a y factor: the unforeseen mishap, like a submerged rock in shoal water, that could rip the bottom out of any plan—bad luck, coincidence, miscalculation. The other was a missing x factor.

There was nothing to be done in advance to forestall a y factor. The

x factor was essential; it had to be added to the equations to make them complete and functional.

The x factor was Annalise.

I could do it for her, but I couldn't do it without her.

I called her the Wednesday after the company audit was completed. She wasn't happy to hear from me, that was plain enough from her voice, but neither did she sound angry or hostile. A little exasperated was all.

"Why are you calling?" she said. "I meant what I said at Perry's."

"I need to see you," I said.

"No, Jordan. It wouldn't do either of us any good."

"As soon as possible. It's important. Very important."

"There's nothing you can say to make me change my mind."

"One hour of your time, that's all I'm asking."

"So you can plead and beg? I couldn't stand it."

"I'm all through with that kind of thing," I said. "What I have to say I think you're going to want to hear."

"And that is?"

"When I see you."

She sighed. "Oh, all right. Tomorrow night at Perry's, after work."

"No," I said. "It has to be your apartment or mine."

"Why? Why are you being so mysterious?"

"I'm not. This talk has to be in person and in private. You'll understand why when you hear it."

"I don't know . . ."

"One hour. You can stop me any time, and I'll leave you alone and never bother you again."

"You mean that?"

"I swear it."

Annalise gave in finally. She'd be home tomorrow night, she said, I could come by for a few minutes then. I said I'd be there at seven.

"You'd better not make me regret this, Jordan."

"If anybody regrets it," I said, "it'll be me."

She wasn't wearing white this time. Blue jeans, an old blue sweater, floppy slippers. Face scrubbed free of makeup, hair tousled. A large glass of white wine in one hand and a flush to her skin and shine to her eyes that told me at least two other glasses had preceded it. All a calculated effort, I was sure, to make herself appear unattractive to me. It didn't work. She could have been caked with dirt and wearing a sack and I still would have wanted her.

Music throbbed through the apartment, the kind of heavy rock I'd told her I didn't much care for. That was intentional, too. She didn't look at me directly when she let me in, didn't ask if I wanted a drink. Just went straight to one of the chairs and sat down. The chair was separated from the other furniture, so that I couldn't sit next to her if that was my intention.

It wasn't. I sat on the couch across from her. "Could you turn the music down a little?"

"It's not that loud."

"It is for what I have to say."

She shrugged and got up to lower the volume on her stereo. When she came back to the chair, she looked at me directly for the first time and what she saw seemed to surprise her. "You look . . . different," she said.

"I am different," I said. "That's why I'm here."

"Well, go ahead, then. I'm listening."

I had already worked out the best approach to take, and on the basis of what she'd told me at Perry's I was reasonably sure I knew how she'd react. But I could have been wrong. People are seldom as predictable as they seem to be; I was living proof of that. It depended on how much she cared for me, if she still cared for me at all, and on just how much larcency there was in her. If she took it badly and sent me packing, I would have to admit she was lost to me and learn to deal with it. And scrap the entire scheme, or revise it to exclude her. To this day, I'm not sure which I would've done.

I said, "The last time we saw each other, you said you were fond of me. Did you mean that?"

"Of course I meant it. I don't say things I don't mean."

"How fond?"

"I can't answer that. Fond is fond."

"Fond enough to be with me if I could give you money, luxury, travel, excitement?"

"Be with you?"

"Long-term. Exclusively."

"Oh, God, I don't know. What difference does it make?"

"Answer the question, Annalise."

I said it sharply, more sharply than I'd ever spoken to her. She narrowed her eyes and bit her lip before she said, "I don't love you the way you love me, you know that. I don't know that I ever could."

"But you could try. Given the right circumstances."

"Will it make you feel better if I say yes?"

"If you mean it."

"All right. Yes, I could be with you. It just isn't possible."

"It is possible."

"I don't see how."

"You said you'd didn't care what you had to do to get the things you want, as long as you got them. Did you mean that?"

"I meant it."

"What would you do for more than half a million dollars?"

Her mouth came open. "Did you say . . . half a million?"

"More. Enough to keep both of us in style for the rest of our lives."

"My God," she said.

"Would you go away with me?"

"Go away where?"

"Anywhere a long way from here. The tropics. Tahiti, the Caribbean."

She was interested by this time. Puzzled, wary, but definitely interested. Leaning forward in the chair, the tip of her tongue moving back and forth over her upper lip. "If you had that much money . . . yes, I'd go away with you."

"Would you wait twelve to fifteen months for the opportunity?"

"Why so long?"

"It's necessary. No more than fifteen months."

"I'd wait longer," Annalise said. "I've waited for something like that all my life."

"Would you make an unbreakable commitment to me during that year?"

"What do you mean, unbreakable commitment?"

"I'm not talking about dating. In fact, I'd want you to keep on seeing other men."

"I don't understand."

"You will. What I mean is a commitment of trust. Mutual trust. Yours would be to trust me to make all the decisions and to do exactly as I say without question."

"As long as I knew what was happening and I had input into where we'd go to live."

"You'll know. And we'll decide together on the destination."

"Then yes. I'd do anything you told me to."

"Would you marry me?"

Her expression changed. She said, "Oh, shit, Jordan. Is that what this is all about? Some devious way of proposing?"

"No. It's part of the larger proposal, another necessary part."

"How can marriage be necessary?"

"In order to make the rest of it work."

"The rest of what? Can't you get to the point?"

"I am getting to it. Just answer the question: would you marry me for more than half a million dollars and a brand-new life?"

"Yes." Without hesitation.

"Would you become an accessory to a major crime?"

Long stare. "What kind of crime? What have you done?"

"I haven't done anything yet."

"What are you thinking of doing?"

"I've as much as told you," I said. "Commit a major crime for all that money."

"Steal half a million dollars?"

"Yes."

"For God's sake, how? Not with a gun or anything like that?"

"Absolutely not. No violence of any kind."

"Then *how?*"

"I have a plan. A detailed, mostly risk-free plan."

". . . You're serious, aren't you."

"Very serious. Dead serious."

She emptied her glass, got up and went to a sideboard to refill it.

I said, "Do you want to hear the rest of it?"

"Yes."

When she sat down again she looked at me in a new way, with a kind of awe, as if she were seeing me for the first time. Her face was flushed, but now it wasn't all the result of the wine. What I'd told her so far hadn't turned her off; she'd taken it just as I'd hoped she would. Excited, eager. Hooked. I could see it in her eyes.

"Half a million dollars," she said. "You really think you can get your hands on that much money?"

"I know I can. That's the easy part. The hard part is getting away with it, disappearing without a trace."

"And you know how to do that?"

"Yes. I can get the money on my own, but I can't do the rest without help. Your help. There's no other way."

She was too restless to sit still; she got up again and paced the room, taking sips of wine, thinking about it. After a time she said, "We'd go to prison if we were caught. I couldn't stand to be locked up."

"I won't lie to you," I said. "Something could go wrong. But I don't believe it will. Not the way I have it worked out."

"Famous last words."

"The risk to you is much less than it is to me. Even if we were caught, you wouldn't know the details of the theft because I won't reveal them to you; you could plead ignorance and I'd back you up, swear you had no prior knowledge that I was going to commit a crime. The most you'd be charged with is aiding and abetting. A good lawyer would probably be able to get you off with a suspended sentence."

She kept pacing. Her glass was empty again; she drained the bottle into it.

"How long have you been hatching this scheme?"

"Not long," I said. "Three weeks."

"Since the last time we saw each other."

"About that."

"So you could have me? That's why, isn't it?"

"Yes. For you and for the money."

"You want me that much?"

"I've never wanted anything more in my life."

She sat down beside me, set the wineglass on the table. Her eyes were very bright, like a bird's eyes, and smoky hot.

"Half a million dollars," she said again.

"More."

"For me."

"Yes."

"You're crazy," she said and took my face between her hands and kissed me, hard. Then she drew back and her eyes burned into mine.

"My God!" she said.

"Annalise," I said.

"For me."

"Yes."

"More than half a million dollars."

"Yes."

She kissed me again, hard enough this time to draw blood from my lower lip, pressing close, her arms tight around my neck, her tongue exploring my mouth. She was trembling, her body quivering as if controlled by invisible electrodes.

That kiss went on for a long time, hot and wet, her breathing coming faster. Then she twisted away and took my hands and pulled us both to our feet. "Crazy," she said again, and led me into the bedroom.

She had a marvelous body. Taut-muscled thighs, large nipples and aureoles on the small hard breasts, skin soft as a baby's. I was so excited that first time I came in less than a minute. She couldn't have been satisfied—her body was still quivering—but she didn't seem to mind. She held me with arms and legs, tight. It was a long time before either of us spoke.

"Jordan?"

"Yes."

"You weren't lying just to get me into bed? You *can* do it?"

"I can do it."

"Will you? Go through with it, I mean?"

"Yes. Will you?"

"Yes. Jesus, yes!"

Her hands moved on me again. Expert hands, expert mouth, expert body, guiding me, showing me new things, making it last until release was an excruciating mixture of pleasure and pain. Sounds trite, I know, putting it like that, but that was how it was for me.

And that's another thing love is. Bottom line.

Love is the best fuck you ever had.

SAN FRANCISCO

1977–1978

I N ORDER TO UNDERSTAND my plan, you have to look at it in historical perspective. The two linked equations were designed according to the laws and business practices existing in the late seventies, and my own experiences in the years preceding 1977. They were flawless in that regard, and that was why they worked. They wouldn't work today. Since 1978, laws have been changed and computerization has completely revamped the way in which large corporations like Amthor Associates and their accounting and comptroller departments operate.

Would I be able to commit and get away with the same crime today, given those changes?

Oh, yes, I think so. If now were then, I would be as proficient in the use of computers and accounting technology as I was in adding machines and ledger books. And there are always loopholes in the law to be ferreted out and utilized. It might take me longer now to devise a foolproof scheme to steal more than half a million dollars, and to establish a new and untraceable identity, but it could be done. If you're deliberate enough, resourceful enough, shrewd enough, almost anything is possible.

I put my plan into operation immediately after that first night with Annalise. You might think I was taking a lot on faith, going forward based on a verbal agreement and a single night of sex, and I suppose I was. She might have changed her mind, backed out at any time before she became an actual accessory. But our involvement together, as I'd told her, *had* to be based on mutual trust. She had to believe I would be able to embezzle the money and that we'd get away with it safely; I had to believe that she wanted the life I'd promised her enough, and cared for me enough, not to back out and to do exactly as she was told. That was the key to the success of the plan.

The fact that I worked in the accounts payable section of Amthor's accounting department was what made the theft viable. Amthor was a large firm, with branches in three other cities and literally hundreds of subcontractors and suppliers spread out across the country and in Mexico and Central America. All of the accounting was done in the San Francisco office, and invoices poured in in large quantities every month. Part of my job, and that of two other accountants, was to check these invoices against existing bids and allocations and, if all was in order, to stamp them with a payment authorization and pass them on to the comptroller's office. Some of the invoices were paid by check, others through direct bank deposit by invoice number. The choice was up to the individual supplier or contractor.

So then, step one: After work on three consecutive evenings I drove to one of the photocopy and job printing stores that dotted the city. In each I ordered a small quantity of invoice forms in different styles and formats, imprinted with six different company names. I still remember all of them, and that the three primaries were Darwin Electrical Contractors, M. & D. Supply, Inc., and West Valley Construction. I provided Bay Area addresses for each—three in San Francisco, two in the East Bay, one on the Peninsula; the cities were genuine, the street addresses made up. There was virtually no risk in this, because I saw to it the addresses never had cause to be checked. Once I had the printed invoices,

I took two days of sick leave and went around to various banks in San Francisco, Oakland, and San Mateo and opened business accounts in each of the company names. On the bank forms I listed myself, under my own name, as sole proprietor and requested that all statements and notifications of deposit be sent to my home address.

Step two: On the next Friday after close of business, I flew to Portland, Oregon, and spent the night in a downtown motel. I picked Portland because it was the nearest good-sized city in another state and yet still relatively close to San Francisco. I paid for the ticket in cash and gave the airline a false name; in those days, remember, you weren't required to show identification to airline or airport personnel and so you could fly under any name you chose. I used the same alias at the motel. These precautions probably weren't necessary, but I took them to ensure that no investigator could ever place me in Portland, a city I hadn't been to before and never visited again.

That Saturday morning I went to the main library, where I requested microfilm files of the Portland *Oregonian* for 1943, the year of my birth. I spent four hours combing through the obituary notices in every issue from January through July before I found what I was looking for. On July 19, a five-month-old infant named Richard James Laidlaw, the son of Carl and Amanda Laidlaw, had died in the Portland suburb of Beaverton. The birthdate and place of birth were also listed as Beaverton. I copied down all the relevant information. Before I left the library for the airport, I looked up the address of the office of vital statistics for Multnomah County, in which both Portland and Beaverton were located, and added it to the data sheet.

Step three: I checked the current San Francisco papers for advertisements for mail receiving and forwarding services, made a list, and then went around to check them out in person. The third one impressed me as the most discreet. I paid their standard fee, giving my name as Richard Laidlaw and asking that any mail addressed to me be held for pickup.

Step four: I wrote a letter to the Multnomah County office of vital statistics requesting a copy of "my" birth certificate and providing all the necessary names and dates. I signed the letter Richard James Laidlaw and gave the mail drop's address as my own. The vital stats office had no reason to cross-check the name against their death records and no legal reason at that time to turn down the request. I wasn't the first to use this method of obtaining a birth certificate in order to establish a false identity, of course. I got the idea from reading about a similar case in Detroit that had come to light the year before. The method was used often enough, in fact, for the regulations and requirements covering the issuance of copies of birth certificates to be eventually changed in most if not all states.

Step five: I bought a secondhand IBM typewriter, the kind that had a ball element and came with extra elements in different type faces. At night in my apartment, I manufactured half a dozen detailed invoices, one for each of the dummy companies, keying each to specific job sites that Amthor was currently operating in various parts of northern and central California and that were guaranteed by size to last more than a year. In two cases there was a distance of several hundred miles between the job sites and the bogus company addresses, but this was not unusual. Amthor hired its subcontractors on a bid basis and its suppliers on a price-break basis, and the costs of relocating workmen and equipment and of long-haul shipping were always factored in.

I kept the total amounts of these first six invoices relatively small; the highest was a little more than $9,000, from Darwin Electric. They were as much a test run as an opening gambit, to satisfy myself that the forgeries were good enough to pass through the comptroller's office without question. Not that I had any doubt of it. In the past I had rubber-stamped invoices in the high five figures, and the comptroller's office had paid them without question.

Step six: At the office I established new accounts in the names of the six dummy companies, then okayed the invoices and sent them along one or two at a time in the daily batches. In each case I noted that the company had requested payment by direct deposit.

A week went by without incident. No one in the comptroller's office asked to see me about any of the new accounts. The invoices were absorbed into the system as easily as any of the legitimate ones.

Notifications of deposit began to arrive from the banks until I had all six. I didn't withdraw any of the money. And wouldn't until much later in the game. I had enough cash in my personal savings account to take care of expenses such as the Portland trip.

Step seven: I created a second set of invoices along the lines of the first set, with larger total amounts—upwards of $10,000 on both the Darwin Electric account and the West Valley Construction account. After two weeks I sent a couple of the invoices through for payment, since it wasn't uncommon for some of the high-overhead independent contractors to bill on a twice-monthly basis; the other phony invoices went in on the monthly schedule. From then on, I increased the sums of some invoices incrementally, while decreasing others so as not to raise any red flags.

Three weeks after I sent the letter to the Multnomah County courthouse, I received the copy of the birth certificate. In a sense that would have horrified Annalise's religious aunt and sister, Richard James Laidlaw—like Jordan Wise—had been reborn.

Step eight: I took another day's sick leave and drove to Sacramento, where I applied for a Social Security card at the local office in the name of Richard James Laidlaw, using the birth certificate as proof of identity. If I'd been asked why a thirty-four-year-old man was applying for his first card, I had a story ready: I had inherited a large sum of money and now that it was almost depleted, I was forced to go job hunting. But the lie wasn't necessary. The bored clerk looked at the application just long enough to make sure I had filled it in properly.

After another three weeks, I had my second piece of new identification. That completed the first phase of the plan; all the factors in the linked equations were now in place and functioning as designed. Nothing more needed to be done until the following spring.

I spent only one more night at Annalise's apartment, shortly after that first night together. From then on, as far as anyone who knew either of us was concerned, we went our separate ways. It was vital that there be no apparent connection between us over the next year, no contact that could ever be traced. We had to appear to be two people who had dated casually for three months and then drifted apart, like thousands of others in the city. Two things made this easy: Our dates and our relationship *had* been casual before the plan. And neither of us had any family or close friends we confided in. Annalise had mentioned me to two women she knew at Kleinfelt's, but only in a general way; she was sure she hadn't told them my full name or where I worked. Even if she had, they were unlikely to remember it after a year's time. The only people I'd spoken to about her, Sanderson and a couple of others right after the wedding reception, weren't likely to remember either.

Of course, I couldn't stay away from her for long. She was a fire in my blood. And she proved to me, whenever we were together, that I had evolved substantially in her estimation. The nice, gentle, unexciting mouse had changed into a romantic figure, a man of mystery and danger. I did everything in my power to keep that image sharp. What she felt for me wasn't love, I didn't delude myself about that, but neither was it mere fondness any longer. I was convinced it would continue to grow and deepen, until one day, maybe, it would be love.

We developed a schedule that suited both of us. Once a week, I called her at her apartment, from a pay phone so the calls could never be traced to my home number. Twice a month, we spent a weekend together at a prearranged place well away from the city—the Monterey Peninsula, the Sierra foothills, the Mendocino coast. We decided on the location in advance, picked a motel or lodge from the Triple A guidebook; I made the reservations by pay phone in an assumed name; we drove there in separate cars. Motel registration cards require a car license number, but no clerk ever bothers to check whether the number you write down is the correct one. And of course I always paid cash for the room, meals, gas.

These weekends added spice to our relationship. Assignations, the secret meetings of conspirators. As soon as we were alone together we'd be at each other in bed—two, often three times before we did anything else. If I'd had any concerns that she was sleeping with the other men she was dating, her passion on those weekends would've knocked it right out of my head. She was mine and that made me want her even more. My sex drive matched hers; I was no longer insecure about my performance. Annalise had been sexually active since the age of sixteen and she was a gifted and patient teacher; she helped me evolve from a student into an innovative disciple.

When we weren't making love, or out playing tourist, we talked about the Plan. Plan with a capital P by then: it was the centerpiece of our lives. I kept her apprised of each step, but only in the most general way. "Everything is in place now," I would say, "and the money is starting to accumulate." And "The birth certificate came this week." And "I'm about to increase the amount of cash coming in each month." I reiterated that it was for her own protection—the less she knew, the better off she was if anything went wrong.

There was another reason, too. Each little morsel I passed on only whetted her appetite for more. Tantalized her, kept her in a constant state of suspense. It grew into a game, a kind of verbal foreplay. I dropped hints, she begged for more details; and when I refused, she offered to do this or that in bed in exchange for another tidbit of information. But I never gave in. There was no need. We were already doing most of what she offered as it was.

The one thing we did discuss in detail, and often, was where we would go to start our new life together. Annalise's first choice was

Paris, then New York, then the French Riviera or one of the Greek islands. None of those places appealed to me. New York was too expensive and the chance of recognition there too great. Paris and the French
Riviera were simply too expensive. More than half a million dollars
was a small fortune in those days, but you could go through it in a hell
of a hurry in overpriced cities or jet-set playgrounds. My objection to
a Greek island, to most locales where English was not the primary language and Americans not the primary inhabitants, was that U.S. expa-
triates with plenty of money and no visible means of support were
liable to stand out. The last thing we could afford to do was to attract
attention.

She was disappointed, but she understood. When I reminded her
that she could pursue her interest in fashion design from anywhere in
the world, we moved on to other choices. Bali was one, Tahiti another.
I liked those better, but they seemed too remote to Annalise. We both
dismissed Hawaii. Too close to San Francisco, too many mainland
tourists. And I still remembered how little I'd enjoyed the vacation trip
to Maui.

The Caribbean, the Virgin Islands had been my selection all along.
They had all the tropical lures of sun and sea and laid-back lifestyle,
they were a long way from California and drew relatively few visitors
from the West Coast, they'd been U.S. possessions since the 1917 purchase from Denmark, and they were inhabited by English-speaking
natives and a large percentage of American expats.

Annalise was dubious at first. "I don't know anything about the Virgin Islands," she said. "Aren't they pretty isolated?"

"Not at all. Close to Puerto Rico. Miami, too, for that matter."

"Virgins. Why are they called that?"

"Columbus named them Santa Ursula y las Once Mil Virgenes on
his second voyage to the Caribbean in 1493. In honor of Saint Ursula
and the Eleven Thousand Virgins, and because there are thousands of
islands in the region."

"Who were all those women?"

"A fourth-century British princess and her sisterhood of maidens. All allegedly raped and massacred in Cologne by marauding Huns."

"Lovely."

"The islands are, yes. Wait until you see the guidebooks."

The Virgins had two other draws for me. One I didn't confide to her because I was afraid it might worry her.

Mixed in with all the positives was an element of risk that held a perverse appeal. The crime of embezzlement as I'd planned mine would violate U.S. banking laws as well as California state laws, and was therefore a federal offense. I would be a federal fugitive; the FBI would come into the case along with state and insurance investigators. If the Plan went off as designed, I had little to fear from any of them. No matter how much manpower went into the investigation, they would have a hell of a time finding me. The perverse appeal lay in the fact that the American Virgins were U.S. federal territory, and that meant the FBI maintained a local branch office there. The prospect of being a federal fugitive living off stolen money in U.S. government territory made me smile every time I thought about it.

The other draw of the Virgin Islands for me I did tell Annalise about. "That part of the Caribbean offers some of the best sailing in the world," I said. "It's the reason a lot of people move there and vacation there."

"Sailing?" she said.

"I've always wanted to own a boat, learn how to sail."

"You never told me that before."

"Just a dream until now."

"Well, I don't know, Jordan—"

"Richard." I'd asked her to call me by that name on these weekend getaways. The sooner it became second nature to her, the less likely she would slip up later on.

"Yes, right—Richard. Somehow I just can't see you in a yachting cap at the wheel of a sailboat."

"Helm," I said.

"What?"

"At the helm of a sailboat. I *can* see myself there, maybe not in a yachting cap but on my own boat. A schooner, maybe even a ketch or yawl. All I have to do is close my eyes."

"Well, I don't much care for boats," she said. "The one time I went out on one, on the Bay, I got seasick."

"The Bay waters tend to be choppy. That's not usually the case in the Caribbean. There's a lot of shoal water down there."

"What's shoal water?"

"Shallow water. Calm and placid. Everybody's a good sailor in the Virgins, they say."

"I'll take your word for it. Personally I prefer dry land."

"You won't feel that way once we get there."

Later, on another of our weekend getaways, I bought her a Virgin Islands guidebook and a coffee-table book of photographs of the U.S. and British Virgins. Annalise's enthusiasm for the region increased when she read through them. Subtropical climate with temperatures that seldom varied from the average of 79 to 88 degrees in the summer and 72 to 82 degrees in the winter, and an annual rainfall of only 27 inches. Sun worshipper's paradise: white-sand beaches, coral reefs, deserted palm-fringed cays, placid waters in ever-changing shades of blue and green. Plus stately homes and old forts and ancient pirate strongholds. Nobody with an imagination and a yen for adventure and excitement could resist this part of the world.

The weekend after Thanksgiving, before the winter snows made driving through the Sierras difficult, we met in South Lake Tahoe and then went down to Carson City together and applied for a marriage license. Annalise Bonner and Richard James Laidlaw were married that afternoon by a justice of the peace.

We had a champagne wedding supper at the Ormsby House, then drove back to South Lake Tahoe and bought another bottle and consummated the union. Afterward we lay in bed and drank champagne and toasted the future.

"How do you like being married?" I asked her.

"So far, it's terrific," she said. "But my God—Annalise Bonner Laidlaw. It doesn't roll trippingly off the tongue, does it?"

"I like it," I said. "It has class. An East Coast, old-money, finishing-school kind of name."

"You think so?"

"Absolutely. Mine's not bad either."

"Well . . . maybe."

I smiled. "Laidlaw is perfect, in fact. I couldn't have found a better surname."

"How do you figure that?"

"Exactly what we're doing, isn't it? Laying the law?"

She burst out laughing. So did I. We laughed so hard she got the hiccups and spilled champagne on my belly. She leaned down and began to lick it off, laughing and hiccuping the whole time, and that led to a second round of lovemaking—"laying each other like we're laying the law," she said, which started us giggling and her hiccuping again right in the middle of it.

I think that weekend may have been our happiest time together. I know it was for me.

We spent Christmas together at a small out-of-the-way inn on the Mendocino coast. I gave her a $300 pair of gold earrings, heart-shaped, with pendants of amethyst—her birthstone. Her presents to me were a yachting cap, not the fancy commodore type with gold braid but a functional Gill sailing hat, and books on sailing for beginners and on cruising the Virgin Islands and Lesser Antilles.

51

New Year's Eve we spent apart, by mutual agreement, to maintain the pretense that we were actively dating others. She accepted an invitation to a party from one of the men she'd been seeing. As for me, there was a plain, friendly secretary in Amthor's design department, whose smiles in my direction I'd interpreted as wistful little signals that she was interested and available. I seem to remember that her name was Joan, but it could have been Jane or Jean. I'd been invited to a party by the newly married Jim Sanderson, and in turn I invited the secretary. We danced, drank champagne, kissed and sang "Auld Lang Syne" to ring in the new year. And every time I looked at her I saw Annalise, only Annalise.

I dated Joan or Jane or Jean four more times over a period of seven weeks. On the last of these she made it plain that I was welcome to stay the night at her apartment, but I couldn't have had sex with her if my life depended on it. I tried to let her down easy—she was a nice person and pleasant enough company—and she took the rejection well enough, but I could tell that she was hurt by it. Alone in the world, hungry for affection . . . a female version of the old Jordan Wise. That Jordan Wise might have learned to care for Joan or Jane or Jean, allowed a relationship to develop. Not the reborn version. Not the faithful and committed married man, Richard Laidlaw.

Establishing a new identity requires more than just paperwork and the altering of a few physical characteristics. You can't simply pretend to be somebody new and different. You have to shed your old personality in layers, the way some snakes shed their skin. Learn how to wear your new one. Change the way you think as well as the way you walk, talk, act in public.

Jordan Wise was an accountant with simple tastes; quiet, passive, uncomfortable in large groups. Richard Laidlaw was a successful executive with expensive tastes, self-confident, aggressive when the need arose, at ease in social situations. Polar opposites in attitude, expectation, mind-set. The first thing I had to learn was how to switch back and forth seamlessly; then, when the time came, I would be able to shed Jordan Wise once and for all. That meant practice, and plenty of it.

Alone at home I worked on a more erect posture, on demonstrative hand gestures, on holding my head at an angle that gave a forward jut to my jawline, on deepening my voice and speaking in terse sentences sprinkled with mild to moderate profanity. The first couple of times I tried out the package on Annalise, she made suggestions for improvement that I incorporated into the Laidlaw personality. Whenever we were together after that, I remained in character until we parted—like an actor perfecting the most challenging role of his life. Now and then she would catch me in an inconsistency. Alone, I worked on correcting it until I was sure it would never crop up again.

None of this was easy, but by the first of March, when the time came to put the second phase of the Plan into operation, I was no longer acting the role of Richard Laidlaw, I *was* Richard Laidlaw.

On a Saturday morning I drove out to Walnut Creek, looked up optometrists in the telephone directory, found one that was open, and called ahead for an appointment, using an assumed name. When I got there I had myself fitted for a pair of inexpensive contact lenses that matched the prescription for my glasses. I asked for the tinted kind, brown. The optometrist commented that I was the first blue-eyed person he'd ever known who wanted brown-tinted contacts. I told him my wife was always needling me, saying she didn't know why she'd married me because she preferred brown-eyed men, so I'd decided to give her a surprise and see what happened. He laughed and dropped the subject. All he really cared about was making the sale. And a cash sale, at that.

At a costume shop in Oakland on the way back, I bought a dark brown theatrical mustache, the can't-tell-it-from-the-real-thing kind that attaches with spirit gum. Not too large or bushy, but thick enough to cover my rather broad upper lip.

It was necessary for Annalise to be in on the rest of phase two. I requested and was given three days off from work, citing personal reasons; she made a similar arrangement with Kleinfelt's. I withdrew $2,000 in cash from the Darwin Electric account and $1,000 in cash from each of the other five dummy accounts. I gave her $2,500, to pay for a round-trip airline ticket to Chicago and to cover a $2,000 cashier's check made out to R. J. Laidlaw, which she obtained at her bank. I also paid cash for my round-trip ticket to Chicago on a different airline.

We flew back there on a Sunday afternoon. I'd picked Chicago for two reasons: it was the largest city in the Midwest, and there were daily flights from O'Hare to Puerto Rico and other Caribbean islands. Mr. and Mrs. Richard Laidlaw were booked into one of the larger, older hotels off the Loop. I took a taxi there as soon as we landed. Annalise rented the car we would need, using her real name and California license—a negligible risk for her.

She had a surprise for me at the hotel. She'd had her hair restyled, the long feathery Farrah Fawcett look replaced by a close-cropped shag cut that changed the shape of her face, gave it a gamine quality.

"Why?" I asked her. "It wasn't necessary."

"I know," she said, "but you're going to change your appearance and I thought I'd do the same. A new look for our new life together. Don't worry, I had it done in Marin County and I bought a wig to match the old style. Nobody in San Francisco will know."

"I'm not worried. Just a little . . . overwhelmed."

"You don't like it," she said, sounding hurt.

"No, no, it's not that. I need to get used to it, that's all."

"Well, I think it's sexy. You can pretend you're making love to a hot new babe tonight."

"I don't want a hot new babe. All I want is you."

We sent down for copies of the local Sunday papers, combed through the ads for mail receiving and forwarding services similar to the one I used in San Francisco, and made a list of half a dozen candidates. From the phone directory, we copied down the addresses of a downtown branch of the Mutual Trust Bank, the U.S. Passport Office, and the nearest office of the department of motor vehicles.

In the morning, first thing, we performed the physical change of Jordan Wise into Richard Laidlaw. She'd brought a bottle of dark brown rinse that would alter hair color but could be easily washed out. I used the rinse, put on the brown-tinted contact lenses and the dark-brown theatrical mustache. Annalise completed the transformation by using a blow dryer and brush to restyle my hair, erasing my usual part and making it appear fuller.

When she was done, we stood side by side in front of the mirror. "It's really amazing," she said, "how much different you look."

"The best disguises are the simple ones. Subtle differences, nothing elaborate."

"I like the new you. You know, now that I see us together like this, I think the Laidlaws are even better looking than Bonner and Wise."

"No question in my case," I said.

The second mail-drop place we went to was just right. Street address rather than a box number, no questions asked, mail to be held on the premises indefinitely until picked up in person by either Mr. or Mrs. Laidlaw. From there we went to the Mutual Trust branch, where we opened a joint checking account with the $2,000 cashier's check, giving the local mail-drop address as our own. We also rented a safe deposit box, into which I put the remaining cash I'd brought along.

Next stop: a photographer's studio near the federal building that specialized in passport photos. We took ours to the passport office, where Richard J. Laidlaw and Annalise Laidlaw applied for passports. They were the first passports for each of us under any name, which simplified the process. Birth certificates were the only form of identification required. Again, we gave the local mail-drop address as our current U.S. mailing address.

That used up all of Monday. Most of Tuesday we spent at the DMV filling out applications for Illinois driver's licenses, having our pictures taken, taking written tests and then behind-the-wheel tests with different examiners. When we left the office, it was with interim licenses in hand.

May.

One of our get-togethers that month was a trip to Las Vegas. Annalise had never been there and wanted to go, and I saw no reason not to oblige her. It would be our only opportunity; once I became a fugitive, I had no intention of ever going within two thousand miles of San Francisco. We were spending a fair amount of money on necessities and incidentals, and we would spend a lot more before the end of September, but I'd factored that into the equation. I could always spread another $10,000 among the final six dummy invoices to cover increased expenditures. Besides, the whole point of the Plan was to live well, travel, see new sights, so why deprive ourselves during the setup year?

We stayed in a motel off the Strip, registering as the Laidlaws and appearing in public in our Laidlaw personas. We ate in four-star restaurants; we saw a musical revue at one of the casinos and Dean Martin at Caesars Palace. Neither of us was much of a gambler, but Annalise played the slot machines and keno and I risked a few bets at the $5 blackjack tables. I won $45 and she had the thrill of hitting a $100 keno ticket.

Good omen. After the Vegas trip, I knew that the Plan was going to work exactly as designed.

Late June.

I'd put in for my annual vacation time well in advance, to ensure that I had the last two weeks of the month. On my first day off I made the rounds of the banks containing the dummy accounts and withdrew $2,000 from each. By then, there was an aggregate of more than $400,000 spread among the six. The next day I drove to the airport and bought a round-trip ticket to Chicago, a trip I was making alone this time. I carried some of the cash in my wallet, some in an envelope in my briefcase; the balance was in a hidden compartment of my checked suitcase. I didn't much like traveling with that much cash or entrusting any of it to TWA's baggage handlers, but it was necessary and there were no problems.

I stayed at the same downtown hotel, transformed myself into Richard Laidlaw the following morning, and was waiting at the Mutual Trust branch when it opened. I deposited $2,000 in the joint checking account and put the rest of the cash in the safe deposit box. From the bank I took a cab to the mail drop. Both passports and both Illinois driver's licenses were waiting.

Another cab delivered me to a downtown travel agency I'd picked out of the phone directory. I booked a round-trip Pan Am flight to Georgetown, Grand Cayman, via San Juan, leaving O'Hare on Sunday morning and returning on Tuesday; I also booked accommodations for two nights at a hotel in Georgetown. I was able to reserve a seat on a Chicago to San Francisco flight Tuesday night, with only a four-hour airport layover. All of this I paid for by check drawn on the Laidlaws' joint account; the price was too steep to fund in cash without the risk of arousing suspicion. The travel agent assured me my tickets would be ready as soon the check cleared, no later than Friday afternoon.

Within walking distance was a car rental agency, where I used Richard Laidlaw's new driver's license to rent a compact for the rest of the week. At the hotel after my arrival I'd combed through the apartments-to-lease ads in the local papers, making a list of several in the metropolitan area. I began canvassing them that afternoon and evening.

I expected the process to take two or three days, possibly longer, but I found what I was looking for on the morning of the second day: a furnished, vacant, one-bedroom apartment in a nondescript building in a lower middle-class South Side neighborhood for $600 a month; and a landlord who was willing to settle for a six-month lease. I gave him a check to cover the first and last months' rent plus a $200 cleaning deposit. He had no objection to letting me have the keys early, "soon as your check clears," or to my arranging for a telephone to be installed right away. I told him my wife and I were moving to Chicago because I had a new job there, and that she would be moving in first while I finished up my old job in Minneapolis. He didn't seem to care; he wasn't the nosy type.

The rest of the week I dealt with the phone company and played tourist. On Friday afternoon, just before closing time, I returned to the Mutual Trust branch and removed $5,000 from the safe deposit box—a sum that didn't exceed the maximum amount of cash that could be brought into the Cayman Islands by a nonresident.

The flights to Puerto Rico and then to Grand Cayman were uneventful. Richard Laidlaw's new passport passed inspection and I went through customs without incident. As soon as I could on Monday, I went to one of the larger banks and, with half of the $5,000, opened an account under the Laidlaw name. At a different bank, I used the other half to open a second account in the name of Wise Investments, Inc., Richard James Laidlaw of Chicago, Illinois, U.S.A., sole proprietor, and arranged for all monies that came in to that account to be immediately transferred to the first one. My passport was the only identification required.

The two separate accounts guaranteed untraceability. Bank accounts in the Caymans are sealed, just like those in Swiss banks, a fact that in those days wasn't as well known as it is today. Not even government agencies like the FBI and the IRS can gain access to personal information related to them. Monies held in Caymans banks are also free of corporation and other taxes and are not subject to exchange controls, which allows free transfer of funds in and out of the islands. Richard Laidlaw would have no U.S. tax liability on the sums he moved from the Caymans to his bank on St. Thomas, because that money was already his; he would be simply transferring assets.

The rest of my time on Grand Cayman I soaked up the heat and local attractions, and the blue-water vistas from my hotel balcony—an invigorating foretaste of what was to come. The tropical sun and humidity didn't bother me. From that brief exposure, I knew I would thrive on them.

I still had two vacation days left when I got back to San Francisco. I spent these making the rounds of the six banks and arranging for wire transfers of half the funds in each dummy to the new Wise Investments account in the Caymans. Only one of the bank officers commented on the procedure, but his main concern was the loss of business to his bank, not the transfer itself. The completed transactions fattened the Wise account to more than $250,000.

That weekend I saw Annalise, gave her a report on the Chicago portion of the trip, and handed over her passport and Illinois license and the keys to the South Side apartment. For her protection, I didn't tell her about the trip to Grand Cayman or the new accounts.

July.

Annalise gave notice at Kleinfelt's, saying that she was moving to Seattle at the end of the month to get married. Her apartment was rented on a month-to-month basis, so there was no lease to break; she gave notice there as well. Over that month, she disposed of nearly all her personal belongings, either selling them to acquaintances or giving them away to Goodwill. She kept only the clothing and personal items she could fit into two large suitcases and one small carry-on bag. She held on to her car until the thirtieth, then sold it for the Blue Book price to a Van Ness Avenue dealership. On the thirty-first, she rode a cab to the airport and bought a one-way ticket to Chicago, as before paying in cash and using an assumed name.

The previous weekend was our last together during the preliminary stages. We met at a small hotel on the Monterey coast and wallowed in bed most of the two days. She was nervous and excited about the move, and this translated into tremendous sexual energy. I was worn out by the time we were ready to leave.

"I'm going to miss you so much," she said. "Two and a half months seems like an eternity."

"They'll go by faster than you think. We'll talk on the phone at least once a week."

"I can't make love to the phone."

"Well, you could, but it would probably be painful."

She laughed and nipped my neck. "Messy, too."

I said, "I'll be thinking of you all the time."

"Same here."

"And of how'll it be for us on St. Thomas."

"And of all that lovely money."

August.

I called Annalise from a pay phone the day after she flew to Chicago, to make sure she'd arrived safely and gotten settled into the apartment. She didn't like the place. Statement of fact, not a complaint. There wasn't much about it for anybody to like. I'd explained why I picked it and why it was important for her to establish residence in Chicago well in advance of October 1. She'd be bored and antsy back there alone, but she'd manage all right.

I increased the amounts on each of that month's dummy invoices, to bring the aggregate close to $500,000. The last set, to be put through the following month, would push it well over the half-million-dollar mark, to a final total of $600,000. My motive now wasn't greed so much as added security. The more we had, the more I could invest for the future, and the better our new life would be.

Later in the month, I made a careful inspection of my belongings, to be certain I left nothing behind that might help the authorities. There were no recent snapshots or posed photographs of me—no one to take any, no reason for the taking. I did find an envelope of old, mostly black-and-white photos my parents had taken. I'd forgotten I had them, wasn't sure why I'd bothered to save them; I had no sentimental attachment to my family or my past. The photos of me were infant and childhood images, mostly. Three had been snapped in my mid-teens; they showed a four-eyed kid I barely recognized or remembered. Shuffling through them had a depressing effect. I tossed the lot into the trash.

I had also saved my high school senior yearbook. My graduation photo was a fair likeness, but in those days I'd worn nerdy horn-rimmed glasses and my hair was in a stiff butch cut that made my ears look larger than they were. Nearly all of the senior-class pix had multiple caption lines; mine had only two. "Activities: Math club. Ambition: To do something important someday."

I laughed long and hard when I read the second line. Oh, Jordan, you teenage schmuck, if you'd only known! I ripped that page out and tore it into little pieces and flushed the pieces down the toilet. The rest of the yearbook went into the trash with the old photos. Investigators would be able to track down another copy, but why make it easy for them?

The only other picture of me in existence was my driver's license photo, four years old. A copy would be on file with the DMV, but it was another fair-only likeness. Average height, average weight, average build, no distinguishing marks or characteristics other than the blue eyes and glasses. Mr. Average. Richard Laidlaw was somebody, Jordan Wise could be anybody.

One other group of items needed to be disposed of. I boxed up the books on the Virgin Islands and my small collection of sailing and seafaring adventure books, and took them around to a trio of secondhand shops, where I traded them for a variety of nondescript fiction and nonfiction hardcovers and paperbacks. These I took back to the apartment and set out on the shelves.

In a new bookstore I bought a history of Mexico and a travel guide to Mexico City. I cracked their spines and thumb-marked and creased some of the pages to make them appear well-read, then tucked them in among the other books. That was the first step in the final phase of the Plan—the laying of a false trail that would lead nowhere.

September.

The closer it got to the end of the month, the more relaxed I became. No trouble sleeping, no worries, not a single tense moment. There is something about overseeing a daring and dangerous scheme like mine, watching all the disparate factors mesh perfectly, that gives you a godlike feeling of power and invincibility. Outwardly I was the same quiet, nondescript individual I'd always been, a small man going about his daily routine among larger men. Inwardly I stood apart from them, towered above them, like a minor deity observing the actions of mere mortals with an amused, winking, sometimes gloating eye.

Annalise grew more and more anxious as time passed. I had to call her two and then three times a week to reassure her, keep her calm and focused. It wasn't that she was losing her nerve; it was the enforced waiting, alone in that shabby apartment in a strange city, imagining all sorts of disaster scenarios in spite of her better judgment. She would be fine when the time came for her part in the final phase, a role that was absolutely vital.

I created, okayed, and passed on the final set of invoices, the last of them on the fifteenth, to ensure payment before the end of the month. As soon as I received notification of deposit from all six banks, I went around to each and closed the account, requesting wire transfers of the funds to the Wise Investments account in the Caymans. To forestall questions and suspicions, and to add an element of confusion for the

FBI and insurance investigators, I gave each bank officer a different explanation for the closure and transfer: I was retiring, I was selling the business and buying another, I was moving to New York, Florida, Cozumel, Grand Cayman.

The total score, including the few hundred dollars I had left in my own savings and checking accounts, was $602,496.

I made my last call to Annalise in Chicago on Wednesday, the twenty-seventh. She said, sounding a little breathless, "I leave for Phoenix at noon tomorrow. The woman at the airline said there are plenty of seats, but I made a reservation anyway. Just to be sure."

"Good."

"Did you make yours in San Diego?"

"All taken care of. The name of the motel is—?"

"Greenbriar."

"Phone number?"

She recited it from memory.

"The name I'll be using?"

"Philip Smith."

"Name and address of the garage?"

"Mainline Parking, 1490 Alvarado."

"Details of your route?"

"All memorized. I'll take the maps along, but I don't think I'll need to look at them again."

"Time to call me?"

"Six o'clock Saturday night."

"Sooner if you're ready early," I said. "I'll make sure to be in the room from five o'clock on."

"God, Richard, it's almost over, isn't it?" She had been calling me Richard for months by then, without a slip; Jordan Wise had already ceased to exist for her. "Almost over!"

"This phase. There's still one more."

"I know, but it won't be bad once you're here. I miss you like crazy."

I said I missed her the same way, and we told each to be careful driving. Just before she hung up she said, "Richard, I want you to know . . ." and there was a pause, and then for the first time she said, "I love you."

I held those three words close the rest of the day, took them to bed with me that night.

Friday, September 30.

Jordan Wise went to Amthor Associates for the last time, sat at his desk in Accounting for the last time, finished preparing for the annual October audit for the last time. He went to lunch with Jim Sanderson, exchanged the usual tired complaints with him and the other drudges. And throughout the long, busy day, he stood apart and looked down at them from his superior height and smiled at their dull normalcy and winked at their foolish weekend plans and gloated at the thought of their reactions when they found out what he had done.

At five o'clock he said good-bye to them for the last time, rode the elevator down to the lobby, walked to the parking garage where he had left his car with his one suitcase and one briefcase already locked in the trunk, drove out into the Friday-evening-commute traffic.

And disappeared.

SAN DIEGO AND CHICAGO

1978

R ICHARD LAIDLAW DROVE STRAIGHT through to Santa Barbara, with brief stops for gas and a coffee-shop sandwich. Good-bye, Jordan Wise.

There was no hurry, but no reason to dawdle, either. The Plan called for me to be in and out of San Diego no later than Sunday morning. That would leave me another three days, of what I figured to be a five-day grace period, to put two thousand miles between me and California. My failure to show up or call in would not raise any alarm bells at Amthor on Monday or Tuesday, and the auditors weren't likely to catch on to the fraud, or the company executives to notify the authorities, until sometime Wednesday at the earliest. That meant late Wednesday or Thursday before a fugitive warrant was issued and the story broke in the media.

An exhilarating feeling of freedom rode with me that night. I was completely relaxed; driving seemed effortless, the usual Friday-evening traffic snarls a source of amusement rather than irritation. All my senses were heightened: colors and the light-shot darkness intensely vivid, night smells crisp, the classical music on the radio as tonally clear and stirring as if I were sitting close to the orchestra during a live performance.

It was after ten when I stopped at a motel on the southern edge of Santa Barbara. At eight A.M. Saturday, I was back on the highway. Traffic through the San Fernando Valley and LA was relatively light and I made good time. I stopped only once, for gas in Orange County, and rolled into San Diego shortly past noon. I had lunch in Old Town, drove around for a while to kill time, and checked into the Greenbriar Motel as Philip Smith at three thirty.

Annalise called fifteen minutes early, at a quarter to six. She sounded relieved when I answered promptly. "Everything went all right, then?"

"Just as I drew it up."

"I knew it would, but you can't help worrying a little."

I smiled at that. "No, you can't."

"I should've left Phoenix a little earlier than I did," she said. "Desert driving really wears you out."

"What time did you get in?"

"After three."

"You're at the airport motel now?"

"Straight from the garage."

"But you're not calling from your room?"

"Come on, Richard, you know I wouldn't make a mistake like that. I'm in a pay phone in the main terminal lounge. I took the motel shuttle over here."

"What kind of car did you buy?"

"Nineteen seventy-three Mercury Cougar. Blue and white. I had to pay a little more than we planned—almost thirteen hundred dollars. I could've bought something cheaper from one of the smaller lots, but you said there was less risk of getting a lemon from a large dealership."

"The price doesn't matter," I said. "The important thing is that it's reliable."

"Well, so far. Good gas mileage, too."

"Parked where in the garage?"

"Second floor, space number two fifty-six. The keys are in a magnetic holder under the right front fender, the registration's locked in the glove compartment, the parking ticket is on the dash. And there's a full tank of gas. I filled up just before I parked."

"That should do it, then. You're booked on the nine o'clock flight to Chicago?"

"I've already picked up my ticket. Richard?"

"Yes, baby?"

"I hate being this close and not seeing you. I want you so much."

I wanted her, too. But my hunger was not as great as hers after the long separation, not at this point. It was still a long way to Chicago, and there was plenty to do before I got there. First things first. We'd be together soon enough, and I said as much.

"I know we will," she said, "but that doesn't make it any easier *now*. Get to Chicago as quickly as you can, okay? Take a more direct route."

I said, "I will," but I knew I wouldn't. Every factor to that point had been carried out with perfect precision. There was no compelling reason to change any of the remaining moves. If I did that, I might be inviting bad luck.

Before nine A.M. on Sunday I packed my suitcase, leaving out the theatrical mustache and spirit gum and the bottle of dark-brown hair dye I'd bought in San Francisco. The suitcase went onto the backseat of my car. I put out the "Do Not Disturb" sign and locked the door to Philip Smith's room, keeping the key. Then I drove the short five blocks to the Mainline Parking Garage.

This early, the second floor had no sign of life and was mostly empty of parked cars. I pulled into the space next to the one marked 256. The Mercury Cougar had a coating of dust, but was otherwise nondescript and in good condition for its age. The tires had plenty of tread, I noticed as I went around to the front and collected the keys. I opened the trunk, transferred my suitcase inside, locked it again, and then drove my car down to the first-floor exit. The sleepy attendant took my money without even glancing at me.

From the garage I headed to the airport, which in San Diego fronts on the bay and is virtually downtown; flights in and out pass over and between some of the taller skyscrapers. I left the car in long-term parking, locked but with the keys on the floor inside and empty of anything I didn't want found in it. A shuttle bus took me to the main terminal, where I boarded another bus that brought me back into the city center. By then I was hungry; I took the time to eat breakfast in a café on Broadway. It was a short walk from there to the Greenbriar Motel.

In Philip Smith's room, I washed and dyed my hair, dried it, combed it. Put on the mustache and the tinted contact lenses. Tucked the bottles of dye and spirit gum into my jacket pocket. Left the room key on the dresser; I'd paid cash in advance, so there was no need to go through the usual checkout ritual. The courtyard was deserted when I stepped out of the room. I walked the five blocks to Mainline Parking. When I drove the Mercury down, the attendant in the exit booth paid no more attention to me than he had earlier.

Like Annalise, I had memorized all the necessary street and freeway routes. Even after twenty-seven years, I could tell you my course out of the city with reasonable accuracy. It was a few minutes past noon when I turned off Highway 8 onto Highway 15, heading north—right on schedule.

The long drive from San Diego to Chicago was one of the y factors in the equation. The unexpected is always a possibility during a two-thousand-mile cross-country driving trip. A chance accident. Some sort of mechanical problem with the car that couldn't be fixed. Annalise had bought the Mercury from a reputable dealer, it had performed for her on the desert drive from Phoenix, and it seemed to handle well enough for me as I wheeled north through Escondido and Riverside. But it had 67,000 miles on the odometer and there was no way of knowing whether the engine and transmission had been mistreated by a previous owner or whether it would hold up for the duration.

All I could do was take normal precautions and trust my judgment and my instincts. Which meant driving carefully and defensively, keeping to a sedate twenty-five on city streets, never exceeding the posted freeway speed limits, observing all traffic laws to a fault. And I checked oil and water levels and tire pressure every time I pulled into a service station to refill the gas tank.

That first day I followed Highway 15 on its eastern loop through Barstow and across the Mojave Desert into Nevada. It was late afternoon when I reached Las Vegas. I wasn't tired and the car continued to run smoothly; I could have kept on going all the way through Nevada, maybe even across the southwestern corner of Arizona into Utah. Instead, I stopped at a motel on the eastern outskirts of Vegas, and had dinner before putting through a collect call to Annalise from a pay phone to make sure she'd gotten back all right and to let her know where I was.

The run to Chicago took four more days. I could have made it in three if I'd pushed it, but the Plan called for four. Too many hours behind the wheel invites mistakes in judgment.

Monday: across Nevada and the northwestern corner of Arizona, then up the middle of Utah to Salt Lake City and Highway 80. I found a bookstore in a shopping center near my motel and bought a new, comprehensive Virgin Islands guidebook and another book on Caribbean cruising, to replace the ones I'd had to give up. Appetite-whetters, and far more enjoyable nighttime diversions than anything television had to offer.

Tuesday: straight across Wyoming and southern Nebraska. In a motel coffee shop outside North Platte, the young waitress and the middle-aged cashier both smiled at me—genuine smiles, not the meaningless lip-stretch variety most women give male strangers. Jordan Wise had been insubstantial, as transparent as a jellyfish; women of all ages looked right through him, never saw him at all. Richard Laidlaw was solid, with the kind of self-assured swagger that comes from a strong nature. Women saw him, all right, and felt his power, and responded accordingly.

Wednesday: northeast to Omaha, through Iowa to Des Moines. The Merc was still running smoothly, the time spent on highways and city streets uneventful.

Thursday: Chicago.

It was late afternoon when I reached the city, almost five by the time I got to the South Side apartment. I'd called Annalise the night before, with an approximate arrival time; she was waiting for me with champagne on ice and candles burning and her fine body naked under a terrycloth robe. Thirty seconds after I walked in, the robe was off and she had my fly unzipped and my cock in her hand.

The story had broken in the media that morning. Annalise had scouted a newsdealer not far from the apartment that sold out-of-town newspapers, and all week she'd kept an eye on the Chicago papers and on both San Francisco rags, the morning *Chronicle* and the afternoon *Examiner.* The crime hadn't made much of a splash in the Midwest; the *Tribune* carried a brief account on an inside page. In the *Chronicle,* of course, it was front-page news. We lay in bed, sipping champagne as I read the account.

Boldface headline: HUGE AMTHOR EMBEZZLEMENT. Smaller sub-head: "Accountant Vanishes with Six-Figure Sum." Jordan Wise's driver's license photo hadn't been released yet, just his Everyman description. The auditors had discovered the theft on Wednesday, confirmed the scope of it by late afternoon, and were still working to assess the total amount of the loss. Both the local authorities and the FBI had been called in and a fugitive warrant had been issued. Amthor officials were shocked, stunned. A vice president was quoted as saying, "There is no way we could have anticipated anything like this. In the ten years Wise worked for Amthor, he had a spotless record."

Annalise clung to me, her eyes as bright and hot as the candle flames. "It says the theft might run upwards of three hundred thousand."

"Early estimate. It'll take them a while to come up with the full amount."

"How much is it, exactly?"

"Six hundred and two thousand, four hundred and ninety-six dollars."

"My God!" She jabbed her finger at the boldface headline. "You did it, Richard, you did it!"

"We did it," I said.

"No, all I did was what you told me to. The Plan was yours. You made us rich!"

"Did you ever doubt I would?"

"Never. Sometimes I wished the time would go by faster, but that's all. I thought the year would never end."

"You won't have to wait much longer."

"Six more weeks," Annalise said. "And six hundred thousand dollars. Just thinking about all that money gives me chills." She wasn't exaggerating. Her arms were covered with goosebumps. "Tell me the details. You said you would."

"Right now?"

"I'm dying to know. Everything. Don't leave anything out."

I explained each of the factors that I'd kept from her. She pouted a little when I told her about the two Cayman accounts.

"You didn't put my name on them? Why not?"

"Same reason I withheld the details. For your protection in case anything goes wrong."

"But we can add it now, can't we? After we get to St. Thomas?"

"There's no reason to," I said. "We'll have a joint bank account and

73

I'll arrange for regular transfers of funds—more than enough to cover anything we'll want or need."

"Well . . ."

"Just let me handle the financial end. You reap the rewards. And keep making me happy in and out of bed."

"Oh, I'll do that, all right," she promised. She reached down for me again. "You'll be the happiest man in the entire Caribbean."

The crime remained front-page news in the San Francisco papers for two more days. I can still quote those headlines verbatim too: AMTHOR THEFT TOPS HALF-MILLION MARK. WISE MANHUNT INTENSIFIES. The *Chronicle* carried the driver's license photo on Friday, the evening *Examiner* in their Saturday edition. Annalise laughed when she brought the *Chronicle* and pointed out the photo. "That doesn't look anything like Jordan," she said, "much less Richard." She was right. The newsprint reproduction was grainy, the oh-so-average features made even more indistinguishable. I barely recognized the face myself.

Grudging superlatives littered the articles. Bold. Daring. Ingenious. Brilliant. And my favorite: audacious. Each was like a sip of strong wine. So were the quotes from law enforcement officials and Amthor executives and employees. "Pursuing several strong leads to Wise's whereabouts." "Won't rest until he's apprehended." "Prosecute him to the fullest extent of the law." One, by Jim Sanderson, made me laugh out loud: "I worked with Jordan for nearly ten years. He was such a quiet, unassuming guy. I still can't believe he had the nerve to do something like this."

News stories the next two days, mainly rehashes, ran on inside pages. Then Jordan Wise was back on the front page again, down toward the bottom with a smaller headline: "Embezzler's Car Found." FBI officials, the account said, were working to trace Wise's activities after his car was found abandoned at San Diego International Airport. Speculation

74

as to his present whereabouts ran along the false trail I'd laid: he had either taken a flight under an assumed name or used some other means of transportation to leave the area, with Mexico his most likely destination.

That was the last of the front-page stories. Inside pages off and on again for a time—"No New Leads in Wise Case"—and then, less than two weeks after the story broke, nothing at all. The FBI doesn't advertise its frustrations; neither do other law enforcement agencies. And there are too many new crimes, too many world crises and natural disasters, too much political chicanery for one man's white-collar crime, even one that has netted him $600,000, to feed the public's hunger for sensationalism for long.

We were home free.

During the first week I stayed put inside the apartment, reading, listening to music, while Annalise ran all the errands. A precaution, mainly. The local papers had also run the driver's license photo, on inside pages, and though there was no reason for anyone in Chicago to think Jordan Wise might be in their midst, it was safer not to be seen in public just yet. The other reason I stayed in was that I was growing a mustache to match the shape and thickness of the theatrical one. After seven days it had filled out enough to look right when colored with the dark-brown hair dye.

My first day out I went to the Mutual Trust branch and arranged for the transfer of $17,000 from the Caymans account to our joint checking account. After that I began going out with Annalise at night, twice that second week, to dinner in dimly lighted restaurants and then to a neighborhood movie theater. If anyone paid attention to us, it was only admiring male looks aimed at her. Alongside Annalise, I was virtually invisible.

Living with her in the close confines of the apartment was a spartan dry run for our life together on St. Thomas. We hadn't spent more than three consecutive days together at any point during the previous year, and those weekend getaways had been all fun and games. It took us a while to get used to being with each other on a daily basis.

Everyone has habits that amuse or irritate others, little idiosyncrasies that don't crop up in casual circumstances. I'd known that she was something of a neatness freak, but not that she was compulsive about it. She was constantly straightening, arranging, picking up, and she chastised me every time I left a glass or dish unwashed or an article of clothing lying around. She drank a little too much, Scotch as well as wine; kept prodding me to get high with her, turned pouty when I didn't and playful to the point of silliness when I did. She was easily bored, used sex to ward off boredom and restlessness, had a tendency to become sullen when she didn't get her way. On the plus side, she was easy to talk to, knowledgeable about more subjects than I'd imagined and filled with an endearing, almost childlike enthusiasm whenever she talked about the Caribbean or showed off one of her new dress designs. At times, in spite of myself, I felt toward her as I'd felt toward Jim Sanderson and the other Amthor employees—as if she were a mortal and I was a higher power, benign and tolerant in my love for her, but superior nonetheless.

The longer I stayed cooped up in that confined space and that downscale neighborhood, the more sympathy I had for Annalise. Three weeks was bad enough; three months must have been torturous. Cabin fever breeds friction, and when we began to get on each other's nerves, snap at each other for no good reason, I got us out of there. It was almost the end of October. There was no need to delay rejoining society on a regular basis.

Over the next three weeks we took day trips in and around Chicago—to museums, the Adler Planetarium, Jackson Park, Monroe Harbor, the wealthy suburbs of Lake Forest and Evanston. We made overnight trips to Milwaukee and the sand dunes region along Lake Michigan. We went to movies, plays, the Chicago Symphony at Orchestra Hall. We shopped at Marshall Field's and a couple of the

76

exclusive women's shops on Michigan Avenue, so Annalise could buy outfits appropriate for the tropics. On November 15, we saw a travel agent and booked her flight to St. Thomas and hotel accommodations in Charlotte Amalie, and my flight to join her a month later. We were two people among millions, faceless, unnoticed, safe and secure enough, yet buoyed by the ever-present danger of recognition. It was that note of danger, as much as escape from the apartment, that put us back on the same close-knit plane as before. The friction disappeared. So did my feeling of superiority.

As the day of her leaving approached, she was like a kid in her excitement. She talked nonstop, making plans, discussing the kind of home we should have and where it should be located and what amenities it should have. I wanted her to pick it out, make all the preliminary arrangements—that was part of the reason for her moving to St. Thomas a month ahead of me. I kept telling her I'd be happy anywhere she was happy, and I meant it. Living space and all its trappings mattered more to her than they did to me.

Two days before her flight, we took the Mercury to a South Side dealership and sold it for $800 cash. Another $1,500 to cover her immediate expenses in St. Thomas came out of our joint safe deposit box. Our last night together we made love three times, and in the morning I rode the taxi with her to O'Hare to see her off.

She called the following night at a prearranged time, full of news and glowing praise. She'd opened a bank account, her first order of business, and she already had an appointment with a real estate agent to look at houses for lease. She loved the island, the weather, everything about the Caribbean. "You were right, Richard," she said. "We're going to be so happy here."

The next morning I went to the Mutual Trust branch and had $15,000 wired to our new account in Charlotte Amalie. Then I called a small brokerage house I'd picked out and made an appointment with an investment counselor. The broker turned out to be discreet as well as knowledgable, the more so when I told him how much money I intended to invest. We spent two hours discussing various possibilities and the current state of the stock market, and he gave me a stack of literature and performance charts to comb through.

Annalise called again that night. "I found the perfect house for us," she said. "Absolutely perfect!"

"Tell me about it."

"It's on the hillside above town, the oldest and most exclusive residential district on the island. A seventy-five-year-old villa just dripping with charm. Tile floors, beam ceilings, everything you could want, including a small garden and a cobblestoned terrace with a fabulous view of the harbor. Cobblestones! Can you believe that? Of course it's small, only two bedrooms, and the garden has been neglected, but we could put up with that."

"Sure we could."

"It's only been available since the end of last month and the agent says it won't last long. And it's vacant, I could move in right away." She paused before she said, "But there's one drawback."

"Let me guess. It's expensive."

"Yes. Because of the view and the location."

"How expensive?"

"Twenty-five hundred a month on a two-year fixed lease. Can we afford that much?"

"I don't see why not."

"Richard! Do you mean it? Are you sure?"

I said, "I'll never deny you anything you really want, you know that."

She said, "God, I love you!"

The apartment was lonely as hell without her. I got out as often as I could, shopped, went to movies, wandered through parks, took bus rides to various parts of the city. In the evenings I made a careful study of the literature and charts the investment counselor had given me, and an informed decision as to which mutual funds and blue-chip stocks best suited Annalise's and my long-term needs. Then I arranged another meeting with the broker and opened an account for the purchase of the selected funds and stocks with a wire transfer of $150,000 from Richard Laidlaw's Cayman account. I told him that I would be moving shortly to the Virgin Islands and requested that all dividend checks be sent to the Cayman account, all business correspondence to me at my new address in Charlotte Amalie.

The portfolio was fairly conservative, with as much guarantee as it was possible to have of substantial income. A third of the dividends would be reinvested in more shares and mutual funds; the balance would supplement the cost of our new lifestyle. Later, once I was sure I had made the right investment choices, and over a period of time, I planned to invest another $150,000. Eventually we might be able to live comfortably off the dividends alone, preserving what was left in the Cayman account for special needs. Richard Laidlaw would have to pay income tax on dividends that exceeded $600 per year, to prevent the IRS from sniffing around, but the annual tariff wouldn't amount to much even in windfall years.

There was not much else left for me to do in Chicago. I informed the landlord at the end of November that I would be vacating the premises on December 15. A few days before I was due to leave, I closed the Mutual Trust account and had the remaining balance wired to the bank in Charlotte Amalie; I also emptied the safe deposit box of the last of the cash and turned in the key.

One final errand. In an exclusive jewelry store in the Loop I bought Annalise's Christmas present: a $2,000 white-gold wedding ring with a two-carat diamond setting, to replace the plain gold band I'd given her after our Nevada marriage.

She called four more times during that period. She had leased the house, moved in, hired a gardener to cure the garden's neglect. She'd bought a car for a good price, a two-year-old Mini, "a cute little thing, what everybody down here drives." She'd met some of our neighbors and become friendly with one couple in particular, the Verrikers, Royce and Maureen. "He was born here; his people came down from Miami before World War II. He's a divorce lawyer, but not the sleazy kind. St. Thomas is sort of the Reno of the Caribbean, a lot of women come here to get divorces, did you know that? That's how he met Maureen, she was one of his clients five years ago." She'd been invited to a party at the home of another couple, the Kyles, where she'd met several other locals. "I told everyone about you, the story that you made enough in the stock market so we could move down here, I mean, and that you'll be here before Christmas. They can't wait to meet you."

Chicago had stifled her, but in St. Thomas she had found her element—established herself among the kind of people she related to and the kind of society she aspired to belong to. Her natural charm and friendliness led everyone to accept her without question, which in turn would lead them to accept me.

Her enthusiasm was infectious. As the day of departure neared, I grew more and more eager. My bags were packed a day early. I didn't sleep much the night before—left the shabby confines of the apartment and took a taxi to O'Hare four hours before my flight.

How did I feel that day?

Like I had the world by the tail, man. Like I could ride it anywhere, ride it forever, and nothing and nobody could ever tear me loose.

ST. THOMAS

1978–1982

ANNALISE WAS THERE to meet me when my flight arrived at Truman Airport on St. Thomas. The trades weren't blowing that day and the overheated air dripped with humidity, but she somehow managed to look cool and fresh in a white skirt and madras blouse and white straw hat. She was tanning already, too. I kissed her passionately right there in the lobby and I didn't give a damn what anyone thought about it.

The Mini she'd bought was bright blue. It had a tendency to make farting noises when you started the engine, but it ran efficiently enough. She drove us down off the plateau where the airport was located, into heavy traffic that was mostly tourist-related—tour vans and buses, taxis, rental cars.

Tourists were the island's major drawback then, same as now. There weren't nearly as many in those days, but still they clogged the airport, Lindbergh Beach across the street, the roads into Charlotte Amalie, the waterfront, and the downtown shopping streets. The seventies building boom—villas, condos, a couple of big resorts—was partly responsible. You could lay the rest of the blame on the damn cruise ship industry. St. Thomas was a primary lure because of the size of its harbor and the fact that it's a duty-free port where you can buy Swiss watches, Irish linen, French perfumes, Italian weapons, single-malt Scotches, Caribbean rums, and a hundred other things at bargain prices.

"It gets really bad when five or six cruise ships come in at once," Annalise said as we drove. "One of the first things the Verrikers told me was to stay away from downtown on those days. The only locals who like the tourists are the shopkeepers."

Despite the overcrowding, the island for me was still the tropical paradise the guidebooks made it out to be. Once you got past the ramshackle native quarter, you encountered lush tropical vegetation and old-world charm just about everywhere you looked. Frenchtown, for instance—Cha-Cha Town to the locals—where the descendants of the first Huguenot settlers on St. Barthélemy lived in small, brightly colored frame houses that had been passed down from generation to generation. They were fishermen, mostly, who spoke an ancient Norman dialect and wore square, flat-topped straw cha-cha hats and had little to do with the other white residents.

I had my first look at Charlotte Amalie from half a mile across the bay. A mix of new and ancient commercial buildings set along the curve of the waterfront, private homes spread in a wide arc halfway up the surrounding mountains—red roofs and whitewashed stucco walls sunstruck and shimmering in the humid heat. The broad harbor, the offshore islands, the turquoise blue of the Caribbean dotted with sails stretching out beyond. It's not easy to describe what I felt, seeing it for the first time. The best I can do is call it a sense of rightness, of belonging, as if I were meant to be there. As if my previous life had been a waiting or trial period, everything I'd done a rite of passage. I tried to put this into words for Annalise, but she didn't understand. She just smiled and nodded.

We dropped down to Veterans Highway and drove in along the harbor past the airboat terminal, the slips for the Tortola ferries and glass-bottom excursion boats, the anchored yachts at the King's Wharf marina. Annalise pointed out landmarks along the way. One was Fort

Christian, a looming pink-plaster pile guarded by a couple of ancient cannon, built in 1671 by the Danes who'd been the first whites to settle the island. It was not only a tourist attraction, which housed a museum in what had once been the dungeon; it was also, in those days, where police headquarters and the local jail were located.

Near King's Wharf, Annalise turned onto one of the uphill streets. We climbed across Dronningens Gade, the main drag, and up past the old slave market and then around Berg Hill into the residential district. The streets up there were narrow, mostly one-way, forming a maze of curves, loops, angles. It had taken Annalise half a dozen trips before she could make all the right turns without consulting the real estate agent's instruction sheet.

We emerged finally onto a twisty little street called Quartz Gade. The handful of villas along it were on large lots carved out of the hillside below street level; all had red tile roofs and lush gardens and either steep driveways or covered parking platforms. She indicated one as belonging to the Kyles, Gavin and Robin, and a larger one on the hillside above, flanked by huge flamboyant trees, as the Verrikers' home.

Our place was down toward the end. White stucco, red tile roof, walls draped in crimson and purple bougainvillea; driveway and one-car garage set at right angles to the house. There were high stucco walls on both sides. The wall on the east side flanked a steep set of stairs that led down to the next street and beyond. The steps were wide and made of ship-ballast brick imported by the Danes during the mid-1800s; they'd been built because the pitch on some of the hills was too steep for streets and cars and also to provide residents with direct foot access to the shopping district. There were several of these long public staircases in Charlotte Amalie. Once I got to know their locations, I mapped out a series of shortcut routes to and from our villa. The return climb could be a bitch in the heat of the day, even though the crow-flies distance was only about a quarter of a mile, but we got used to it and used the stairs fairly often to keep in shape.

The villa was built of stone and stucco, and the thick walls cooled the interior. Annalise had said it was small, but that was a matter of perspective. Six rooms, all good-sized, the living room and master bedroom long and wide with high, beamed ceilings. Whitewashed walls hung with tapestries and pictures by local artists. Beige tile floors. Massive old furniture. All the modern conveniences.

Two sets of heavy, jalousied doors opened from the living room onto a wide cobbled terrace that ran the width of the house. Two more sets of doors gave access from the master bedroom to the terrace and to a narrow side veranda. The garden ran downhill some fifty yards: coconut palms and guava trees, oleander, hibiscus, white ginger. The view was spectacular. From one point or another on the terrace you could see most of the harbor, Hassel Island and its mountaintop fort, a section of Water Island, the Caribbean in the distance.

When we finished the tour, Annalise said expectantly, "Well? What do you think?"

"As advertised. You couldn't have made a better choice."

"I just love it. I knew you would, too." She kissed me. "So what do you want to do now, as if I didn't know?"

"A shower first," I said. "And something cold to drink."

"You go ahead. I'll make us a couple of rum punches."

I was in the shower, soaping off, when she brought the drinks. Brought them naked into the tiled stall. We drank standing close together under the cool stream of water, not sipping but gulping, and then we took turns with the bar of soap. That kind of foreplay doesn't last long or allow for a time-out to towel dry and hop into bed. Our first round of lovemaking in our new home was started and finished standing up in the shower.

Over the next ten days we christened all the other rooms. The terrace and the side veranda and the garden, too, each of those after dark in deference to public decency.

★ ★ ★

I met Royce and Maureen Verriker the next day, and the Kyles and some of the other members of the white establishment at a Christmas party the Verrikers hosted that weekend. Only about 10 percent of the island population was white—U.S. expats, and descendants of U.S., Danish, and French settlers—so it was a fairly small and close-knit community.

Richard Laidlaw was more comfortable in a party atmosphere, among strangers, than Jordan Wise had ever been; better able to mix and make small talk. But that doesn't mean that I liked it. Annalise was genuinely at ease, smiling, laughing, charming everyone, enjoying the attention, but a part of me stood off and observed what she and the others did and said and then took cues from them so I could make all the appropriate responses.

Royce Verriker was a few years older than me, tall, lean, with a mop of sun-bleached hair and intense gray eyes. Very suave, very glib: if I hadn't known he was a lawyer, I would have guessed it on the first try. When he and I talked, he asked a lot of questions, not prying, just displaying interest. I gave him all the rehearsed answers—successful Chicago tool-and-die manufacturer, made a bundle in the stock market, decided to sell my business and retire young, moved down here to live the good life in the sun. He smiled and said he envied me. He also said, "I imagine Annalise has told you that my specialty is domestic law. But if you ever need any other kind of legal help or advice, my door is always open." I thanked him and said I'd keep that in mind. Typical lawyer. Cut him open and he would bleed green for money and brown for bullshit.

His wife, Maureen, was a slender, thirtyish redhead, the dark-complected rather than the pale-skinned variety. One of those pretty cameo faces, but with oddly sad eyes. A little reserved until you got to know her, pleasant and gracious. She and Annalise had hit it off from the first and were already friends. She wore a skintight blue dress that night—and low-cut blouses and tight pullovers and skimpy bikinis at other times—that called attention to overlarge breasts. The way she dressed was Verriker's idea, not hers; he was the one, she'd told Annalise, who wanted to show off her boobs.

Gavin and Robin Kyle were both architects pushing forty, owners of their own firm. A study in contrasts, those two. He was short, on the tubby side, with sparse hair the color of ginger ale, and a gossip-monger who liked to hear himself talk; she was six inches taller, skinny, had thick dark hair, and seldom spoke more than two sentences in a row. I liked them both. Despite Gavin's constant chatter, most of what he had to say was interesting and amusing.

The guest I related to best, though, was Jack Scanlon, the middle-aged manager of a cement plant. That was because he was a day sailor, the only person there who had any but a passing interest in sailing. He owned a twenty-four-foot sloop that he kept at the marina adjacent to the West India dock. When I told him I was planning to learn to sail, hoped to buy a boat of my own one day, he invited me to join him on a day cruise after the holidays.

St. Thomas is a small island, just thirty square miles. Annalise had al-ready seen some of it, but we explored it all together, one end to the other, in a handful of day and night excursions.

Some of its attractions appealed to both of us. The views from atop Crown Mountain and the Drake's Seat overlook, of the sixty-odd reefs, islets and islands that ring St. Thomas, and on clear days, of the British Virgins and some of the Puerto Rican archipelago. Coral World, an underwater observation tower where you could see all sorts of exotic marine life and coral formations. Blackbeard's Castle, atop Government Hill—a sprawling, three-hundred-year-old, cannon-guarded fortress that had been turned into a luxury inn and restaurant. Annalise liked it for the cuisine, which was among the best on the island. I liked it for its architecture and its history. Local legend had it that Edward Teach, the pirate known as Blackbeard, used the five-story masonry tower as a lookout post for the merchant ships carrying rum, cotton, and spices he later ambushed. I felt a certain kinship with the old buccaneer, and his supposed use of St. Thomas as a safe haven amused me.

But for the most part, Annalise's and my tastes differed. She preferred Market Square, the remodeled Danish warehouses along Dronningens Gade that dispensed all the duty-free goods, the palm-fringed beaches at Magens Bay, Coki Bay, Secret Harbor, and Sapphire Bay, and the raucous nightlife. I preferred the marina next to the West India dock, with its slips for two hundred luxury yachts, and the working waterfronts at Red Hook and Frenchtown and Sub Base harbor where you could hire charter boats or catch ferries or buy fresh fish and shellfish or watch the pelicans and flamingoes on their fishing rounds. The narrow, winding, old-world streets of Frenchtown. The bluff above Nazareth Bay, where you had the best view of St. John three miles across Pillsbury Sound. The ancient French cemetery on Harwood Highway with its decaying walls and rusted iron gates, its gnarled old trees and peeling whitewashed tombs.

And the sunsets.

Christ, the sunsets.

They impressed me more than anything else. Annalise was already starting to take them for granted by the time I got there, but I never have. They still stir me, even after twenty-seven years. Bright gold, dark gold, burnished copper, old rose, fiery orange, lavender and pink and saffron and deep purple . . . all the colors and some gradations and combinations you can't imagine until you see them. Plus thousands of intricate cloud shapes and formations to reflect the colors and the dying light. Most travelers will tell you that Caribbean sunsets are the most spectacular in the world; I don't see how anybody can dispute it. Doesn't matter where you watch one—backyard terrace, restaurant patio, mountaintop, deck of a boat at sea, even through an open-air window in a back-island café like Jocko's. Each is unique, and nearly all of them are magnificent.

Our different tastes weren't a problem in those early days. We'd come down here to enjoy ourselves, do whatever made us happy. It wasn't necessary to agree on all our pleasures, to share them in lockstep. There was plenty for us to do as a couple. So why shouldn't we each have time to ourselves, some private space of our own?

Annalise was thrilled and a little overwhelmed by her present on Christmas morning. She cried when I slipped the diamond wedding band on her finger, the first of the two times I ever saw her shed a tear.

I seemed to have passed muster with the Verrikers. They invited us to a New Year's Eve dance at the Royal Bay Club, one of the members-only, whites-only places that they and the Kyles belonged to. It took up a full block down near the marina. The old, whitewashed main build-ing housed a bar lounge with leather chairs and card and chess tables and a private library, and a ballroom large enough for a five-piece or-chestra and a ring of tables around the dance floor. A smaller building at the rear contained handball courts, men's and women's saunas, and locker room facilities. Outside there were tennis and badminton courts.

At one point during the evening, while the women were in the ladies' room, Verriker asked me if I played handball. I said no, nor ten-nis or golf, explaining it by saying I'd been too busy making a living to get involved in sports.

"Great game, handball," he said. "Keeps you fit. I could teach you the basics in one session, if you're interested."

I wasn't, but I said, "Sure, I'd like that."

"Members have unlimited use of the courts whenever they're free. All the other facilities, too. How would you and Annalise like to join?"

I pretended to be flattered and asked casually what becoming members entailed, if there was some sort of screening process. No, he said, the club wasn't that exclusive. Strictly social. There were no hard and fast rules for membership; financial status and background were of no importance. As long as you were able to pay the yearly dues of $500, and had the sponsorship of a member, your acceptance was pretty much a given. And he'd be glad to sponsor us.

So I accepted with a show of gratitude. The more firmly entrenched we became in island society, the less likely our new identities would ever be questioned or breached.

I went sailing three times with Jack Scanlon on his little sloop, *Manjack*. Annalise came along the first time. The sea was calm that morning, when we left the harbor, but a strong wind kicked up later in the day as we were tacking out of Caneel Bay on St. John, and it got a little rough. She was seasick and shaky by the time we docked. Never again, she said afterward. I thought that once I had my own boat, something larger and made for smoother sailing like a ketch or yawl, I might be able to change her mind. But until then I wouldn't try. You can't force somebody to love the things you love, any more than you can force them to love you.

That first sailing experience had just the opposite effect on me. I took to it immediately, as I'd been sure I would. Had my sea legs from the start. From my reading I'd already internalized much of the basic information and language of the sea. I knew that sloops and catamarans had a single mast, ketches and yawls two masts, and that most modern sailboats were Marconi rigged. That's a triangular rigging with the sails spread by two spars, with a lower boom that extends past the mast and a second that runs at an angle from the forward end of the boom to the masthead; Depression-era sailors gave it the Marconi name because the stays and shrouds holding up the mast reminded them of the first radio towers set up by the Italian inventor. I knew the names of all the sails, the meaning of such terms as luff and kedge and reef points, and I could define jibstay, lapstrake, burgee, spinnaker, genoa, freeboard, lubber line. I knew that a boat will sail in three basic ways—before the wind on a run, with the wind abeam on a reach, and close-hauled or toward the wind; that the wind fills the sails from both sides, on either a starboard tack or a port tack. I knew a lot of facts about sailing, or thought I did, but I didn't know a damn thing until I learned the working application of those terms and principles.

Scanlon was a fairly good small-craft sailor, though he'd only been at it about four years, and those day cruises were more exhilarating than anything I'd done except for the Amthor crime and making love with Annalise. Standing on *Manjack*'s deck, hanging onto one of the stays while she ran with the wind, the sea creaming up around the bow and back along the hull, the wind singing in the sails . . . I'd had no other experience quite like it.

I learned a few rudimentary lessons from watching Scanlon and following his instructions. The first time he let me trim the jib, I did it without hesitation or mistake. But he wasn't much of a teacher overall because he was still learning himself, and because he was a day sailor and a twenty-four-foot sloop was all he ever aspired to own and operate. He wasn't offended when I asked him if he could recommend someone more knowledgeable and more experienced I could pay for private lessons.

I discovered Arundel Cane Rum at a rum tasting in early January. The hosts were a British couple, the Potters, rum connoisseurs and historians who lived out on the West End and delighted in throwing this kind of shindig for newcomers to the island. The invitation came through the Kyles, who were both rum drinkers, and we went with them. There were a dozen or so others there in addition to the Potters, among them another recent arrival, a London banker named Horler.

You think of rum as being light or dark, with varying degrees of alcohol content, and mainly as an ingredient in mixed drinks. I did, anyway, until that day. But there are a lot of different varieties, each with characteristics as distinctive as those separating single-malt Scotches. Rum has been made in the Caribbean since the seventeenth century, from fermented molasses, cane syrup, or fresh sugar-cane juice derived from a multitude of species and hybrids of cane. Originally it was distilled in clay pots, then in single-pot stills that look like teakettles with long spouts, and finally in single-, double-, and mutiple-column continuous stills. Some blends are rich and heavy, others carbon filtered to produce a clear spirit; some are aged for up to four years, others not aged at all. The taste of each depends on the raw ingredients, the bottled strength, its barrel time or lack of it, the distillation purity and the length of fermentation. A rum drinker's preference is highly individualistic. There are no universal standards or measures for judgment.

The Potters gave a little lecture that included this information (and later I did some studying of the subject on my own) and then proceeded to demonstrate. They had more than sixty varieties arranged on sideboards around their big living room. From Puerto Rico, the British Virgins, Martinique, Barbados, St. Lucia, Marie-Galante. Well-known labels such as Bacardi and Pusser's, and obscure brands like Buccaneer, Blackbeard's Five-Star, Cockspur, Jack Iron, and Rhum Vieux du Père Labat. Various potencies, light and dark, from Mount Gay Eclipse's 154-proof, 80 percent alcohol rocket fuel down to the milder 80-proof, 40 percent alcohol content types. There was water and ice and cane syrup, as most distilleries provided in their tasting rooms, but we were encouraged to try at least a few of the rums straight for a better evaluation of the flavor.

We were also encouraged to follow a little ritual on each tasting. Read the label first, to determine how strong the rum was and how long it had been aged and what it was distilled from. Pour a little into a glass and hold the glass up to the light so as to judge the color or clearness. Swirl the rum in the bottom of the glass. Take a deep breath, exhale, then lift the glass to the nose to assess the delicate flavors in the aroma. Repeat the process if you liked what you smelled the first time; if you didn't like it, you probably wouldn't care for the taste, so just move on to the next. Sip a little and roll it on the tongue, then savor it and mentally compare your impression of the taste with the aroma.

I'd drunk rum before that day, but it wasn't until I began sampling and comparing that I began to really appreciate it. It was all good, but I preferred the mature, dark types. Most of the women were partial to the light and clear. And most of the men, predictably, preferred the 151-proof Cruzan and 154-proof Mount Gay Eclipse. I agreed with them, more or less, though I had yet to find one I really liked until I came to the bottle of Arundel Cane Rum.

The label said it was distilled from pure cane juice and aged in oak casks. That it had been distilled and blended by the Callwood family in the Caribbean's oldest continuously operating pot distillery in Cane Garden Bay, Tortola. The first sniff hooked me; two more confirmed its character. The taste was as close to ambrosial as anything I'd ever had. Nobody else seemed to find it as special as I did, which proved the dictum about personal preference.

Potter told me Arundel Estate had been in operation for four hundred years, the last two hundred in the hands of the Callwood family. It was the only distillery still operating on Tortola, the only licensed one in the eastern Caribbean that used a single-pot still, and one of the few that made rum directly from sugar-cane juice from locally grown green cane. They manufactured both white and dark, the light kind mainly for local islanders. The thick, rich dark was what I'd tasted.

The next day I went to one of the larger liquor stores in Charlotte Amalie and bought six bottles of dark Arundel Cane, all they had in stock.

From the day of the Potters' tasting in 1979, I've never willingly drunk any other kind of rum. Iced usually, straight or with a little water occasionally. And never, never in punches or collinses or any other concoction that would dilute and spoil the flavor.

The first private sailing lessons I took were from an acquaintance of Jack Scanlon's who skippered a private yacht for a local government official and kept a schooner of his own at Red Hook. After half a dozen sessions, I moved on to a grizzled ex-navy, ex–charter fisherman and working drunk who claimed to've sailed the Caribbean for more than forty years. Less than a month of him was all I could stand.

I felt I'd learned pretty well what little seamanship I'd been given, but I wasn't satisfied with the quality or content of the instruction. Practical enough, but dry and basic, lacking in detail and lore—skimpy value for the money I laid out. They paid lip service to my ability to absorb information and put it to use, but not for a moment did either of them act as though I had the makings of an equal. They treated me with the disdain, the thinly concealed contempt commercial boatmen have for the idle rich. Deaf ears when I tried to tell them I had no interest in racing cutters or sport cats or any other kind of craft, or in being a day sailor like Jack Scanlon or one of the aimlessly cruising weekend yacht owners more interested in partying than seamanship. Mocking little smiles when I said I wanted to be more than a hobby sailor, to eventually singlehand my own ketch or yawl. And eyes that looked through me most of the time we were together, the way people had once looked through Jordan Wise.

So I went looking for someone reliable who'd teach me as I wanted to be taught. I'd been to a couple of the boatyards in the Red Hook area, to soak up the atmosphere and to look at the boats they had for sale, and the owner of Marsten Marine, Dick Marsten, had been friendly and unpatronizing. I sought him out. He didn't hesitate when I asked him for a recommendation.

"Bone's the man you want," he said.

"Who's he?"

"Fellow who works for me now and then. Does odd jobs, takes on day charters and gives lessons when the mood suits him."

"Temperamental?"

"Too strong a word," Marsten said. "He's his own man, marches to his own drummer. And there's no better sailor in this part of the world."

"Where can I find him?"

"He rents a slip at the Sub Base harbor marina. Ask anybody over there. They all know him."

"Bone," I said. "His last name?"

"His only name, far as I know. Just Bone."

The Sub Base harbor area, west of Frenchtown and named for the submarine base that had operated there during the Second World War, wasn't half as picturesque as the Charlotte Amalie or Frenchtown harbors. The Water Island ferry was located there, but for the most part what you saw were tramp steamers and charter fishing boats and sloops and schooners and ketches of various sizes and condition. Bone's boat was a forty-foot gaff-rigged ketch, old but well-maintained, humorlessly named *Conch Out*. C-o-n-c-h, like the shellfish. That was where I found him, on his ketch, giving the deck a coat of gray nonskid paint.

I don't know why I was surprised when I first saw him. His name, maybe. A bone is white, and I guess I expected a white man. He was black. The color of milk chocolate, actually. A Bahamian native, I found out later, from Nassau Island. Big man, not so much tall as broad and solid, beefy through the shoulders and torso and across the hips, with short legs and heavy thighs, like a tree split at the crotch into a pair of thick boles. There were flecks of gray in the grizzled beard he wore; otherwise you wouldn't have had a clue as to his age. His skin was smooth and unlined except for a few sun wrinkles around his eyes. He had two gold-crowned teeth, one upper and one lower, that glinted whenever he smiled. Which wasn't often, and not at all on our first meeting. Mostly his expression was flat and unreadable. I took this to be the usual stoic native reserve until I got to know him. In fact, he was neither stoic nor reserved; the expression masked an almost fierce dignity. Bone was an intensely proud man, and smarter than ninety-nine percent of the white men circumstances now and then forced him to serve.

I introduced myself, told him that Marsten had referred me and why I was there. He studied me for half a minute, squinting in the sun glare, taking my measure, before he said in his lilting Bahamian accent, "Where you come from, mon?"

"Chicago," I said. "But I live here now."

"St. Thomas?"

"Yes."

"Own a boat?" He pronounced it "bow-ut."

"Not yet. I intend to buy one, but not until I'm ready for the responsibility—not until I'm a good enough sailor."

Bone studied me again. Then he said, "Come over in the shade," and went ahead without waiting for me. He sat down on the mushroom bitt that the ketch's bow was tied to, took out a stubby briar and a cracked oilskin pouch, and loaded the bowl with tobacco as black as tar. The aroma, when he set fire to the shag, had a molasseslike sweetness. His movements were deliberate, economical, efficient. He used words the same way, as if he had a limited supply stored up and was parceling them out a few at a time.

"How much you been on sailboats?" he asked.

"Not much. Taking private lessons the past two months."

"Who from?"

"A couple of boatmen at Red Hook." I named them.

"Why you want somebody else?"

"They weren't teaching me what I want to know."

"What you want to know?"

"All there is about boats and the sea," I said. "I told you the kind of sailor I want to be."

"Let me hear what you learned so far."

"Everything?"

"Everything you know."

I told him that, too. I thought it would take some time; I thought I was crammed full of basic knowledge. But when I laid it all out, it sounded pretty thin. Just the bare rudiments.

"I know I've got a lot to learn," I admitted. "That's why I'm here. I'm serious about this, Mr. Bone."

"Not Mister," he said. "Just Bone."

"Will you work with me?"

"This ketch," he said, "she's a fussy old woman, sometimes. Hard to get along with. Some say the same about her cap'n."

"I'm not looking for an easy time of it. When I buy a boat of my own, it won't be new and it won't be fancy."

"So you say now."

"I mean it, Bone. What do you say?"

"You take orders from a black mon, no argument?"

"You're the master, I'm the new hand. I know my place."

He sucked on his pipe, thinking about it.

"I'll pay you well," I said. "More than whatever you usually charge for lessons."

"What I charge depends."

"On what?"

"How hard you want to work."

"As hard as I know how, for as long as it takes."

"Might take a long time," Bone said. "Might take more time than you or I got."

"Meaning I might never be a sailor?"

"Some men born to it, some not."

"It's in my blood, Bone. I honestly believe that. I just never had the opportunity until now."

He almost smiled. "We'll find out," he said.

★   ★   ★

98

I could not have hooked up with a better sailor or better man than Bone.

He didn't just live on that ketch of his; he treated her the way I tried to treat Annalise, as a friend, a lover, an extension of himself. He pampered her, handled her with great care and gentleness. Growled at her now and then when she didn't cooperate, but never with any real anger. He knew more about sailing and the sea than any man I've ever met; now and then he'd surprise me with such obscure facts as the origin of the term starboard (a corruption of the Norse word *steerboard,* from the days when Viking dragon ships had right-side rudders). And he had an aptitude for practical instruction. He taught me more in a week than the others had in two months.

I spent full days with him once or twice a week when he was in port and not working at one of his other sources of income. Every now and then he'd sail off by himself—"going out," he called it, the real meaning of the ketch's name—and stay away for a week or two, one time for more than a month. He never said where he'd been or what he'd done on these trips. Long, solitary cruises, probably, and visits to his native Nassau. But I never asked him. It was his business, not mine or anybody else's. His own man, Dick Marsten had said. That was Bone in a nutshell.

Some days we'd go out on a sail. Short practice runs around some of the little islands like Thatch Cay and Hans-Lollik Island that surround St. Thomas; longer trips to Great Tobago or Jost Van Dyke or around St. John. In all kinds of conditions except for heavy-weather seas. Other days we'd stay in the harbor and work on the ketch—sanding, painting, reeving new main and mizzen halyards, cleaning the head and the bilge, checking oil, gas, and water lines, doing a hundred other small chores that go into the maintenance and smooth operation of a sailboat—

He was doing what? Using me as a workhorse and taking pay for it?

No. Hell, no. You couldn't be more wrong.

After the first couple of weeks he wouldn't accept a dime for the dockside days, even though I kept offering—and he did most of the chores himself, with little enough help from me. He let me pay him the going rate for lessons on sail days, and buy gasoline and other provisions, but that was all. Money didn't mean much to Bone. Almost all of what he got from me or from his other labors went into the ketch, and what was left over into the few small creature comforts he allowed himself.

Mostly, he taught by example rather than words. He'd perform this or that task, or series of tasks, and he expected me to watch carefully and internalize what I was seeing and understand the reasons for it and be able to perform the same task on my own when the time came. The Red Hook boatmen had insulted my intelligence; Bone accepted it and counted on it. He didn't talk down to me, or look through me. From the first he treated me with the same respect I accorded him.

Over a period of several months I learned the proper way to rig and trim sails and the fine points of docking and anchoring. How to read geodesic charts and tide tables, how to use compass roses and track a course—easy for me because of my mathematical turn of mind. How to read water depth and gauge the weather and navigate by shooting sun and stars and by dead reckoning. How to whip the ends of manila line to prevent raveling, make an eye splice, tie a clove hitch. The right and wrong ways to dock a boat under power and under sail. All the running rules and safety rules. All the little things that could go wrong on a boat and how to safeguard against them. What to do in this or that type of emergency. What essential tools and repair materials to keep on board. These and a hundred, a thousand more.

Often he'd spring a question on me, by way of a test. Is a jib the strongest pulling sail per square foot of area? (No. A jib's main function is to increase the power of the mains'l.) If you're running downwind, how do you prevent a dangerous jibe? (Rig a secure boom vang.) What's a long fetch? (The fetch is the distance the wind blows over unobstructed water; a long fetch can create dangerously high waves.) Why should a sail be set smooth and at the same time as stiff as possible? (The wind doesn't just flow onto the sail, it flows off it as well. Every little wrinkle or hard spot sets up eddies on both sides that break up the windflow and reduce the sail's efficiency.)

Bone also taught me about sharks. He had a thing about them, an odd mixture of hate and reverence. "A shark, mon, he's all stomach and never full. He don't care what he eats and he's always hungry. Sailor falls into deep water and can't get back on board, chances are he'll be some shark's supper." Another time he said, "Sharks, they like to race a boat sometimes. Some mon keep a rifle on board, every time he see a fin he shoot at it. Think it's fun to watch other sharks tear up a wounded one. Don't you do that. Bad luck to kill a shark for fun. Bad luck to kill anything lives in the sea you don't plan to eat."

He had amazing patience to go with his fierce dignity. When I made a mistake, as I did often enough in the beginning, he'd shake his head or growl in the same mild way he growled at the ketch. That was all. He never once raised his voice in anger. Not even after the worst of my screwups, the day I was responsible for blowing out the ketch's mains'l.

That day we were over in the Virgin's Gangway, the narrows between St. John and Tortola, and a squall began making up to eastward. Bone decided not to shorten down any more than we had to, so we left all the sails on and turned in a couple of reefs in the main and mizzen. Just as we were finishing the main, the squall hit us and Bone ran back to the wheel to keep her into the wind. My job was to tie in the last few points and raise sail again, and I had the halyard taut and was throwing it on the winch. The wind and drumming rain kept me from hearing Bone's shouted order to slack off. I slid the handle into the winch and took a turn, and all of a sudden the mains'l split all the way across. I realized what I'd done wrong before Bone had to tell me. I'd mixed up a pair of reef points, tied one from the first row to another on the opposite side in the second row; that had pulled the sail out of shape and put all the strain in one place.

One growl and a quick hard glare was all I got for my stupidity. Bone had another mains'l on board, fortunately, and the squall passed and we didn't have any trouble getting the new one up. Afterward, ashamed of myself, I kept trying to apologize, but he wouldn't listen to it. All he said was, "You'll never do that again, Mr. Laidlaw." It was a statement, not a question. And he was right, I never did anything that sloppy again.

After each day with Bone I wrote out a list of what I'd learned, to make sure I didn't forget even the smallest detail, and on the days I didn't see him I pored over the lists and star charts and geodesic charts that I'd bought myself. I plotted courses and made increasingly complex calculations—a whole new set of equations—and then embarked on imaginary voyages and dealt with various kinds of situations. I approached these studies with the same intensity as I had my accounting courses at Golden Gate University and the Amthor crime. The only difference was that this time, what awaited me on graduation wasn't a well-paid job or $600,000. It was a boat of my own.

Day-to-day living on a tropical island is not the same as it is on the mainland. Time slows down. The heat and humidity induce torpor and indolence. You don't keep regular hours or eat balanced meals. You have a tendency to drink too much, lie around too much, and when you play, to play too hard. Routine translates to boredom, unless it involves something you're passionate about. So you make an effort to see new places, develop new interests. And in my case, to be more social.

Our first year on St. Thomas, and most of the second year, we took the ferry to St. John a couple of times a month to eat and shop in Cruz Bay, to soak up sun on the powdery white sand beaches at Maho and Trunk and Hawknest bays. Now and then we took the longer ferry ride to Tortola, where we visited the Arundel Estate distillery and Annalise bought an antique music box and I bought a small brassbound mahogany chest that was supposed to have come from a Soper's End pirate's den. She didn't seem to mind riding on the larger ferryboats; it was only the pitch and roll of small craft that made her seasick.

We flew to Puerto Rico and spent five days exploring San Juan and the outlying areas. We took interisland flights to St. Croix, Culebra, St. Martin. We went snorkeling and tried scuba diving in Coki Bay. We attended parties, gave a couple of parties of our own. At the Royal Bay Club I played handball with Verriker and she played tennis with Maureen. One or two evenings a week we ate out and then went to Bamboushay, Annalise's favorite nightclub, named for an old Calypso tourist phrase that means "Have yourself a fat old time"—a dark, noisy place that featured steel Calypso and Fungi bands and exotic native dancers. In April there was Carnival week—music and dancing, masquerades, costumed stiltwalkers representing the legendary West Indian spirits called jumbees—and the St. Thomas Yacht Club's annual regatta.

Some afternoons when it wasn't too hot and the trades were blowing soft, we played sex games. In one corner of the living room there was a daybed that Annalise had piled high with white throw pillows trimmed in blue. We opened the jalousied doors in that corner and moved the daybed over close to the sill, so that it commanded a view of the harbor and the sea beyond. Then we'd take turns sitting propped up naked against the pillows, while the other—

Christ, why did I bring that up? I don't want to talk about that.

Some things—

No, forget it, I'm not going to say any more.

Annalise liked the beaches more than I did; too many tourists to suit me. On the days I worked or sailed with Bone, she'd go to Magens or Coki or Sapphire alone or with Maureen or one of the other nonworking wives; swim, sunbathe, sit under an umbrella with her sketchpad designing swimsuits and beach attire. Occasionally she and Maureen would take an off-island trip together, or spend an evening at Bamboushay when I preferred to sit home with an iced Arundel and watch the sunset and the harbor lights.

No one asked any questions about our past life that we couldn't answer with a few simple lies. No tourist or island resident looked at me as anything but another well-to-do expat. We spent money, but not as much as you might think. The cost of living wasn't all that high on St. Thomas in the late seventies and early eighties. And the return on my investments had exceeded expectations, so much so that I added another $100,000 in blue chip stocks to the portfolio.

I can't say exactly when Bone and I stopped being just tutor and pupil and became friends. It was a gradual thing, built on mutual respect and ease in each other's company and our shared passion for boats and the sea. One of those curious, not quite explicable, almost symbiotic relationships that occasionally develop between like-minded men of different races and cultures. But I can tell you when I first realized it and knew that he felt the same way.

It was a day near the approach of hurricane season in '80. The kind of humid day where you can almost see the moisture dripping in the air, feel it wet in your lungs every time you breathe. We'd been belowdecks on *Conch Out* all afternoon, installing a rebuilt chemical toilet and a new water line in the head, and when we finished we were dehydrated and sweating like pigs. I suggested we head over to one of the waterfront taverns for a cold beer, as we'd done a few times before. Bone nodded, but when we were up on the seawall he asked if I'd brought my car today. I said I had, and he said, "How about we go to another place I know."

The place was on the edge of the native quarter, a rust-spotted Quonset hut that must have dated to the early years of World War II. The only indication that it was a tavern was a painted sign over the entrance that read "Bar"; if it had a name, I never heard Bone or anyone else mention it. And if any curious tourist had ever walked in, he'd likely have turned right around and walked out again. The interior was dark, with a plank bar and mismatched tables and chairs and a pair of vintage ceiling fans that did little to stir the sluggish air. The customers were mostly Thomian blacks, one of whom turned out to be an Obeah woman who dispensed charms for love and luck and to ward off jumbees. You had the feeling that trouble brewed there now and then, and that you wouldn't want to be around when it did.

The dozen or so drinkers that day wouldn't have tolerated me half so well if I hadn't been with Bone. They all knew him; a few spoke to him; the bartender called him by name. This was his regular watering hole. I understood that was why he'd brought me there: he'd decided to let me into a corner of his private world. For a native black man to do this for a white expat was not only an expression of friendship but a privilege, and I didn't treat it lightly. He bought the first round and when I bought the second he raised his glass in a toast and for the first time called me Richard instead of "mon" or Mr. Laidlaw.

After that day, he wouldn't take any more money from me except for gas, oil, and provisions when the two of us went to sea together. "No, Richard," he said when I offered. "Remember when you first come to see me? You said you have sailing in your blood, I said we'll find out. Now we both know. Bone won't take pay from a mon same as him."

We went to the Bar fairly often. And now and then to one of the native cafés for fish chowder or conch fritters or callaloo. Sometimes we talked, sometimes we just sat and drank beer or iced rum. Occasionally he would reveal snippets about himself and his past. He'd been married twice; his first wife had died and he refused to talk about his second, even to speak her name. He had a teenage daughter, Isola, he visited from time to time in Nassau. He'd attended college for a year before the sea called him. He'd once worked as a deckhand on a Panama-bound tramp steamer, once been approached to smuggle a ketch-load of weapons to a group of Puerto Rican insurgents (he wouldn't say whether he'd actually done it), once spent two years island-hopping his way around the Caribbean.

I envied him his free spirit and his adventures, and part of me wished I could tell him about the one bold, daring adventure in my life. It was just as well that I couldn't. For all his knockabout ways, Bone had a strong moral code to go with his intelligence and his dignity. He might have understood what had led me to do what I'd done, but he'd have thought less of me and probably severed our friendship. Would he have turned me in? No. He wasn't the kind to involve himself with the law. His duty was to himself and those he cared about, not to white or black society.

After a while I was more or less accepted by the Bar regulars, though I wouldn't have wanted to walk in alone after dark. In Bone's company I felt as comfortable there as I did at the Royal Bay Club. I was acquainted with a lot of white people on the island by then, the Verrikers and the Kyles and Jack Scanlon and Dick Marsten and several others, but the only man I considered a friend was a West Indian black sailor with a single name.

Bone.

He was the only real friend I ever had, before or since.

Hurricanes are always a concern when you live in the Caribbean. The hurricane season runs from June through November, but historically more storms—and the worst ones—occur in September than any other month. Most are Category 1 or 2, sustained winds of 74 up to 110 miles per hour, and if any of the islands is in the path of the blow, you can expect relatively minor damage such as flooding and what the official notices refer to as "moderate defoliation of shrubs and trees."

There was a Caribbean hurricane that first year, in early August. Hurricane Allen, I think it was. A monster blow, so intense that it reached Category 5 status—sustained winds of more than 156 m.p.h.—three different times over a period of about five days. Its central pressure was one of the lowest of all time, around twenty-seven inches when it was south of Puerto Rico. For a while it looked as though it might hammer the Virgins, and there were all sorts of storm warnings and preparations. But the eye stayed out over open water, bypassing us and howling up through the Lesser Antilles, where it weakened off Haiti and Jamaica; it didn't cross land until somewhere near Brownsville, Texas. We did get a taste of it, though: high winds and heavy rain for a couple of days.

Annalise was terrified the whole time. Her appetite for danger didn't extend to hurricanes. She'd been through earthquakes, as most native Californians have, but they were a tolerable threat because they came suddenly and were over in a minute or two. With a hurricane, you had plenty of advance warning and dire predictions of how much devastation to expect, and then, when it came howling and screaming like a bombing blitz, you had to ride it out over a long period. She wouldn't leave the villa, or let me take down the storm shutters and open the jalousies, until the day after the winds died down and the rains stopped.

I didn't say anything to her, but I had just the opposite reaction to Hurricane Allen. There is something in the elemental fury and frenzy of a tropical storm that excites a matching wildness in me. Still does to this day. An appeal to the dark side, I suppose. Yes, definitely an appeal to my dark side.

Annalise was jealous of my relationship with Bone. It threatened her somehow, in ways other than the time I spent with him—irrational ways. She hadn't liked him when I first introduced them, a reaction based on nothing I could see that passed between them. He was polite to her, on his dignity, as he was with everybody he met for the first time and especially with whites. And yet all she had to say about him afterward was "God, he's ugly, isn't he?" It occurred to me that she might be prejudiced. I didn't want to believe it and I never spoke to her about it, and she never said anything to me, but now I'm convinced she was. She avoided native Thomians other than service and trades people, and looking back, I can see that there was a kind of condescension in the way she treated blacks.

Once he suggested we take *Conch Out* on a three-day run to St. Croix, and that night I told Annalise about it and asked her to join us. With Bone's blessing, I said, a poor choice of words.

"His blessing!" she said. "Well, isn't that big of him!"

"He thought you might like to go along. So did I."

"Well, I don't want to. You know how I feel about small boats."

"It's only three days. And the weather forecast—"

"Three days. Lovely. Cozy. Just you and Bone now."

"What does that mean?"

"If I didn't know you so well," she said, "I'd think the two of you were sleeping together."

"For God's sake, Annalise."

"Well? You spend more time with him than you do with me."

"That's not true."

"Oh, isn't it? Sure seems that way."

"You know how much sailing means to me—"

"And what about the things that are important to me? Like visiting other parts of the world. Like trying to get a foot in the door of the fashion industry. I haven't given up on that idea, even if you think I have . . ."

There was more in the same vein. And it was no use arguing or trying to reason with her when she was in one of those moods. I'd had a few stings from her sharp tongue in Chicago, and a few more that were even more barbed down here. It gave her a hard, nasty edge that I didn't like at all.

If she'd used that tongue on me regularly, I'd've confronted her about it. But she didn't. She seemed to sense how often and how much she could provoke me, and she never went beyond the limits of my tolerance. Most of the time she was the same soft, sexy, loving woman she'd been that year in San Francisco and the first several months on St. Thomas. It was only Bone and the time I spent with him, and not getting her way when she had her heart set on something, that brought out the bitch in her.

In February of '81 I had a call from Dick Marsten. I'd told him I was interested in buying a boat of my own, and he had one in the yard, he said, that I might want to take a look at. A twenty-five-year-old yawl, thirty-four feet at the waterline, that had just come over from St. John. You don't see many yawls down here anymore, but there were still a few around in those days. This one had been built in Connecticut, run for a time on Long Island Sound, then sailed down in the fifties. Her owner had been ill for some time and she'd been neglected as a result, but she was still a sound vessel. The owner had died recently and his heirs were looking for a quick sale. So the price was right—not exactly a steal at $16,000, but still something of a bargain.

I'd been counting on a ketch, but that was because it was the type of sailboat I was familiar with; the only difference between the two is that the mizzen is smaller on a yawl, and stepped behind the wheel. So I said I'd come down, and when I went I took Bone with me. The yawl was out of the water for scraping, and she looked old and frowsy sitting there in the hot sun. There were a lot of things wrong with her. Her hull and deckhouse needed painting, the spars and brightwork sanding down and varnishing; the halyards would have to be replaced, the tracks and slides overhauled, a new bilge pump put in, and any number of smaller repairs made above- and belowdecks. But she had nice lines, a plumb stem and broad beam, a clean-running stern without too much overhang, and lifelines that had been rigged in heavy bolted stanchions.

When I asked Bone what he thought of her, he said, "Good salty sea boat. Built strong, caulked tight. Hull's solid. Engine got to have an overhaul, but it should be okay. Tell you better when I hear it run."

"How long to put her back in shape?"

"Hard to say. Lot of work to be done."

"Six months?"

"Maybe longer."

"Is she worth the asking price?"

"Seems so to me. You want her?"

An odd feeling had come over me as we examined the yawl. The same sort of feeling I'd had for Annalise in the beginning, without the sexual element—an intense possessive need that I now understood was the first stirrings of love.

"Yes," I said, "I want her."

"Then you better buy her," Bone said. Then, as if he'd intuited what I was thinking, "Right boat for a mon like the right woman. Grab her quick before somebody else take her away."

"Will you help me with the repairs?"

His two gold teeth flashed in one of his rare smiles. "Nothing Bone likes better than shining up a good salty sea boat."

The $16,000 price was firm, but I wouldn't have tried to haggle anyway. We signed the papers that same day, in Marsten's office. When I told Annalise that night, she wasn't pleased I'd gone ahead with the deal without talking to her first, but she didn't turn bitchy about it. Not then. I took her out to dinner and Bamboushay to celebrate.

The next day I went to the harbormaster's office, reregistered the yawl in Richard Laidlaw's name, and arranged for slip space not far from Bone's at the Sub Base harbor marina. Once she was barnacle-free and had been relaunched, Bone and I ran her over to Sub Base harbor under power. The auxiliary diesel labored somewhat, but he was satisfied with its durability. The first thing we did after we got her there was to paint a new name over the old one on the transom. She'd been *Moonlight Lady;* now she was *Annalise.*

I thought Annalise would be pleased when I brought her down to show off the yawl. Wrong. Her reaction was distaste, scorn. The bitch coming out in her then, as if it were the end product of a long brood since I'd told her about the purchase.

"This is what you named after me?" she said. "This is what you spent sixteen thousand dollars on?"

"She's rough around the edges," I admitted, "but Bone says she—"

"Bone says. Bone says."

"She needs work, that's all. A lot of hard work."

"So you'll be spending even more time down here."

"It's going to take some time, yes."

"You and Bone."

"I asked him to help me. What's wrong with that?"

"Oh, nothing. Nothing at all." Heavy sigh. "I suppose now you'll never take me to Paris. Or even to New York."

Paris again, New York again. She'd been pestering me about a long trip to both cities, and I kept putting her off. The FBI wouldn't have forgotten about Jordan Wise after only two and a half years; there was still a risk in traveling on the mainland and in Europe. But it was a small risk, I couldn't deny that. And now that I had what I'd always wanted, and the way she was reacting to it . . .

"All right," I said.

"All right?"

"We'll go to New York. We'll go to Paris."

"When?"

"This summer. June or July."

Fast change. The bitch vanished; she was soft and sweet again. "Richard! You mean it?"

"Yes."

"Promise? You won't try to back out?"

"No. We'll start making arrangements right away. But you have to promise me something in return. When the repair work is finished and the *Annalise* is ready for a shakedown cruise, you'll come along. No fuss, no argument."

111

"When will that be?"

"At least six months. Maybe not until the end of the year."

"Just the two of us?"

"Well, maybe. Bone might have to join us."

"Why, for God's sake?"

"I don't know when I'll be ready to sail a boat this size by myself. It could be another year or two before I can singlehand. If Bone does come along, he won't bother us. You'll hardly even know he's there."

"So you say."

"Will you promise?"

"Yes, I promise," she said. Then she said, "New York, Paris. Monte Carlo, too? I've always wanted to go to Monte Carlo. And London? Oh, God, I can't wait!"

Jack Scanlon came down to see the yawl. So did another boat owner I'd met, and the Kyles. Royce Verriker wasn't interested. "I hear you bought yourself a boat," he said when I saw him at the Royal Bay Club. "A fixer-upper that's taking up a lot of your time."

"I wouldn't describe her as a fixer-upper," I said. "She's got a good pedigree. She just hasn't been taken care of."

"Well, everybody needs a hobby."

"It's more to me than a hobby."

"Sure, I understand. Every man needs a vice, too." He winked at me. "Mine's making money."

The repair work went slowly. Among other tasks, the spars had to be sanded down to the wood; that meant hoisting up in a bosun's chair, and I've never been fond of heights. I put in two and sometimes three days a week, much of that time by myself. Bone helped when he wasn't working on *Conch Out,* or at Marsten Marine or taking out a day charter, or when he hadn't been seized by the need to be alone at sea for an extended period. I offered to pay him longshoremen's day wages to work on *Annalise* on a regular basis, but he still wouldn't take money from me. He didn't make friends any more easily than I did and he had his own ideas, stubborn and prideful, about what was acceptable in a friendship and what wasn't.

At the rate the repairs were progressing, and with the off-island trip with Annalise coming up, there wasn't much chance the yawl would be ready for cruising until the end of the year. And maybe not even then.

We flew to New York via Miami the first week in June. We were away a total of three weeks. Five days in Manhattan: museums, restaurants, a couple of Broadway shows. I would've liked to hear a performance of the New York Philharmonic, but they were dark for the season. Annalise took one entire day to make the rounds of large fashion houses like Gloria Vanderbilt and Calvin Klein, as well as a couple of the smaller ones, lugging a portfolio of her designs and trying to wangle an audience with one of the head designers. I thought she was being naive, that she wouldn't get past the receptionist in any of the houses, and I was right. But the turnaways didn't dampen her enthusiasm. She left designs at two or three places, and held on to the belief that they were good enough to generate interest somewhere.

Six days in Paris, three in Monte Carlo, five in London. Annalise loved them all. For me the whole trip was an exhausting and uncomfortable experience. The cities were interesting enough, but not to my taste. Too many people, too many eyes. Every time we went through passport and customs checks, I felt exposed and vulnerable. I imagined policemen were watching me, thinking that I looked familiar. Ordinary citizens, too. In London a tourist pointed a camera in my direction, and I ducked and turned away before I realized it wasn't me but one of the double-decker buses behind me that he was interested in. If Annalise noticed my discomfort, she ignored it because she was having such a good time.

I was relieved to get back to St. Thomas. The island was my safe harbor, the Caribbean my comfort zone. An illusion, sure; I could've been recognized there just as easily as in New York or London or Europe. But everybody has a place where he feels secure, a lifestyle that suits him perfectly, and this was mine. More of a home, after only two and a half years, than Los Alegres or San Francisco had ever been.

I slept for fourteen hours and then went down to the harbor and talked Bone into a day sail on *Conch Out*. I needed time on a boat on the open sea to unwind and resettle.

It wasn't long after our return that things began to deteriorate rapidly between Annalise and me.

She was still on a high from the trip and she started lobbying for us to move to New York—"not immediately, in a year or two." I told her it wasn't going to happen, and why it wasn't going to happen. At first she pouted. Then, when the high faded and sank into a low, she turned broody and distant.

One set of the designs she'd distributed in New York came back stuffed in a envelope with no note and postage due. The others were never returned. This depressed her, started her drinking more than she had before. And the drinking brought out the bitch again.

"I'm never going to get anywhere with my designs living down here. If we were in New York I could talk to people, meet somebody who'd look at them and see the potential and give me a chance. Or I could enroll in Pratt Institute and eventually get a referral from them."

"How many times have we been over this?" I said. "New York is too expensive. And the weather is miserable."

"Somewhere outside the city, then."

"Same negatives apply."

"I suppose you want to stay here for the rest of our lives."

"That was the plan, wasn't it? We're settled now, we're safe here—"

"We'd be safe in New York, after all this time. That's just an excuse."

"Don't you like St. Thomas anymore?"

"You want the truth? No, not very much."

"Why? What's changed?"

"Nothing's changed, that's the point. There's not enough to do on an island this small—half the time I'm bored to tears. But you don't even notice. You don't seem to care about my feelings, my needs. All you care about is that goddamn boat of yours. And your black buddy Bone."

"That's not true, Annalise."

"Isn't it? Makes me wonder if you still love me. Or if now I'm just somebody you keep around to screw when you feel like it. . . ."

She drank more and more; I hardly ever saw her without a glass in her hand. We went out together less often. There were long silences whenever we were together. Our sex life slacked off, to the point where I was spending much more time on *Annalise* than I was on Annalise. It didn't seem to bother her. Before, she'd been in a constant state of heat, and the aggressor at least half the time; now the aggressiveness stopped altogether. She was still cooperative enough when I initiated lovemaking, but without any of the wantonness that had always made it special between us. She was the dutiful wife, nothing more.

I kept trying to put us back together, giving her little presents, surprising her with an evening at a restaurant she liked on St. John. Nothing worked. The rift between us kept on widening. But I refused to believe it was permanent. Denial. I needed us to be all right, so we'd be all right. Every marriage has its rocky periods, I told myself, and this was ours—a bad patch that would smooth itself out sooner or later.

There were other problems, too. By the end of hurricane season, she was no longer spending time with Maureen Verriker. When I asked her about it, all she'd say was a curt "The friendship's run its course." She wasn't seeing much of her other friends, either, the apparent reason being that she'd made a new one at Sapphire Bay she liked more. JoEllen something—Hall, I think—an artist who lived out near Red Hook.

I didn't care for JoEllen. She was from somewhere in Florida, one of the divorcées who stayed on to make a new life for herself. It wasn't much of a life, as far as I could see. She was fortyish, loud, bawdy—the bohemian type who dressed sloppily in shorts and a loose halter that kept threatening to expose one or the other of a pair of juiceless brown tits. A polar opposite to Annalise in every way except for their shared fondness for sun, steel and scratch bands, and rum punches. Beach buddies, drinking buddies. JoEllen lived hand to mouth on what she earned from seascapes and island scenes aimed at the tourist trade. Annalise thought the oils and watercolors were better than they were, just as she thought her fashion designs were better than they were. She saw JoEllen as another yet-to-be-discovered genius. JoEllen saw her as a regular source of free drinks and small loans.

They hung out together three or four days a week, sometimes well into the night. Once Annalise didn't get home until after midnight. I was waiting up for her and I heard her squeal the Mini into the driveway, veer off the pavement, and slaughter half a dozen plantings on the way down. She wasn't just drunk—she was glassy-eyed, slack-jawed, jelly-legged plastered.

I was furious. "What the hell's the matter with you, driving in that condition?" I yelled at her. "What if you'd had an accident, run over somebody?"

"Well, I didn't."

"But you could have. You could've been stopped, arrested, thrown in jail. Any kind of serious trouble, the police might do a background check, and then we'd be finished. We can't afford to call attention to ourselves, we can't afford to lose control—not ever. How many times have we been over that?"

"A million. Two million. That's your favorite word—control. You know what you are? A control freak, that's what you are."

"That's not true, I've never tried to control you—"

"Oh, bullshit, Richard. You've been controlling me for four god-damn years. Do this, don't do that, don't take chances, don't take risks. What's that if not controlling?"

"Being sensible. Being careful. Trying to keep us safe."

"Careful, right. Another of your favorite words. You don't sound like Richard anymore, you know that? You sound like that tight-assed accountant back in San Francisco, Jordan what's his name."

"Now who's spouting bullshit?"

"You are. Control, careful, sensible, safe. What happened to all the excitement you promised me?"

"Haven't you had enough already?"

"No! I'll never have enough. I told you a long time ago how it was with me. I can't stand the way we've been living, all safe and careful. I want to take risks again, live on the edge again. Feel alive again."

"There's a big difference between living on the edge and crossing the line. We're fugitives, for Christ's sake."

"*You're* a fugitive, not me. I don't know anything about what Jordan Wise did, I only know Richard Laidlaw. Remember?"

"If we're caught, no matter what you say or I say, you could still be convicted as an accessory. You think your life is dull and confining now? Imagine how it'd be in a prison cell!"

That was the first big fight we had, but not the last. She was contrite when she sobered up, and for a while she reined herself in. She still hung out with JoEllen, but there were no more drunk-driving inci-dents; I told her I'd take the car keys away from her and cut off her access to the joint bank account if she ever came home loaded again.

But then the holidays rolled up, and there was the night of the Ver-rikers' annual Christmas party.

Annalise didn't want to go, which would've been all right with me, but at the last minute she changed her mind. She and Maureen were stiff with each other when we arrived, avoided each other after that. At one point I asked Verriker what the problem was between them; he shrugged and said, "Beats me." Usually at parties Annalise was animated and charming, and restrained in her drinking. At this one she kept refilling her glass at the punchbowl, and the more she drank, the more erratic her behavior became.

I didn't realize how drunk she was until she dropped and shattered her glass on the floor tiles and then upset somebody's plate of hors d'oeuvres. I was trying to ease her out of there without making a scene, when she said, in a voice loud enough for Verriker and some of the other guests to hear, "Oh, for Christ's sake, why can't you just let me enjoy myself? So I spilled a drink and some food, so what? I'm not gonna spill the beans, you know. Secrets are safe with me, yours, everybody's. My lips're sealed."

"Be quiet!" I snapped at her.

"Whoops," she said. "Oh, shit."

Verriker said, "Maybe you'd better take her home, Richard."

"Yeah. Right away."

I dragged her out of there. When I got her into the house I caught her arms and shook her, hard. "Are you crazy? Are you trying to get us caught?"

"God, no." She wasn't fighting me. The night air had sobered her a little; she seemed horrified by what she'd done. "I don't know what happened. . . . It just slipped out. . . ."

"How many other times has something 'just slipped out'? To Maureen, to JoEllen, to Christ knows who else?"

"Never—never! First and last time, I swear."

"It better be the last time," I said. "I mean it, Annalise. Don't ever get drunk enough in public to make a slip like that again. If you do . . ."

She swore she wouldn't. Over Christmas and New Year's she controlled her drinking, stayed home most evenings. We still weren't spending a lot of time in each other's company—work on the yawl was nearing completion and I was putting in long hours at the marina—but when we were together, she seemed to make an effort to be reasonable and good-natured. No more pressure about moving, no more bitchy behavior, a couple of sessions in bed that she didn't treat as duty fucks. I felt relieved. It looked as if she'd gotten her perspective back and the bad patch was beginning to smooth out at last.

Work on *Annalise* was finally done at the end of January.

She was a thing of beauty by then, a sight to make you catch your breath when you stood off on the stringpiece and looked at her in the slanting rays of the sun. Her spars and brightwork, her hull and deckhouse gleamed with thick coats of varnish and blue and white paint, her brass was shined to a high gloss, her new Dacron sails had a freshly laundered dazzle when unfurled. The ship-to-shore radio worked fine. The overhauled auxiliary diesel ran without a hitch during every ten-minute test run. In the cockpit, all the gauges and dials were in perfect working order and the new compass sat bright and shiny in its gimbals. Belowdecks, the marine refrigerator and primus stove in the tiny galley were in order, the ventilators and new bilge pump worked fine, every fitting and connection had passed muster.

And she was mine, all mine.

January and February are usually optimum cruising months in the eastern Caribbean. Clear weather, light winds, calm seas. I picked an arbitrary sail date, the twenty-eighth, which fit into Bone's schedule. Then I gave Annalise a full week's advance notice. She wasn't thrilled at the prospect of four days on a thirty-four-foot yawl, but when I reminded her of her promise, she agreed to honor it. I asked her if she wanted to come down to the harbor early and see what all the months of hard work had accomplished; she said no, she'd wait and be surprised on the twenty-eighth. I thought about inviting Jack Scanlon and the

Kyles for a look, decided it could wait until after the shakedown voyage. The only people I really cared to share the yawl with until then were Annalise and Bone.

I plotted out a course that would take us south around St. John, up through Flanagan Passage into Sir Francis Drake Channel, along the east coast of Virgin Gorda and out across the Hawks Bill Bank; we'd swing north by northeast near Horseshoe Reef and run due east through deep water outside the dangerous coral heads that ring Anegada, then drop down across the Kingfish Banks and home to St. Thomas through the Virgin's Gangway. Bone approved. It would be a good long test of *Annalise*'s seaworthiness, and there were anchorages on Tortola, Guana Island, and Virgin Gorda, and a safe harbor at Anegada for emergencies or if any of us felt like an overnight stop.

The long-range forecast promised perfect sailing weather for the four-day period beginning on the twenty-eighth. The day before, Bone and I loaded in stores, topped off the fuel and water tanks, put fresh linens on one of the vee bunks up forward for him and on the double berth in the main cabin for Annalise and me. I ran the engine for ten minutes one more time, even though there hadn't been any tendency toward overheating; the gauge held steady at 140 degrees. Fussily, I even rechecked the gland nut in the stuffing box for any looseness that might cause leakage.

At six that night, the yawl was ready for sea.

At six the next morning, Annalise refused to go along.

She didn't feel well, she said. She thought maybe she was coming down with something, she said. It made her seasick just thinking about being out on the water, she said. I suspected that she was faking, but she sounded so apologetic and sincere, I didn't call her on it. I offered to postpone the trip; she said no, she felt bad enough as it was, she didn't want to deprive me of my pleasure. Why didn't Bone and I just go ahead, she'd come along next time, swear to God she would. I was disappointed and a little upset, but what could I do short of branding her a liar and shanghaiing her? She kept urging me to go, and so finally I went.

As soon as the yawl was out of the harbor and under sail, tacking up against a light southeasterly breeze, I forgot my disappointment and I forgot Annalise. Reality isn't always as wonderful as the anticipation of it, but in this case it was even better. *Annalise* handled like a dream. There is no other feeling like standing at the helm of your own boat, the wind in your face and the sea smell in your nostrils, listening to the hiss of the water and the wind-fattened sheets singing and the lines, shrouds, and stays thrumming in accompaniment. It's more than just exhilaration, a rush or a high. It's freedom and wonder and a kind of pure and innocent joy. I've never put much stock in religion, but there's something spiritual about it, too, an almost mystical connection of man to nature. If there is a God, the closest I've ever gotten or will ever get to Him is the days and nights I spent on that yawl at sea.

We were out four full days, and it was superb sailing the entire time. Running down the trades at four and five knots, the deep water an ever-changing mosaic of blues and greens topped by foaming crests, puffy white trade-wind clouds that never banked or darkened. Even the routine of sea-keeping—checking the chafe points on sheets and sails, restowing shifted supplies, all the other little chores—was a pleasure. We stood watch and watch, four hours on and four hours off; the man on watch steered and trimmed sail, the man off watch did the cooking and bilge-pumping and slept when he could.

We didn't talk much; there was no need for conversation. All your senses are heightened at sea, your thoughts clear and sharp, and you'd much rather tune in on them than on spoken words. The nights were even better than the days, with the vast, star-shot sky draped low overhead and the water sometimes black as oil, sometimes glistening with starshine and luminescent moon tracks.

121

When we got back to St. Thomas I docked the yawl without a bump, whisper smooth. Bone said, "Good job, Cap'n"—he'd taken to calling me Cap'n on the cruise, a term of respect—and I grinned and nodded. I felt as I had the afternoon I walked out of Amthor Associates for the last time. Apart from ordinary men, above them at a great height. Happier, more content than they could ever be.

The illusion, the delusion, lasted until I walked through the front door of the Quartz Gade villa.

And found that Annalise was gone.

No warning. No explanation, no good-byes.

Gone from the house, gone from the island—destination unknown. Vanished into thin air, just as Jordan Wise had vanished from San Francisco.

Everything of value that she could pack into her three suitcases went with her. Jewelry, hers and mine both. Clothing. The antique music box and a handful of gold doubloons we'd bought on St. Martin and all the gold and silver trinkets. The only thing she left behind was the brass-bound pirate's chest, and that was only because it was too bulky and too heavy to be easily transported.

Money, too?

Oh, hell, yes. All the cash from the safe deposit box, everything in the joint bank account, more than $26,000. If any of the stocks had been negotiable for her, they would've been gone as well. If she'd had access to the Cayman account, she'd have plundered that and left me with exactly the same amount she had left in the joint account.

One dollar.

One fucking dollar.

And there wasn't a damn thing I could do about it.

ST. THOMAS

1982

THE FIRST WEEK was very bad.

I didn't leave the house, didn't bathe or shave or bother to get dressed except for a pair of shorts. I drank steadily, without ever getting to the blotting-out stage, until the supply of liquor ran out. I raged at her. I raged at myself for misjudging her and for being too stupid to see it coming, and because maybe part of it was my fault for neglecting her, and because there was still some residual love left in me in spite of what she'd done. The phone rang three times during that week and I answered each time, thinking it might be Annalise, and when I heard somebody else's voice I hung up without saying a word.

When I couldn't stand the empty house or my own miserable company any longer, I cleaned up and got out of there. I needed to talk to somebody, and the only one I could confide in was Bone.

He listened to me unload as much as I dared to, without interrupting. His face showed no emotion, but I could tell that he empathized; we were friends and he'd gone through the same kind of thing himself with the second wife whose name he wouldn't mention. He didn't offer any bullshit advice, as most men would have. All he said was, "You hurting bad, Richard. Mon hurts like that, only one thing to do. Go out. Let wind and sea wash out the poison."

I said, "Will you go with me?"

"No, mon. No place for Bone on that kind of trip."

"Alone? I couldn't do it. I'm not ready to singlehand."

"You're ready," he said. "You never be more ready."

The next day I put in fresh stores, fuel, water. Then I painted a new name on the yawl's transom and reregistered her with the harbormaster's office. Annalise was gone; I wanted *Annalise* gone, too. Her new name, picked at random, was *Windrunner*.

The day after that, I left early into a stiff wind and an uncertain forecast. I had no idea where I was going. If I succeeded as a singlehander, fine. If I screwed up badly enough so that the yawl lost a mast or broached and went down, so be it. I didn't much care then, either way.

I set sail to windward on a starboard tack and let the trades take me wherever they felt like. I had a little trouble handling her at first, without Bone's sure hand with the rigging and the Dacron, and came close once to a bad jibe. But the lessons I'd learned from him, plus instinct and applied skill, allowed me to regain and maintain control.

The not-caring didn't last long. Singlehanding a thirty-four-foot yawl is work, hard work, and requires constant vigilance even under optimum conditions. When you have a passion for sailing, the work soon translates to pleasure and then to that sense of exhilarating freedom. I *could* singlehand. I was on my own boat, alone on the open sea. Everything else diminishes after a while, loses some of its importance—even betrayal and a suddenly brutalized love.

By nightfall I was no longer running aimlessly. I reckoned my position by compass and celestial navigation, used the nautical almanacs and logarithmic tables to chart a course that would take *Windrunner* on a broad loop around St. Croix, and put her on the right coordinates.

The weather held until the afternoon of the third day, when I encountered a rain squall off East Point on the northeastern tip of

St. Croix. That was the only real test of my seamanship that I faced. A following breeze had risen, and before long the swells steepened and there was a rough cross chop. Then, as the wind increased, I saw the squall line moving in dark and fast. I double-checked the hatches, lashed down the loose gear, then went forward to replace the genoa with a working jib, again to reef in the main, and one more time to replace the working jib with the storm jib. Rain burst over the yawl in a blinding tropical downpour. The squall lasted about an hour, but despite the driving rain and thrashing sea it wasn't bad as Caribbean blows go. *Windrunner* showed no desire to broach, and I rode it out with the wheel tied down and a lifeline fastened around my waist and clipped to a backstay.

I stayed out five and a half days. At night I slept on the cushions in the cockpit aft. Every morning I pumped the bilges, ran the auxiliary for an hour to charge the batteries, checked the sails and halyards. I shot the sun at noon and took star sights at dusk and dawn, and kept a daily log. The yawl sailed herself with the wind abeam or on the quarter; those times I ran a piece of the sheet from a cleat on the lee coaming to the wheel's king spoke to keep her off the wind, and made my meals and lazed on deck, communing with the towering emptiness of sea and sky. I saw schools of flying fish, and what I was sure was the dorsal fin of a trailing shark. I passed deserted cays and other boats with their sails bellied fat, and avoided reefs, and once made five knots running close-hauled against the wind.

Bone was right, as usual.

When I sailed back into the harbor at Charlotte Amalie, the poison was gone.

The second dose came two weeks later.

I was all right then. But I wouldn't have been if I hadn't purged myself of the first dose with that long singlehand voyage.

I don't know why I picked that Tuesday to make my last visit to the Royal Bay Club. I don't believe in predestination, cosmic manipulation, any of that crap. It was a random choice of day and time to clean out my locker and cancel my membership. I'd never really felt comfortable at the club, and now there was no longer any need to keep up appearances. Since my return I'd managed to avoid the Verrikers and Kyles and other members, and I intended to keep on avoiding them; the last thing I wanted to have to deal with was pity.

The club was usually more or less deserted in the middle of the afternoon, the hottest part of the day. I expected to be in and out in a few minutes. The fact that Gavin Kyle happened to be in the lounge, and I happened to overhear him talking to the British banker, Horler, was sheer coincidence.

The steward wasn't in his customary cubicle at the front entrance, so I walked into the lounge looking for him. Gavin and Horler were at the bar. I would have done a quick about-face before they saw me, except that voices carry in a mostly empty room. When I heard Gavin use my name, I stopped and listened.

"You can't help but feel sorry for Laidlaw," he was saying in his gossipy way. "He doesn't know how much better off he is without that bitch. She—"

I was on the move by then, straight toward them. Horler spotted me first and jabbed Gavin with his knee. When Gavin saw me, his moon face warped in on itself as if squeezed from within. He squirmed visibly on his stool.

"Go ahead," I said. "Don't let me stop you."

"Christ, Richard, I—"

"Let's hear the rest of it."

Horler muttered an excuse and made a hasty exit. Gavin gulped his drink and started to get up, but I held him down with a hand on his shoulder. His eyes pleaded with me, as if he were a dog about to be kicked.

"I'm not going to make a scene," I said. "I'll just buy you a drink and we'll chat a little."

"I don't blame you for being pissed—"

"I'm not pissed. What're you drinking?"

". . . Scotch and soda."

I ordered another round for him, a double shot of Arundel for myself. Then I said, "What did you mean, I'm better off without that bitch?"

"I've got a big mouth," he said. "Robin says so, and she's usually right about my shortcomings."

"What did you mean?"

"You don't really want to hear it."

"Why is Annalise a bitch? Why am I better off?"

The drinks came and he slugged half of his. "All right, you asked for it," he said, not quite looking at me. "She wasn't faithful to you. She . . . well, not for a long time."

It was several seconds before I asked, "How long a time?"

"At least six months."

"How many men?"

"I'm not sure. Two that I know of."

"The first?"

"Does it matter?"

"You, Gavin?"

"Christ! I don't play around. Never have, never will."

"Who, then?"

"If I tell you . . . what're you going to do?"

"Nothing," I said. What could I do that wouldn't call attention to me? "I'm not the confrontational type. Or the violent type. I just need to know."

I watched him struggle with it for half a minute. Then he said, "Screw it, I don't owe him any favors," and swallowed some of his fresh drink. "Royce Verriker."

Verriker. I felt a rush of hatred for him. *Every man needs a vice; mine is making money.* And making friends' wives.

"How do you know?"

"I saw him going into your house one afternoon," Gavin said. "When you were out and Maureen was away visiting in San Juan."

"It could've been innocent."

"It wasn't. I asked him about it later on and he owned up."

"Just like that, he owned up?"

"You don't know Royce like I do. He's a shit when it comes to women. Likes to brag about his conquests. He never bragged to you?"

"No. But then he wouldn't, would he, if he was screwing Annalise."

Gavin made the rest of his Scotch disappear. "He's been like that ever since I've known him. Dozens of women—that divorce practice of his is tailor-made."

"How long did it go on with him and Annalise?"

"A while. Until he met somebody new, I guess."

"Does Maureen know what he is?"

"Hell, how could she not know? She either doesn't care or just turns a blind eye because she loves him."

So that was the cause of the rift between her and Annalise, the reason they'd stopped being friends. Had Annalise felt any shame? Probably not. Did she feel any over running out on me? Probably not.

"Who else besides Verriker?" I asked him.

"Nobody you or I know. Some rich tourist from New York."

"Name?"

"Jackson, Johnson, something like that. Manufacturer of women's clothing. Down here for the sport fishing, stayed at the old Grand."

"How do you know about him?"

"It was right before she left you," Gavin said. "A week or so. By then she wasn't bothering to be discreet about it. Snuggling up to him in public, spent at least one night in his room while you were off on your cruise."

"When did he go back north?"

"I can't tell you that. You'd have to ask at the hotel." Pause. "You think she ran off with him?"

Of course she'd run off with him. A women's clothing manufacturer from New York? She'd have sat naked on his lap on the plane for an opportunity like that.

Gavin said, "Richard, man, you're not thinking of going after her and this guy? Trying to get her back?"

"No," I said.

He seemed relieved. "That's the right attitude. What you heard me say to Horler . . . well, it's a fact. You really are better off without her."

He was right.

I had no doubt of it by then.

In an odd way, finding out the full scope of Annalise's betrayal made it easier for me to get on with my life. You might think that I hated her then, but I didn't. Nor did I have any love left. I felt nothing at all for her. It was as if someone who had once been very close to me had died, and I'd gone through a short period of bereavement, and then I was able to move ahead with no emotional baggage.

At first I tried to figure out how and where it had all gone wrong, if there was a turning point, any specific incident that had led to her betrayal. But of course there wasn't. It was a gradual thing. She had been right when she accused me of evolving back into Jordan Wise, but she'd been undergoing a metamorphosis of her own. We were two divergent life forms, changing in opposing ways—that was what had doomed our relationship. It wouldn't have mattered if I'd realized it along the way. I couldn't have stopped it. The deterioration, the decay, was inevitable.

I could see all this now with an objective eye, as if across a chasm. I understood Annalise as I never had before. And I understood myself, as an individual and in relation to her.

She'd given me a lot to be thankful for since that night in her apartment in San Francisco. Four years of greater passion and stimulation than I'd ever known. St. Thomas and the sea and sailing and Bone's friendship. But I hadn't given her all she'd wanted. She had never been content living here. Or content with me. From the first, I was a means to an end, a source of satisfaction for her cravings—an integral part of a package deal. If she'd ever felt love for me, even a little, it had been for that reason and that reason alone. That was why she'd stayed with me as long as she had.

Verriker had been a dalliance, a way to relieve the restless boredom. The New York clothing manufacturer had been a ready-to-wear excuse. When I refused to satisfy the most important of her hungers, a shot at the New York fashion world, she ran off with the first man who could offer it to her. She'd been gone a long time before she actually left.

What it boiled down to was that I couldn't have held on to her because I'd never really had her in the first place. That was what hurt the most. Even at the moments of our deepest connection, in and out of bed, she'd never really been mine in the way that I'd been hers. I don't mean love—I mean the extension and commingling of self, the absorption of one persona into the other that creates a bonded third. Or, hell, maybe I do mean love. Maybe that's another thing love is, the only definition that's not strictly personal.

If I hated anybody during that time, it was myself for not understanding sooner. Love is blind—the platitude makers got that one right. Blind and stupid and short-sighted. I accepted that, and accepted that I was a fool for believing otherwise. That was why, when the hurt went away, the rest of the emotion went with it.

Did I stay in the villa? Yes. I would have moved out right away, except that the lease ran until December; I'd been paying the rent in six-month increments to take advantage of a discount offered by the owners. Giving it up immediately would have meant breaking the lease and taking a heavy financial hit, because one condition of the discount was that the biannual payments were nonrefundable. I'd been so careful with money up to then, I couldn't bring myself to throw away thousands of dollars for no good reason.

Aside from a short period of adjustment, I had no trouble learning to be alone again. I slept at the villa most nights, but I spent very little time there otherwise. Days, except when there was a storm, I was at Sub Base harbor or Frenchtown or the native quarter, or out on *Windrunner.* In port I worked on the yawl's upkeep or just sat on deck reading and listening to music. Sometimes Bone would join me; sometimes I would join him on *Conch Out.* I ate all my meals alone or with him on one boat or the other, or in Harry's Dockside Café or one of the native eateries. Now and then I would drive over to Red Hook to see Dick Marsten, or up to the top of Crown Mountain for a sunset watch, or out to Coki Bay or Sapphire Bay for a swim and some snorkeling among the coral reefs. Once at Sapphire I helped a native kid with a speargun drag a big moray eel in from the reefs offshore—an ugly creature with a body like a bar of white iron and foxlike jaws, that even dead scared hell out of a couple of female tourists.

St. Thomas crawled with unattached and willing women; it would have been easy enough to pick one up for a one-night stand. But I had no interest in playing that kind of game. No interest in female companionship, no interest in sex. My libido had reverted to what it was before I met Annalise. Maybe that would change eventually, I thought, and maybe it wouldn't. It didn't seem to matter much either way.

What mattered was doing as I pleased twenty-four hours a day, every day, with no encumbrances. I didn't have to attend any more parties, play any more handball, dance in any more nightclubs or eat in any more expensive restaurants or take any more lengthy trips that didn't involve sailing. I let my hair get long and shaggy and I grew a beard to go with my mustache. I saw none of the people who no longer cared to see me. The only one of that crowd who ever came around, once, was Jack Scanlon. I didn't encourage him and he never came again.

After a while I came to realize that I not only preferred this way of life to the one I'd had with Annalise, but that it was actually a relief to be alone again. You can change your financial status, your environment, your perspective, but you can't change your basic nature. After three years or thirty, you're still the same person. Jordan Wise had led a quiet, contemplative, mostly celibate, loner's existence in San Francisco; Richard Laidlaw, without Annalise, gravitated to the same on St. Thomas. She had been only half right when she accused me of evolving back into my former self. I'd never really been anything else.

I thought about her less and less. And when I did, it was only to wonder, with detached curiosity, whether she was still with the manufacturer, whether her intro into the fashion industry had paid off, whether she had any regrets, whether she ever thought of me. I didn't wish her ill and I didn't wish her well—I didn't care one way or the other.

Out of sight, out of heart, out of mind.

Gone.

On one of the solo voyages on *Windrunner*, I discovered an island. A tiny cay, actually, out near the Kingfish Banks, so small and low-lying it didn't have a name on the charts. It was about the size of a couple of football fields, humped in the middle, not much more than a sandspit formed by the action of wind and sea. One day it would probably disappear if a Category 4 or 5 hurricane passed anywhere near it.

Curiosity and the fact that the day was clear and the seas calm led me to explore it. I hunted up a gap in the reef that surrounds almost every cay, large or small, eased in as close as I dared under power, and then weighed anchor and put the dinghy over and rowed in the rest of the way. There was nothing on the cay other than a few twisted screw palms, scatters of broken coral and shells, some tiny, almost translucent crabs, and a noisy colony of nesting terns and frigate birds. It was a beautiful place, quiet except for the birds and the murmur of the sea, lonely unless you were a loner yourself. There were tidepools and a little lagoon among the reefs on the leeward side, the water so clear you could see the dark red starfish on the bottom sand and the multicolored fish darting in and out among the lace and brain coral. I stripped down and had a swim in the lagoon. Later, in the tidepools, I caught a brace of yellow-and-black-mottled crayfish and pried loose a couple of dozen mussels.

Fine, lazy afternoon, so much enjoyed that I returned twice over the next few months for more of the same. On the third trip, I decided the spit-kit needed a name and christened it Laidlaw Cay. When I told Bone about it, he laughed and said, "Next thing, you gonna want to move out there and build a house."

"Nope. I was thinking of burying my loot on it like one of the old buccaneers."

"Not you, mon. No pirate blood in you."

That made me laugh. That's what you think, my friend, I thought. That's what you think!

On the first of November I gave six weeks' notice that I would not be renewing the villa's lease. That was fine with the real estate agent: rental prices were climbing—there were a lot of new expats moving in, and other wealthy people looking for vacation homes—and the owners would be able to command a much higher lease price from the next tenant. He asked whether I wanted him to find me a smaller house or apartment, but I said no. I was spending so much time on *Windrunner*, I figured I would try living on her once the lease expired. Her main cabin was large enough to hold all my possessions. Surprisingly few possessions, I found when I took stock of them—clothing, a small collection of books, the brass-bound chest, a few odds and ends. And I could rent a parking space for the Mini cheap.

All the prospects looked good. Life looked good. Uncomplicated. Comfortable.

Then, without warning, the bottom fell out again.

I was having lunch alone in Harry's Dockside Café. A day like any other day. The place wasn't crowded and I was at a corner table, looking out through the open-air window while I ate, admiring a racing yawl with a balloon spinnaker, hull down on the horizon, tacking in search of a steady breeze. The scrape of the chair opposite pulled my gaze around. A man I didn't know sat down and fed me a lopsided smile around a thin, dark-brown cheroot.

He was about my age, late thirties, short but muscular, and hard-looking in an indolent way. Thick biceps bulged the sleeves of the blue pullover he wore. Fair hair, blue eyes, a sideways bend in his nose that indicated it once had been broken and the break hadn't healed properly. Pale skin that marked him as a snowbird, the local name for northern tourists who flock to the Caribbean in the winter months. He seemed vaguely familiar, but I couldn't quite place him.

"What's that you're eating?" he said.

"Fish chowder."

"Looks greasy. How's it taste?"

"It tastes fine," I said. "Even better without cigar smoke."

He tapped ash on the floor. "I don't like fish," he said. "That's all you get down here, fish and more fish."

"Try one of the downtown restaurants."

"They serve meat in this place? Any kind of red meat?"

"Look, I really don't want company—"

"Maybe I'll just have a beer."

"Have it at another table."

"I like this one."

He sat watching me, smoking, while I spooned up the chowder. I could feel his eyes on my face, like bugs crawling; they were making me uncomfortable. I pushed the bowl away and started to get up.

"Hold on there," he said. "Let's talk a little."

"I don't think so. I've got work to do—"

"The work can wait. My name's Cutter, Fred Cutter."

"Good for you."

"And you're Richard Laidlaw."

". . . You know me?"

"I know a lot of things about you."

"What do you want? Are you selling something?"

"Might say that."

"Well, whatever it is, I'm not interested. I don't need anything."

"You need what I'm selling. You just don't know it yet."

"All right, what is it you think I need?"

"Silence," Cutter said.

"What?"

"Richard Laidlaw's a good name," he said, "but I like Jordan Wise better."

I could feel the muscles pull as my back stiffened. I went cold all over. "You must have me mixed up with somebody else."

"I don't think so. Not anymore." The lopsided smile was broader. My control had slipped for only a second or two, but that was long enough for him to see it. "I thought I recognized you when we bumped into each other yesterday morning. I wasn't a hundred percent sure, with the beard and the long hair. Now . . . I'm sure."

Outside my bank on Dronningens Gade, that was where I'd seen him before. We'd almost collided on the sidewalk when I walked out.

I said, "I've never heard of anybody named Jordan Wise."

"You're not from San Francisco, either, I suppose?"

"That's right, I'm not."

"I used to live in Frisco myself," Cutter said. "Worked for an insurance company in the same building as Amthor Associates. I saw you a few times in the elevators, the lobby, remembered you when the story broke in the papers. Everybody figured you disappeared into Mexico, but no, you came down here instead. Real clever, the way you pulled off the whole deal."

Crazy coincidence. The y factor. Three years, all the traveling in the Caribbean, to New York, Paris, Monte Carlo, London, and recognition happens right here in Charlotte Amalie.

"I've never even been to San Francisco," I said. "I'm from Chicago."

"Uh-huh. Retired tool-and-die manufacturer, made a killing in the stock market, sold your business and showed up here three years ago. Out of the same blue Jordan Wise disappeared into."

"If you know all that about me . . ."

"I know that's your cover story. I made it my business to find out."

"You want me to prove I'm Richard Laidlaw? My passport says so. So does my driver's license."

"Sure they do," Cutter said. "The way you had the embezzlement and the disappearance planned out so smooth, you had to've arranged for some pretty good false ID."

He was leaning forward, his voice low, confidential, but I couldn't stop myself from glancing around at the other tables. Nobody was paying any attention to us. He didn't want to be overheard any more than I did.

"Pretty good," he said, "but not perfect. Wouldn't stand up to a background check. And then there's fingerprints. The FBI must have yours on file."

"If you're so sure of yourself, why come to me? Why not just go to the FBI and turn me in?"

"Well, I'll tell you, Jordan, I thought about doing that. Might be a reward or something, even after four years. But then I thought, no, why not give you a break? I admire the way you pulled off that big score of yours. Real clever, like I said."

"Blackmail."

"I don't like that word. Call it a business deal. You thought I was a salesman when I first sat down, okay, that's what I am. I sell silence and you're in the market. I'm happy, Richard Laidlaw stays free and happy, too. Simple."

"How much, Cutter?"

"Well, I don't know yet. I'm not sure just what to charge."

"How much?"

"I mean, what I have to offer is a one-of-a-kind commodity, right? I don't want to sell it too cheap. Then again, I don't want to set a price so high it puts a strain on the deal."

"I'm not as well off as you might think," I said. "I've already spent a lot of what I came here with."

"Not all that much, you haven't. I told you, I did some checking up. You'd be surprised how much you can find out about somebody in twenty-four hours, if you see the right people and ask the right questions."

"All right. You've made your point."

"Tell you what," Cutter said. "I'll give it some thought and let you know. You going to be around that boat of yours the rest of the day?"

"Yes."

"Maybe I'll drop by later. Or else give you a call at home tonight."

"I'll be there after six."

"Good man." He pushed his chair back, then leaned toward me again. "One thing, Jordan—"

"Don't call me that. That's not my name."

"Sure. One thing, Richard. Don't go getting any ideas about trying to run. You wouldn't get very far."

"I won't run."

"Just so we understand each other. If you're not on the boat when I come around, or not home when I call, I won't waste any time having a talk with the FBI."

He stood up. "Well, it's been a pleasure. Later." The lopsided grin again, and he was gone.

He didn't show up at the yawl. I didn't expect him to. Old psychological ploy: once you've got somebody on the hook, let him squirm for a while—make sure he's good and caught.

I squirmed plenty at first. Panic kept rising and I had to struggle to hold it down. Once I thought, To hell with Cutter, to hell with the FBI, go straight downtown and clean out the bank account and catch the first plane out of St. Thomas, no matter what its destination. Or sail the yawl to Puerto Rico and charter a small plane or catch a commercial flight before the alarm went out. But without a careful plan and enough time to implement it, running was a fool's game. They'd catch me quick, and that kind of caught meant federal prison until I was too old to care anymore. Even if I'd had time to make a plan, where would I go and how would I establish a new identity? St. Thomas was the only place I wanted to be. Richard Laidlaw was the only man I wanted to be.

Eventually I stopped squirming. Bitter resignation set in. Pay Cutter his blood money, whatever the amount, and hope he wouldn't come back too often. What else could I do?

He didn't call that night either. I drank too much, waiting, but there was no more inclination to panic. He'd call in the morning, early—I knew that before I went to bed. The bastard was too eager for his payoff to let me squirm for long.

The phone rang at seven fifteen. I'd been up two hours by then. "I thought it over," he said, "and five thousand seems like a nice round number. What do you think?"

"I can afford that," I said.

"Sure you can. Cash, nothing larger than a hundred."

"When and where?"

"How about I come up to your house tonight around eight o'clock? That way we can do our business in private."

"I'll have the money waiting."

"Good man. You know, I think we'll get along just fine."

Five thousand dollars. Not nearly as much of a bite as I'd expected. He'd want more later—blackmailers never stop bleeding their victims—but if he limited the amounts to five thousand and spread them far enough apart, it would be a tolerable price to pay to keep my freedom.

It was almost eight thirty before the doorbell rang. Muggy night, overcast, storm clouds making up on the horizon; the barometer had been falling steadily since mid-afternoon. A salt-laden northwest wind was already blowing at around twenty knots. I had the doors and jalousies open and all the fans running, but the house still sweltered with a sauna-like stickiness.

Cutter wasn't late on purpose, it turned out. His face had a dark-red flush, and he was breathing heavily and wiping away a coating of sweat, when I opened the door. The yellow shirt he wore over white ducks showed dark stains under the arms and down the front.

"Whew," he said, "that's some goddamn climb. That last set of steps almost did me in."

"You walked up here?"

"No point in renting a car. I won't be on this island much longer and I'd probably have gotten lost anyway. But I'd've grabbed a hack if I'd known what a ballbuster of a hike it was."

I led him into the living room. He stood fanning himself with his hand, looking around. "No air conditioning?"

"No. Just the ceiling fans."

"How the hell do you stand the humidity? It's like a fucking oven in here."

"You get used to it."

"Not me, brother. All those clouds piling up, smells like rain."

"Storm forecast for tonight."

"Well, I'm not hoofing it down those steps in the rain. You can drive me back to my hotel." He went to the open terrace doors, stepped out briefly as if to make sure there was nobody lurking around out there, and came back inside. "I could use a cold beer," he said.

"I don't have any beer."

"A drink, then. Gin and tonic, vodka tonic, something cold."

"Only liquor I have in the house is rum."

"Rum. All right then, rum. What've have you got to mix it with? Tonic, juice?"

"Water and ice, that's all."

"Christ. You're some host, you know that?"

At the sideboard I poured twice from the cut-glass decanter of Arundel, added ice cubes to my glass, ice and water to his. He took a long pull, made a face.

"I don't know what you see in this stuff," he said. "Tastes like cough medicine to me."

"Don't drink it if you don't like it."

"Let's get down to business. Where's the money?"

"Manila envelope on the coffee table."

He moved over there, scooped it up, sat down with it in one of the rattan chairs. I followed him, perched on the sofa, and watched him open the envelope, dump the rubber-banded packets onto his lap, riffle through each one. Then he let me see his crooked grin.

"Five thousand on the nose, all fifties and hundreds. I figured you'd come through, but I had to be sure. Good man, Jordan."

"I asked you not to call me that."

"Yeah, okay, whatever." Cutter put the money back into the envelope, slugged more of his drink and then rolled the wet glass across his forehead. He was still oozing sweat, his face still red-flushed with prickly heat; the wet spots on his yellow shirt hadn't dried any. "How the hell can you stand this climate? Even at night, you can hardly breathe."

"It isn't always this muggy."

"Well, you can have it. Closing in on winter up north, but I'd rather freeze my ass off than suffocate any day."

"Where do you live, up north?"

"Uh-uh," he said, "you don't need to know that. All you need to know is what I tell you. Now here's the deal, Jordan. Tomorrow—"

"Richard. My name is Richard."

"Jordan, Richard, who the hell cares?"

"I care," I said.

"Just shut up and listen. I wasn't going to spring this on you for another day or two, but I've had enough of this shithole. I'm leaving as soon as I can rebook my flight. And when I go, I'm taking the second installment with me."

I tightened up inside. "What do you mean, second installment?"

"You think all I wanted was a paltry five thousand? Uh-uh. This was just a test."

"How much more?"

"Another twenty-five."

"Twenty-five thousand!"

"Nonnegotiable and no arguments. Then I'll go away and you can stay here and keep on drying out like old shoe leather."

"Until the next time, the next installment."

"Don't worry about that," Cutter said. "You just go back to your bank tomorrow and draw out the twenty-five thousand and have it waiting for me here when I call you. Fifties and hundreds, same as the first installment."

"I don't have that much in my account."

"Then get it from the one in the Cayman Islands. A wire transfer doesn't take long."

". . . How did you know about the Cayman account?"

"How do you think? Same way I found out everything else about you."

"Not by asking around, you didn't," I said. "Nobody on this island knows about that account but me and my bank, and they wouldn't give out the information."

"Well, somebody else knows."

I got it then. All at once, like a rocket going off inside my head. Crazy coincidence, hell. Y factor, hell. Y plus x equals xy squared—that was the real equation here. My hands had started to shake. I pressed them together, hard, between my knees.

"Annalise," I said.

His face bunched into a scowl. "Who?"

"Blue eyes. Jesus, I should've known. She always was partial to men with blue eyes."

"Huh?"

"*She* told you. That's how you knew about the Cayman account. About Jordan Wise. About the steps from downtown, too—you couldn't have figured out the way up here just from looking at a city map, or been able to find this house in the dark. You're not from San Francisco, you never laid eyes on me before that bump in front of the bank. She told you where to find me, told you everything. You're in this together, you and Annalise."

He didn't try to deny it. "Oh, what the hell," he said. "She didn't want you to know, but you figured it out anyway and I don't give a shit. That's right, me and Annalise."

"How long have you known her?" I could barely get the words out.

"Three months, if it matters."

"Living together?"

"Uh-uh. I had enough of that."

"What about her?"

"What do you care?"

"Where does she live? New York City?"

"Never mind where. None of your business anymore." The grin was back on his mouth. Now that the truth was out, he was openly enjoying himself. "She's some piece," he said.

"Some piece."

"You were lucky to hang on to her as long as you did, you know that? Woman like her." The grin widened into a smirk. "Really something in bed, isn't she? Man, she could suck the varnish off a table leg."

I couldn't look at his face any longer. I lowered my gaze to the front of his shirt, fixed it there. You could almost see the sweat stain spreading. The shape, if you looked long enough, seemed oddly trapezoidal.

"She come down here with you?"

"No way. She's had it with this island."

"The blackmail—her idea?"

"Mine," Cutter said. "We were drinking one night, she had a little too much and dropped your name, and I dragged the whole story out of her. But she didn't try to talk me out of it, I'll tell you that. She needs money, same as me."

"Why does she need money?"

"Dumb question, Jordan. Everybody needs money. The shittier your job, the more you need."

"What kind of shitty job?"

"Quit trying to pump me. You got all the information you're going to."

I had something else I wanted to say, something I wanted him to tell her, but the words seemed clogged in my throat. Even after another swallow of rum I couldn't push them out.

Cutter pasted one of his dark-brown cheroots into a corner of his mouth, left it there unlighted. His drink was gone; he rolled the tumbler over his forehead again, then tapped the melting ice cubes into his mouth and began to chew them, the cigar bobbing up and down with the motion of his jaws. The sound he made was like glass being crushed.

He said, chewing, "So you'll go down to your bank tomorrow and get the twenty-five thousand, right? No arguments?"

"Yes."

"Good man." He took the cheroot out of his mouth, scowled at it, spat out a shred of tobacco, and extended the empty glass. "Do this again, Jordan. Tastes like crap, but at least it's wet. Then you can drive me back to my hotel."

I got up slowly, took his glass, went around behind him and across to the sideboard. The shaking had stopped; my hands were steady. I put ice in the glass, picked up the heavy decanter. And then I just stood there.

Annalise. Annalise and Fred Cutter. The twenty-six thousand she took with her—gone or almost gone. The clothing manufacturer, the shot at being a fashion designer—gone, too. A different kind of life on the edge now, after only eight months. Back to working at shitty jobs, like the one she'd had in San Francisco. Bedding down with a muscle-bound halfwit, resorting to blackmail. Scraping bottom.

Outside, the wind was rising. I could hear it making a frenzied rattle in the palm fronds, feel its sultry breath swirling in through the open terrace doors.

"Hey," Cutter said, "hurry up with that drink. I'm dying over here."

I turned around. He was leaning forward, rubbing slick off his face again. There was a wet spot on the back of his shirt, too, between the shoulder blades. Another geometric shape, this one a ragged-edged circle with a darker circle in the middle where the cloth stuck to his skin. It reminded me of something, but I couldn't think what it was. Couldn't seem to think clearly at all.

Twenty-six thousand. Five thousand. Another twenty-five thousand. And more bites to come, little ones and big ones until they bled me dry.

Screaming, that wind. Like jumbees in the night.

Some piece. Great in bed. Suck the varnish off a table leg. Lucky to hang on to her as long as you did.

It was as if the coming storm, the jumbees, were inside me now. Blowing hot and wild. Screaming.

Cutter and his *Good man, good man.* Cutter and his smarmy grin. Cutter the lowlife blackmailer. Hurry up, I'm dying over here—

I don't remember crossing the room.

146

I don't remember hitting him with the decanter.

One second I was standing in front of the sideboard, looking over at him, the storm wind shrieking inside my head, and the next I was beside the chair staring down at him on the floor. The back of his head was crushed and there was blood mixed with rum streaked over the fair hair, blood and rum on the floor, blood and gore on the decanter and spattered across my shirtfront.

I knew then what that sweat stain on the back of his shirt reminded me of.

It looked exactly like a target.

Either I dropped the decanter or it slipped out of my hand, I don't know which. The sound of it hitting the tile floor dragged my gaze away from Cutter. An edge of the heavy cut glass had gouged a triangular chip out of a tile.

Now how am I going to fix that? I thought.

I kept on standing there. Looking at him again, at what I'd done to him. The wildness was still inside me, but it had mutated into a near panic overlain with numbness—

What? Yes, I know that sounds contradictory, but it's an accurate description. All the crazy rage and fear held down under the weight of dazed confusion, like a lid on a bubbling pot.

Time seemed to have gone out of whack, to stop and stutter with long spaces between the ticking seconds. I couldn't think; my mind was a wasteland. Then I grew aware of something moving on my cheek, like a fly walking. I raised a hand, brushed at it. The fingers came away wet and sticky. When I looked at them I saw that they were smeared with blood and something else, a whitish gelatinous substance that must have been brain matter. That broke the spell.

Bile pumped thick and hot into the back of my throat. I ran blindly for the bathroom, barely made it to my knees in front of the toilet before the vomit came spewing out. I puked until there was nothing left but strings of saliva. It left me weak but calmer. I flushed the toilet,

147

rinsed my mouth. Washed the blood off my hands and face. Pulled my shirt off, found more blood spots on my chest and neck and washed those off. Better still by the time I finished, both the wildness and the numbness starting to fade. I went back through the living room, not looking at what lay sprawled on the floor, and out onto the terrace.

The storm clouds were a dark, fast-moving mass, the wind blustery and hot, the air thick with moisture. When the rains came, the downpour would be heavy for a while but the storm wouldn't last long; before morning the skies would be clear again. You get so you don't need the Caribbean Weather Center to gauge the severity and length of each blow, from squalls to hurricanes. I had developed a mariner's eye, ear, and feel for any barometric change and what it meant.

I sat on one of the wrought-iron chairs, letting the wind fan my naked torso, listening to it moan in the palms and guava trees while I ordered my thoughts. I was all right by then, my mind working more or less clearly again. It seemed incredible that I could have killed a man, any man; that in the span of a few seconds I had gone from blackmail victim to taker of human life. But the fact didn't have as profound an effect on me as I would have believed beforehand. Didn't frighten or disgust or even sicken me any longer. Temporary insanity, irresistible impulse. The product of circumstances and of my dark side. I was sorry it had happened, if not sorry that the life I'd taken was Fred Cutter's, but it was done and I couldn't undo it. The only thing to do now was to find ways to protect myself from the consequences.

I approached it as I'd approached the Amthor crime: as a series of mathematical problems—three of them—to be broken down and solved one at a time, by a combination of logic and creative planning.

First and most important: what to do with the body.

Limited options, on an island of just thirty square miles. The optimum solution would be to take it off the rock, dump it at sea, and let the sharks have it. But that wasn't possible. No way could I transport a dead man onto *Windrunner* without being seen. The slips at the Sub Base harbor were well lighted at night, and there was a watchman on duty and others like Bone who lived on their boats.

Wait until late and leave the body in Frenchtown or out near one of the beaches? Crime was becoming a problem on the island, and there were occasional acts of violence against tourists; Cutter's death might pass for a mugging or a drug deal gone bad. No, that was no good either. The last thing I wanted was a murder investigation. Suppose one of my neighbors had seen him come here? Suppose he'd mentioned Richard Laidlaw to someone at his hotel, or at the harbor the day before? If he had, and the police found it out, it would bring them straight to my door.

Hide the body in the jungle? There were stretches of dense growth on both Crown Mountain and St. Peter's Mountain, and there'd be very little late-night traffic on the roads during or after a storm. I wouldn't have to carry the body far to conceal it. But the disadvantages outweighed the advantages. It would mean parking on a turnout or overlook—I couldn't just leave the Mini in the middle of the road—and what if a passing police patrol stopped to investigate? Snakes, prowling animals, unseen hazards made a night foray into a tropical jungle dangerous. And even if I managed that part of it, there was no guarantee the remains would stay hidden. Turnout and overlook areas were magnets for road crews, curious tourists, hikers. Dead flesh attracted scavenging animals and carrion birds. If just one human bone surfaced, the rest could be tracked down and identified through forensic means. Even a cold trail might someday lead back to me. I'd always be afraid something like that would happen.

Still, I might have to do it that way. The only other solution I could think of was to cut up the body, get rid of it piecemeal. I liked the irony in that, given the bastard's name, but I knew I didn't have the stomach for such grisly work. Or for that matter, any idea of how to go about it.

I didn't waste any thought on the other two problems. They were secondary concerns until I dealt with the major one. Annalise? No. I wasn't ready to think about her yet. Dangerous to let myself think about her. An emotional overload was what had led me to smash the decanter into Cutter's skull; I couldn't afford to let it happen again and interfere with the job ahead. For the next several hours I had to be as disciplined as I'd been at any time in my life.

The longer I sat there, the icier my resolve and the clearer my thinking. The combination produced another solution to the disposal problem. The best one, if a potential obstacle didn't stand in the way. Bold, clever, audacious—all the adjectives the newspapers had applied to the Amthor crime. I knew I was going to try it. If I were successful, I would have no cause to worry about Fred Cutter's body ever being found.

The blow started shortly after nine. Gusty winds that whipped the trees into a frenzy, scraped palm fronds across the roof tiles, hammered at the closed doors and shutters as if clamoring for admittance; mutters of thunder, flashes of lightning, driving torrents of rain. Even with the jalousies closed I could smell ozone mixed with the sweet fragrances of white ginger and hibiscus.

I had just finished emptying the thing's pockets and rolling it into the yawl's old storm jib that I'd brought home and hadn't gotten around to restitching. *The thing. It.* That was how I was thinking then. What was wrapped in that piece of Dacron wasn't Fred Cutter, wasn't the shell of a man; it was a thing, an it, a large bundle of trash to be hauled away.

I'd also found a roll of duct tape in the garage and I used strips of it to tightly bind the sail in the middle and on both ends so there would be no leaks. The dead weight put a strain on my arms when I lifted it, lugged it into the kitchen. I'd have to use a fireman's carry after this, I thought as I lowered it to the floor near the side door that led out to the garage.

The storage closet yielded a plastic bucket, some rags, a pair of rubber kitchen gloves. I filled the bucket with warm water and dish soap, found a can of cleanser under the sink. In the living room I cleaned off the decanter first and replaced it on the sideboard. There was still some Arundel inside and I badly wanted a drink, but I didn't let myself have one. No more liquor until after the job was done.

On my hands and knees, I scrubbed the red and gray-white spatters, the spilled rum, off the tiles and the chair and table legs. A few blood spots stained the chair fabric; I couldn't get them out no matter how much elbow grease I used. No sense in worrying about it. People spill things on furniture that leave dark stains; the fabric was a brownish weave and you couldn't tell that the spots were blood. No sense in worrying about the gouge in the floor tile, either. If the real estate agent or his cleaning staff noticed the minor damage, the cleaning deposit would cover it.

When I finished, the wind was still howling but the rain had already let up. Fast-moving storm. The worst of it would be over an hour or so past midnight. I emptied the bucket, rinsed it out, washed off the gloves, put the rags in the washing machine with my stained shirt and pants. Then I went into the bedroom and sat on the bed to look through what I'd taken from Cutter's pockets.

Wallet. Folded piece of paper with a crude map and directions to the villa written in Annalise's backslanting hand—all the proof I needed of her duplicity. Folder of traveler's checks. Handful of change. Room key attached to a piece of plastic with Hotel Caribbean embossed on it. The package of cheroots and a book of matches. That was all. No other keys, and no return airline ticket; those things must be in his hotel room.

The wallet contained $72, three snapshots, and a driver's license, social security card, and U.S. Post Office ID all in the name of Frederick Cotler. The address on the license was Hollyoak Street in Yonkers, New York, but the license had been issued in 1977 and the address might or might not be current. There was no street address on the postal identification, but the city was the same.

So his name had been Cotler, not Cutter. A small, sly deception in case I had any intention of trying to track him down.

And he'd worked for the Post Office. A mailman? The fact struck me funny. Annalise and a mailman! Some progression she'd gone through. From an accountant and embezzler to a cheating divorce lawyer to a manufacturer of women's clothing to . . . a mailman. From San Francisco to Chicago to Charlotte Amalie to New York City to . . . Yonkers. From a department store buyer to accomplice in a major embezzlement to thief to blackmailer to . . . what? What next, Annalise? Shoplifter, bag lady, hooker? Somebody else's mistress—a truck driver's, a garbage collector's, a pimp's? Yonkers to Harlem or the Bowery? How low can you sink? Not low enough to suit me. Hell wouldn't be low enough to suit me.

It wasn't funny any longer; the anger had begun to burn hot and bitter again. I forced it down, forced the thoughts of her out of my mind. Cold focus. Rigid control.

None of the snapshots was of Annalise. One depicted a much younger Cotler (I had to think of him by his real name) in a dark blue suit, and an attractive redheaded woman wearing a white gown and holding a bouquet of flowers. Another in color was of the same redhead, older, heavier, staring at the camera with a tight little leer on her mouth and her middle finger upraised just below the point of her chin. The third was an old black-and-white portrait of a graying, sad-eyed woman. Written on the back of that one in ballpoint pen was "Mom, '62." Fred Cotler, the sentimental blackmailer.

Was he still married, screwing Annalise on the side? Possibly, but he hadn't been wearing a wedding ring and he'd implied that he lived alone. And a man would be more likely to keep a photo of an ex-wife giving him the finger than of a current wife making that gesture. Much better for me if he'd been divorced. A wife would likely try to find him when he failed to come home; an ex might never know he'd disappeared, or care if she did know.

I flipped through the folder of traveler's checks. Seven altogether, each in the amount of $50. Except for the "F" and the "C," his signature was an illiterate squiggle like the up-and-down lines on a seismograph or a lie detector graph I'd seen once in a movie. I studied the signature for a time, then located a pen and a pad of paper and tried to duplicate it. The first few attempts, the initials didn't look right, but then I got the hang of it. After a dozen or so, I was able to match the scrawls on the checks fairly closely.

Fatigue had given me a headache, put an abrading graininess in my eyes. I set the alarm clock for two A.M., stripped, shut off the light, and sprawled naked on the bed. I was out in less than a minute.

The alarm dragged me up out of a sticky, restless sleep. I put on the nightstand lamp long enough to take an old pair of blue pants and a dark-blue long-sleeved pullover out of the closet. I dressed in the dark, then rummaged up a clean pair of shorts and a short-sleeved shirt. In the kitchen I reviewed the mental list of items I would need from the house. The flashlight I'd used in the garage earlier. The rubber gloves. A plastic garbage bag. A handful of clean rags. I gathered everything, shut off the light, and went outside.

The wind still blew in noisy gusts but it was no longer raining. Some of the humidity was gone; the air had a fresh, sweet taste, the way it does after a storm has passed. Clouds moved sluggishly across the sky now, thick piles of them—cumulonimbus, not rain-swollen cumulus. Here and there you could see a random star shining faintly in a ragged patch of clear. The only lights showing in the neighboring houses were night lights, tiny islands surrounded by restless dark. It would be another couple of hours, I judged, before the cloud cover broke up enough to free the moon and stars.

I shut myself inside the garage. Gloves, garbage bag, rags, and the change of clothes went into the Mini's trunk. The flash beam picked out a folded section of sailcloth I'd planned to use for patching, and the largest shovel among the gardening tools against the back wall. I added the shovel and the torch to the other stuff in the trunk, put the sailcloth on the roof, and left the passenger door standing open.

Back to the house. It was a struggle getting the thing hoisted and slung over my shoulder. Its joints had stiffened with the onset of rigor mortis; I couldn't make it bend all the way in the middle. The dead weight put a staggering strain on my knees as I carried it outside. I stood braced against the door jamb, looking up at the street, listening. No headlights, no engine sounds, nothing but the calls of night birds flying again after the blow. I moved slowly, to keep from stumbling, as I crossed the few yards to the garage.

I eased the thing through the Mini's open passenger door. Getting the legs and arms bent so it would fit low into the seat, the sailcloth draped over and around it to make it look like a shapeless bundle, was a ten-minute chore. I was running sweat by the time I finished.

I waited until I had the Mini out of the driveway onto Quartz Gade before I switched on the headlamps. There was no traffic; I didn't see an-other car as I came down across Dronningens Gade to Veterans Drive and turned west, and only one, heading in the opposite direction, on the drive to Harwood Highway. The road was deserted in both direc-tions when I made the swing onto the narrow lane that led to the old French cemetery.

What better place to hide a dead thing than in somebody else's grave?

I shut off the lights, coasted up to the closed gates. If the gates had been locked, I would've had no choice but to turn around and head up Crown Mountain. I had neither the tools nor the facility for busting locks, and even if I had I couldn't risk arousing suspicion by breaking and entering. But I'd counted on the gates being unlocked, and they were. The place was ancient, overgrown, not much used anymore. The only reason to lock it up at night was vandalism, and there hadn't been any of that.

The rusted iron squeaked and sprayed me with rain-wet as I pushed the gates open. I ran back to the car. Just as I shut myself inside again, headlights appeared on the main road, coming from the west.

I hunkered down on the seat. For a few seconds the light glare seemed to fill the Mini. If it'd been a police patrol, they'd have stopped, sure as hell, and I would have been as dead as the thing beside me. But it wasn't. The car whooshed past without slowing down.

I let out the breath I'd been holding, straightened up. When the tail-lights passed out of sight, the highway was a shiny black smear empty in both directions. I drove ahead into the cemetery. Got out quickly to close the gates again.

It was thick dark in there, a place of indistinct shapes like figures on a nightmare landscape. Not enough light filtered through the cloud gaps for me to make out more than a few feet of the rutted mud-and-gravel lane, and the mist-streaked windshield made it even harder to see. I rolled down the window, leaned my head out. Better, but I had to move ahead at a crawl.

I'd been to the cemetery a few times to walk around looking at headstones and grave markers, and once when I followed an old-fashioned Cha-Cha funeral procession led by a robed priest, the coffin balanced on a donkey cart. I remembered the layout of the place. Visualized it, fixed it in my mind, before I put the Mini in gear and crept forward.

Rain puddles had formed in the ruts; the tires splashed deep into a couple of them. Twice I lost sight of the verge, veered off onto softer ground and barely managed to correct in time to keep from getting stuck. When I reckoned I'd gone far enough, I stopped and shut off the engine and got out with the flashlight.

Pale shifting rays of moonshine came and went among the clouds, enough for me to orient myself. I was near one of the branch lanes that led toward the rear wall. I set off that way on foot, shielding the flash beam with my hand and aiming it downward. The whitewashed tombs seemed to shine faintly, as if with an inner ghost light; the trees were like shadowy, skeletal figures performing weird gyrations. In the night hush, the sound of dripping water rose above the mutter of the wind. My shoes and pantlegs were sodden before I'd gone fifty yards.

The older section I came to was heavily overgrown with grass and vines and gnarled sapodilla and gumbo-limbo trees, all but forgotten. I prowled a short distance through the tangle until I found what I was looking for, under the sprawling branches of a gumbo-limbo and half hidden from the lane by a scabrous tomb. If it hadn't been for the lean of a wooden marker, you wouldn't have been able to tell that there was a grave beneath the thick grass mat. I shone the torch briefly on the marker. So old that the wood was split and insect-pitted, and whatever had been written on it had completely faded away.

I drove the Mini as close to the grave as I could. I pried the thing out of the passenger seat, using the handle of the shovel to loosen one of the stiffened legs, then carried it through the wet grass and dumped it a dozen feet from the grave. To the car again for the shovel and the piece of Dacron and the rubber gloves. When I had the sailcloth spread on the grass, I paced off a distance of six feet back from the marker and dug the rough, shallow outline of a rectangle six feet long by two feet wide. I cut the inside of the rectangle into small squares. These I dug up in three-inch-deep clods, setting them aside under the tree one by one to preserve the tall stalks of grass. Then I scooped out the new grave, shoveling the muddy soil onto the Dacron.

It was hot, filthy work. But not as hard as you might think. The clearing sky now shed enough moonlight and starshine to give me some visibility. The earth was sandy and moist from the rain; the only difficulty I had was chopping through straggles of tree root. I don't know how long it took to open up that six-by-two rectangle to a depth of six feet. There were no visible lights, no sounds except for the wind and the dripping water and the bite of the shovel into the earth— nothing to make me aware of the passage of time.

The muscles in my back and shoulders were on fire by the time I'd gone deep enough to uncover the buried coffin. There wasn't much left of it, just rotted crumbles of wood; the blade sliced through and clanged against something that sounded like bone. I scraped away shreds of wood and flung the pieces up onto the pile of dirt, widening and deepening the hole a little more. The flashlight was hooked onto my belt; I turned it on to take a quick look at the partly exposed skeleton and the grave walls. Deep enough, wide enough.

I climbed out, wet to the skin and covered in slick mud, a quivering in my arms and legs from the strain of digging. For a little time I sat under the gumbo-limbo with my back against the trunk to rest. When my strength returned, I went to lift the thing again and haul it to the grave. It wouldn't lie flat when I dropped it in, and I had to get down there with it and use the shovel in a couple of ways I'd rather not talk about. It fitted the space well enough when I finished.

I shoveled and scraped most of the dirt back in. Picked up the ends of the sail and dumped in the rest. Firmed it down, replaced the clods of grass, dragged over a couple of dead tree limbs and some brush and vines. You could still see the seams here and there, tell that somebody had been excavating, but you had to be standing right on the spot. From a distance of a few feet there were no visible signs of disturbance; I put the light on briefly to make sure. If nobody came poking around back here in the next week or so, enough new grass would sprout to hide the seams completely.

I shook out the sailcloth, folded it, took it and the shovel back to the Mini. Off with the gloves and filthy clothing, into the garbage bag with them and the rags I used to scrub mud off my arms and face. On with the clean shirt and shorts. I rested again for a time before I started the engine and got the car turned around.

The highway was deserted when I reached the gates. It stayed that way as I rolled through and closed them behind me and turned toward Charlotte Amalie. My hands were steady on the wheel. I drove slowly, carefully. None of the handful of other cars I passed was a police patrol, and none of the drivers paid any attention to me.

Home safe and sound. Exhausted, so relieved I was weak and tingling. I admit to a feeling of exhilaration, too—the kind you can't help but feel after a dangerous job well done.

There were still a few things left to do. In the garage, I dropped the plastic bag into the trash can, rinsed off the shovel and the Dacron in the utility sink and put them away, and hosed mud spatters off the Mini. In the house, I scrubbed down under a long, hot shower. Afterward, I shaved off my beard and mustache, then used a pair of scissors and a hand mirror to trim my hair all around—preparations for the solution to the next problem.

It was full dawn when I crawled into bed for few hours' sleep.

The Hotel Caribbean was a small, old-fashioned hotel on Kronprindsens Gade off Market Square, built before World War II when the Virgins were sleepy islands and the tourist trade was at a relative minimum. It's long gone now. In the early eighties it was staggering along on its last legs, catering to small package-tour groups and individuals who wanted a little island ambiance on the relative cheap. Naturally Fred Cotler had gravitated there; it was the only inexpensive hotel in the downtown area.

The lobby was crowded when I walked in at ten o'clock. It was my first visit to the hotel, so there was little danger of my being recognized as Richard Laidlaw. Shaved, hair trimmed, talcum powder lightening my sun-weathered skin, wearing a Madras shirt and white slacks, I blended right in with the snowbirds. I was even blue-eyed that morning, the first time I'd been out in public without the tinted contacts since I'd been on St. Thomas—unnecessary, but I was still feeling bold.

I crossed straight to the elevators as if I belonged there and rode up to the second floor.

Cotler's room was at the rear. I let myself in with the tagged key. Stuffy little box, its single window overlooking a corner of the hotel garden and most of the gravel parking lot—probably the cheapest accommodations the Hotel Caribbean had to offer. The maid hadn't been there yet that day; the bed was rumpled, the glass-topped teak nightstand littered with cigar ash, an ashtray cradling a couple of cheroot butts, and an empty beer bottle and several wet-rings. The room stank of stale cigar smoke.

I looked in the nightstand drawer first. Empty except for the usual Gideon Bible. In the closet, half a dozen shirts and pants on hangers and an imitation leather suitcase. I opened the suitcase on the bed, checked through all the pockets inside and out. Cotler's American Airlines return ticket was in one of them. Economy fare, the cheapest available judging from the rate. From what I knew of airline practices, economy fares were nonrefundable; if a ticket wasn't used, it was immediately canceled, the passenger's seat was given to somebody else, and no permanent record of the cancellation was kept. I called the American counter at the airport later to make sure.

The rest of Cotler's clothing was in one of the bureau drawers— underwear, socks, T-shirts, an extra belt. The only personal item in the bathroom was his toilet kit, and it contained nothing other than his ring of keys and the usual travel items. The only other place in the room to look was under the bed; I found nothing there but a freshly dead roach. I was satisfied then that Cotler hadn't brought anything with him that pointed to Jordan Wise or Richard Laidlaw. Or to Annalise.

Had he told anyone other than Annalise that he was going to St. Thomas? Probably not. You don't advertise a trip you're making for the sole purpose of extorting money from a fugitive. He could be traced here, of course, once his disappearance was reported, but only if someone cared enough about him to pursue an investigation—someone other than Annalise. The police in places like Yonkers don't have enough manpower to run thorough backchecks on every missing-person case. If Cotler was traced to the island, the odds were good that his trail would lead no farther than the Hotel Caribbean. And I was about to make those odds even better.

I gathered up Cotler's belongings and packed them into the suitcase, double-checking to make sure I had everything before I left the room. Tourists often carry their own bags in a hotel like the Caribbean; I attracted no attention on my way to the desk.

Both clerks, a man and a woman, were native blacks. All to the good. The woman waited on me. Professional smile, and only the briefest of eye contact when I put the key down and said, "Checking out, please."

She got the bill from the file, studied it for a few seconds before making eye contact again. "Is anything wrong, Mr. Cotler?"

"Wrong?"

"Your room is reserved for two more days."

She said it without suspicion. That and her calling me Mr. Cotler put me at ease. There'd been only a slight chance that any of the hotel staff would know I wasn't Fred Cotler; too many tourists come and go for them to equate names with faces. And West Indian blacks tend to regard snowbirds the same way Annalise had regarded natives, though not necessarily for the same reason—not as individuals but as see-through members of a class and race to be dealt with and immediately forgotten. If by some quirk the woman had noticed I wasn't Cotler, I would have told her he'd asked me to check out for him. As it was, I said, "No, no, nothing wrong. Just have to cut the vacation short, is all. Business reasons."

"I'm sorry you'll be leaving us so soon." Taught to say that, and the next by-rote sentence: "Will you need help with your luggage?"

"Not necessary."

She slid the bill around for me to look at. The only charges on it other than the room rate were a $38 bar and room service tab—no long-distance phone calls. The total came to just under $300.

"Will you be paying by credit card, sir?"

"No," I said, "traveler's checks."

I signed all seven left in the folder. She glanced at the top one to make sure the signatures matched—just a glance—and after that looked only at the denomination on the rest as she counted them. She shuffled the checks together, put them into a cash drawer. Gave me another see-through smile along with the change and a copy of the bill.

"Please come and see us again, Mr. Cotler."

Not in this life, I thought, and smiled back at her, and walked out carrying all that was left of Fred Cotler's short visit to St. Thomas.

Two problems solved, provisionally. What happened next was up to luck or fate or whatever you wanted to call it. And up to what Annalise did when Cotler failed to return with the blackmail money.

Annalise.

I let myself think about her then. The anger had gone cold. For the time being I could consider her and her role in all this with unemotional detachment.

I tried to put myself in her position, to think as she would think. She would probably call the Hotel Caribbean eventually, and when she was told that Cotler had checked out, she might call the airline to ask if he'd used his ticket or taken another flight. But they wouldn't tell her anything. Airline passenger manifests are confidential as far as the general public is concerned; government and law enforcement agencies could get the information, no one else. I'd checked on that, too, when I called American and verified their economy cancellation policy.

What would she think then? The obvious was that Cotler had gotten the payoff, maybe even a bigger payoff than they'd planned, and run out on her with it. She might believe that, if she wasn't too sure of him and if he had little money and no other valuables or ties in Yonkers. Even if she had doubts, it wouldn't occur to her that I could be responsible. To her I would always be Jordan Wise, accountant—a passive personality in spite of the Amthor crime and the Richard Laidlaw persona, a man incapable of violence. I would have said the same about myself before Cotler. She wouldn't contact me. Still wouldn't want me to know she was in on the extortion. And she wouldn't go to the police. For all her craving for excitement and danger, and all her drunken antics, Annalise was fiercely self-protective. The same as I was.

Still, she had an unpredictable side. Her sudden disappearance the previous year proved that. It was possible she'd do something unexpected, something brazen and foolish and threatening to both of us.

Time would tell. All I could do was wait and see.

I was too restless to return to my daily routine, and I wasn't about to sit around counting the hours. The Weather Center forecast was for clear skies and winds of from ten to fifteen knots, good sailing weather, so I took *Windrunner* out the next morning. Cotler's suitcase went along with me, hidden inside a large cardboard box for transport and then stowed belowdecks. And when I was out near the Kingfish Banks, no other boats in sight, I weighted it with a couple of heavy and dispensable wrenches and consigned it to the briny deep.

The course I'd set was for Laidlaw Cay. I anchored just inside the reef on the lee side. Swam, fished, watched the nesting terns and frigate birds, napped under one of the screw palms. An hour before sunset I rowed back to the yawl, ate my supper on deck while the rainbow colors appeared and shifted and blended like patterns in a kaleidoscope. After dark, I sat with my back to the deckhouse and sipped Arundel and watched the constellations in the night sky. It was so clear the stars in the Milky Way burned like points of white fire.

Two more days and nights at sea, and the restlessness was gone and I was poison-free again.

Shortly after docking, I talked to Bone. He was the best source I knew of local news. Nothing had happened in the three-plus days I'd been gone that I didn't want to hear about. Later I read through recent issues of the *Virgin Islands Daily News* and the *St. Thomas Source,* just to make sure.

A week passed.

Two weeks.

Still no mention in the papers or on the radio of anything amiss at the old French cemetery. Or of a missing snowbird named Fred Cotler. No one called, or wrote, or came to see me except Bone.

I moved out of the Quartz Gade villa the first week in December. If the cleaning crew noted the gouge in the floor tile or the blood spots on the chair fabric, they didn't report it; I heard nothing from the real estate agent or the absentee owners. A short time later, I received a check for the full amount of the cleaning deposit.

By then I knew I was going to get away with the Cotler crime, too.

ST. THOMAS

1983–1984

I THOUGHT YOU'D ASK about my emotional state in the aftermath of the Cotler crime. Did I have nightmares about what I'd done? Daymares? Did I suffer remorse, guilt, any of the other so-called murderer's torments?

The answers are all no.

My emotional state, once the initial dose of blackmailer's poison had been flushed out, was no different than it had been before Cotler showed up on the island.

I told you I'm not religious; I don't believe in mortal sin or any of the other biblical covenants, or in divine punishment. I do believe that morality, like love, is a private thing defined by and suited to each individual. I've freely admitted to my dark side, but like Bone, I also have my own code of ethics. I've always adhered to that code, and within its boundaries I was and still am a moral man.

No, I *don't* consider myself a murderer. How many of those who have taken a human life, for any reason, ever look at themselves in the mirror and think that they've committed a mortal sin? Damn few. No man, unless he's a homicidal psychotic, ever thinks of himself as an evildoer. If you called him one to his face, chances are he'd be shocked. So would I.

I killed Fred Cotler in a fit of blind rage, for a perfectly justifiable reason. It was an act of self-preservation, not one of murder. How can anyone be expected to feel sorry for having killed to save his own life?

Yes, of course I know the law, the churches, many individuals would consider that a rationalization. Everyone who has killed in hot or cold blood has a reason or an excuse. The human mind is capable of bending and shaping any act to fit any preconceived set of beliefs, of justifying even the most heinous crime. But in most cases, that bending and shaping is the result of the mind's inability to cope with the magnitude of the act; it can continue to function only through a process of denial and self-delusion. I knew exactly what I'd done, and why. I was not self-deluded. I have a very clear understanding of the differences between right and wrong.

I'm not a sociopath. Maybe you think so, but you're wrong. Sociopaths care about no one but themselves, have no empathy for others or capacity for love or belief in the sanctity of human life. I cared about others, good people like Bone; I'd loved Annalise with all my heart; I would never willingly harm anyone who was not a direct threat to my safety and well-being, and then only as a last resort.

Murderer? Evildoer? Sociopath? No. Just a man with a dark side, nothing more and nothing less.

I had to forget Annalise all over again. There was no other reasonable course of action.

Oh, I gave some thought to flying up to New York, tracking her down, confronting her. I could have done that without too much difficulty, I think. But to what purpose? Threats were useless unless I told her what I'd done to Cotler, and that was out of the question. If she believed that I'd killed him, it would only give her a greater hold over me.

Yes, I could have destroyed her as I'd destroyed her lover, but I told you, I couldn't harm anyone except as a last resort. Not even Annalise, as much as I hated her—from love to indifference to hate, full turn. It was a cold hate, locked away and shackled. I could no more have gone hunting her than I could have gone hunting an animal, even a loathsome animal. I'm not made that way.

As I settled back into my day-to-day life, I was able to keep from dwelling on Annalise and her duplicity. With some difficulty at first, then more easily behind a wall of passing days. Only one thing continued to bother me, a nagging worry like a splinter that had worked itself in too deep for extraction.

What if she hooked up with somebody else like Fred Cotler?

What if another blue-eyed bastard showed up someday to bleed me dry?

A complex man with simple tastes.

If I had to describe myself in a single sentence, that would be it.

I didn't realize it until I came to St. Thomas. The simple tastes, I mean. I thought the quiet life I'd led in San Francisco was a result of my job, of lack of funds and resources, of circumstances. What I wanted, I believed then, was what Annalise wanted: all the luxuries and material possessions money could buy. Not so. I didn't miss the Quartz Gade villa or the Royal Bay Club or the company of the elite white community or the parties and nightclubs and expensive restaurants or the dress-up clothes or the trips to far-flung places. The only material possession that really meant anything to me was *Windrunner.* If it hadn't been for Annalise and the misunderstanding of my needs, I wouldn't have had to steal $600,000 from Amthor Associates to finance a new life in the Virgin Islands; I could have done it on not much more than $100,000, and to hell with the stock portfolio and the Cayman Islands bank accounts. As it was, except for an occasional small draw, what was left of the initial bankroll, plus all the dividends, just sat over there accumulating interest. There was nothing I cared to spend money on other than the yawl, no place I cared to go that the yawl couldn't take me.

I liked living on *Windrunner*. The major reason was that she was Annalise-free. The villa had had her taint in it, a faint residue of our life together trapped within its walls. I hadn't felt it so much while I was occupying the place, but once I moved out I realized how subtly oppressive it had been the past year. I was glad I hadn't given it up sooner, because of the nature of the Cotler crime, but to be rid of it finally was like the removal of a weight.

The yawl's main cabin had never seemed cramped when I was out to sea, nor did it seem cramped in port. There was room enough for everything I owned, and it was easy to keep clean and tidy. I kept the galley well stocked and I didn't mind cooking, learned to enjoy it enough so that I ate most of my evening meals on board. Simple meals. West Indian dishes like chowders and bouillabaisses, fried fish, crab sandwiches, an occasional chicken or meat course. I slept better on her, too, than I ever had in the villa. You couldn't ask for a more soothing soporific than the movement of the harbor water, the creak of rigging and old timbers, the familiar odors of salt and creosote.

Once a week or so I took *Windrunner* out for a sail, sometimes on a day trip over by St. John or another nearby island, sometimes on longer cruises. Days when I was in port, I followed the same routine and enjoyed the same small pleasures as I had before the blackmailer's arrival. Evenings were the same, too—the best part of any day for me. Quiet time. Sunsets, Arundel, Calypso and Fungi rhythms, harbor sounds, the boom and cabin lights on the berthed boats like a bright jeweled chain around the marina's dark throat.

I'd gotten to know some of the other residents and now and then one of them would drop by to socialize, or invite me over for a drink or a meal. Other evenings, Bone would show up and we'd drink rum and talk some while he perfumed the darkness with his molasses-sweet pipe tobacco. Or we'd just sit quiet together, absorbing the night. They were all the company I needed or wanted.

Fred Cotler gradually faded out of my consciousness, until it was as if he'd never come to the island in the first place, never dirtied my hands with his blood. I couldn't entirely forget Annalise, but sometimes a full week would go by without a single thought of her entering my head. I felt I couldn't ask for any more than that.

In May '83, shortly after Carnival, I had my fortieth birthday. Bone and I went out to celebrate. We nibbled a few drinks in the Bar, had dinner in a Creole restaurant on the Rue de St. Barthélemy, then set off on a Frenchtown and native-quarter pub crawl.

Somewhere along the way we picked up a couple of women, or the women picked us up—I'm not sure which. They were both native West Indians. One—big, bawdy, skin the color of melted licorice—knew Bone and latched on to him. I can't remember her name. The other one, Pearl, was younger, slimmer, lighter skinned, shy until she took in enough rum to loosen her inhibitions. She was a singer, or wanted to be a singer, and in one of the clubs she joined a loud steel band and sang an old Calypso song called "Don't Stop the Carnival" in a husky Antilles patois.

At some point after midnight we all piled into the Mini, four sardines in a can, and drove down to the Sub Base harbor marina so I could show off *Windrunner*. We partied on board, Pearl singing another song, to radio accompaniment this time, Bone and his woman joining in—the first time I'd heard Bone sing. He didn't have much of a voice, but he made up for it with energy and a high-stepping island dance. They got me up and dancing, something I would not have done if I'd been sober. The rum went down like water, very fast, and time got lost in a heady, rollicking swirl. We were all pretty drunk by then.

I don't remember Bone and the big woman leaving. The four of us were dancing, laughing, drinking, and the next thing I knew, Pearl and I were alone on deck, snuggled together in the moonlight, and I was shaking the last bottle of Arundel and it was empty. She said, "We doan need any more," and kissed me, and murmured snatches of another song in my ear, something soft and intimate, and kissed me again, and pretty soon we were down in the cabin, naked on my bunk.

Mistake.

I wanted her, all right, and I wasn't too far gone, and she was willing and eager. She had a good body, hard and soft at the same time. And pubic hair that was sensuously abrasive, like a fine grade of steel wool. With her help I managed to get an erection, but it was only a three-quarters salute, and neither it nor I lasted very long. Thin, almost painful little spurts.

Afterward I kept telling her how sorry I was, and she held me and said, "Doan worry, doan fret," in a crooning voice. More lost time. Then we were trying again, but it was no use, I was impotent. I apologized again and I think I might have gotten a little maudlin. The last words I remember her saying before I passed out were "It's all right, honey, it's all right." But it wasn't all right, for her or for me. In the morning, when I woke up, she was gone.

I lay in the bunk with my head throbbing, berating myself for getting too drunk to do either of us any good. And not believing the lie, even then. It wasn't the rum. It wasn't Pearl, and it wasn't me.

It was Annalise.

Windrunner was out of the water for more than two weeks that summer, for scraping and minor rudder repairs. I did some of the hull work myself to keep busy. Bone let me bunk with him for the duration, and helped out with painting and varnishing chores after the yawl was relaunched. By way of repayment, I talked him into joining me on a long cruise to the Turks and Caicos. It was an iffy time of year for that kind of sail on the Atlantic, but summer storm activity was light that season and the long-range forecast was favorable. Bone said we'd be all right. I trusted his instincts, with good cause as usual. Other than a couple of light squalls, we had fair weather and light-running seas.

As usual we stood watch and watch, four on and four off, except when there was a weather helm to be held. On clear nights, when one or the other of us wasn't tired enough to sleep, we'd hang out on deck together. Bone still used words sparingly, but at sea he was a little more voluble than on land. Some subjects opened him up more than others. One was boats and sailing, another was the destructive effects on the Virgins of tourism and overpopulation.

St. Thomas was becoming a shadow of the island it had been twenty years ago, he said, when he first came there. The changes were evident to me after just five years. More cruise ships clogging the harbor every season; big new resorts going up and more planned where once there had been quiet bays and pristine beachfront; fancy villas springing up on the north shore and the mountainsides of the West End, to spoil undeveloped forests and fields. Crime, racial friction, environmental problems. The island was losing its appeal for Bone. One day he'd have his fill of the new St. Thomas and move away, he said. He could feel the time coming.

"Where will you go?" I asked him. "Back to the Bahamas?"

"Same things happening there."

"Entire Caribbean's changing, they say. All the islands."

"Not all yet. Some still pretty much the way they were."

"Such as?"

"St. Lucia. The Grenadines—Carriacou."

"How long since you were down there?"

"Two years," Bone said. "Going out again next summer."

"Why next summer?"

"Promised Isola a three-month cruise when her graduates from college. Just the two of us, get to know each other better."

He'd told me once that his daughter was studying to be a marine biologist. I said, "You must be proud of her, Bone."

"Yeah, mon. Her mama be too, if she still here."

I asked him how long it had been since his first wife passed away. He hadn't volunteered the information before.

"Twenty years. Isola was a baby." He sat silent for a time. Then he said, "Dengue fever. Two days sick, that's all. Just two days."

"Must've been hard to deal with," I said.

"Real hard, Cap'n."

"Is that why you left Nassau?"

"Didn't leave then. I stayed two more years." Pain had come into his voice when he spoke of his first wife; now it was replaced by bitterness. "Seemed right for Isola to have a new mama."

"Your second wife."

"Yeah, mon. Bad mistake."

"What happened with her?"

It was a question I'd asked a couple of times without getting an answer. He took so long to respond I thought he was going to stonewall me again. But then he said quick and hard, spitting the words, "You ever see a coral snake? Pretty, mon, pretty snake. But underneath that pretty skin, full of poison."

"She must have hurt you bad."

"Never been hurt worse."

"But you survived."

"Poison don't get in deep enough, that's why."

"I guess we're both lucky that way," I said. "So when you found out the truth about her, that's when you gave Isola to your sister to raise and left Nassau."

"That's when."

"What did you do about the woman?"

"Nothing, Cap'n. What should I do?"

"I don't know. Seems like there ought to be some way to keep a woman like that from hurting somebody else."

"Snake bites you, what you gonna do? Beat on her or get away quick so you can suck out the poison?"

"You could do both."

"Too late then. You can't get all the poison out."

"I suppose you're right."

"Right enough," Bone said. "Only smart thing to do with a snake is stay out of her way, don't let her fangs get in you again."

That was all he'd say about his second wife, then or at any time afterward. I never did find out exactly what it was she'd done to him, and he never once spoke her name.

From time to time I ran into one of the people I'd known when Annalise and I were together. On an island as small as St. Thomas, that kind of thing is unavoidable. Twice I encountered Royce Verriker, once near Emancipation Garden and once on Waterfront Drive during Carnival week. The first time, he spoke to me in his glad-handing way, making a snotty comment on my regrown beard and long hair, and I turned my back on him and walked away; the second time we made a point of ignoring each other. Maureen Verriker passed me without speaking in Market Square. I exchanged stiff hellos with Gavin Kyle in the Dronningens Gade liquor store, and with the Potters, the British rum connoisseurs, at the Yacht Club regatta.

It happened again on a morning in late September, on the dock at the Sub Base harbor marina. I'd just returned from an errand and I didn't notice the sloppily dressed woman until she came up and blocked my way. "Richard Laidlaw? Is that you under all that hair?" She laughed at my blank look. "JoEllen Hall. Remember me?"

I recognized her then. Annalise's drinking buddy, the Red Hook divorcee and not very talented artist. She seemed thinner than the last time I'd seen her, more juiceless, her sun-darkened skin as lined and cracked as old leather. She was there sketching for a new series of paintings, she said. How was I and what was I up to these days? She'd heard I was living on my boat; how come I'd given up the villa? Was I seeing anyone now that I was single again? Nosy questions in her too-loud voice that I answered in monosyllables.

175

After I made my escape, I didn't think any more about her. Just another chance meeting to be quickly forgotten. Only it wasn't. Hell no, it wasn't. JoEllen Hall hadn't been down there to sketch and running into her hadn't been accidental and her questions hadn't been casual. The whole thing was a put-up job—a goddamn scouting mission.

On a Saturday afternoon ten days later I came up the companionway from belowdecks, where I'd been doing some work on the generator, and Annalise was there waiting for me.

I didn't believe it at first. Eyes playing tricks. Mistaken identity. Hallucination. I stopped stone still, staring. No mistake. Annalise. She stood on the stringpiece astern, bathed in sunlight in a way that made her seem to glow, both hands clutching a straw bag, a tentative, nervous smile on her unpainted mouth that came and went like a blinking sign.

"Hello, Richard," she said.

It took me a few seconds to recover from the shock. "Jesus," I said.

"I guess you never thought you'd see me again."

I had no answer for that. I stood flatfooted, the oily rag I'd been using dangling from one hand. She wore white shorts, a white halter top, and a pale-blue-and-white beach shirt. The exposed parts of her were no longer tanned; the pale skin was sun-reddened in places. Her hair was long again, shoulder-length, worn in one of those frizzy-permanent styles. She'd put on a little weight in the past two years; it showed in a puffiness around her cheeks and mouth, a slight bulge at the waist of the shorts. Signs of dissipation in her face, too, veins showing here and there, faint crow's-feet around the eyes, a muscle twitching along her jaw. Her hands kept kneading the straw bag.

She said, "I see you've changed the name of your boat."

"Does that surprise you?"

"I'd be surprised if you hadn't. *Windrunner.* I like that."

I didn't say anything.

"I like the beard, too. And your hair long that way. They give you a sort of sea captain's look."

I didn't say anything.

"Is it all right if I come aboard?"

"Why?"

"To talk."

"We don't have anything to say to each other."

"Yes we do. I have so much to say to you. Is it all right?"

"No," I said.

She chewed her lower lip, head cocked a little to one side, eyes lowered. Her pleading-little-girl look. "It took a lot for me to come here like this, Richard. Please don't turn me away without listening to what I have to say."

"How long have you been on the island?"

"Two days. I've been staying with JoEllen Hall. You remember JoEllen?"

"All too damn well."

"She told me you were living on the boat now."

"Sure she did. Among other things. Good old JoEllen."

"She let me use her car to drive over from Red Hook," Annalise said.

"Why the hell did you come back?"

"To see you."

"What do you want? More money? More of my blood?"

"No. God, no."

"You must want something. You always did."

Struck a nerve. "I deserve that," she said.

"Well? I'm waiting."

"It's hot standing here in the sun. If you don't want to talk on board, can we go to one of the cafés? I'd really like to have a drink."

"I'll bet you would."

"Please, Richard. Just for a few minutes. Listen to what I have to say, then if you want me to I'll go away and never bother you again."

The urge to tell her to fuck off then and there was strong. But I couldn't do it. I had to hear her out, find out what she wanted. For my own protection.

We went to Harry's Dockside Café. Neither of us said anything on the walk over, or when we first sat down at an outside table under one of the brightly colored umbrellas. She couldn't hold eye contact; the few times she tried, the smile would flicker on and then flicker off again after a few seconds and she would look somewhere else.

It felt unreal to be with her again this way, all of a sudden, so close I could reach out and touch her. As if she weren't really there and what I was facing was a holographic projection of her, the image of an intimate stranger. I kept waiting for the anger and the hate to rise up in a choking wave, but it didn't happen. Undercurrents, yes, but that was all. The surface of feeling was curiously flat and empty, like shoal water under a gray-black sky.

No more rum punches for Annalise. She ordered Scotch, a double, no ice. I wanted an Arundel; I settled for beer to keep my head clear. Before the drinks came, she rummaged in her bag, came up with a little amber-colored plastic bottle. The prescription kind, except that it had no label. She shook out a white tablet, swallowed it dry.

I said, "What's that you just took?"

"Valium. For my nerves. Somebody I know got it for me. Not JoEllen—where I was living before."

Scraping bottom, all right. She'd never used drugs of any kind when we were together. "Where was that?"

"New York."

"You always did want to live in the Big Apple. How was it? Exciting?"

"I don't know," she said bitterly. "I never lived there. You were right, I couldn't afford Manhattan."

"Where did you live, then?"

"Long Island. God, what's keeping those drinks?"

They came and she gulped half of hers. The combination of Valium and Scotch worked fast to calm her, restore her poise. Color came back into her cheeks. The smile flicked on again and stayed lit.

"Whoo, that's better," she said. "I'd almost forgotten how twitchy and woozy tropical heat can make you until you get used to it."

I sipped beer and said nothing.

"So," she said. "How have you been, Richard?"

"Fine, until a little while ago. Never better."

"I'm serious."

"So am I."

"Well, I've been miserable," she said.

"Is that right? Things didn't work out with the clothing manufacturer, I take it. What was his name? Jackson? Johnson?"

She took another slug of Scotch. "Johnson. Paul Johnson."

"You don't seem surprised I know about him."

"I'm not. I . . . wasn't very discreet."

"I know about Verriker, too," I said. "Good old Royce."

"Oh, God. How did you—?"

"Does it matter?"

"I guess not. Did you . . . I mean . . ."

"Confront him? No. I'm not confrontational, you know that."

"I don't know why I went to bed with him. I honestly don't."

"Sure you do. He's handsome and glib and charismatic. A stud, too, I hear. I'll bet he was terrific in the sack."

She winced. "Please, Richard."

"How about Paul Johnson? Another stud, another good lay?"

"I don't want to talk about any of that."

"Why not? Sex was always one of your favorite topics."

"You have every right to hate me," she said.

"Don't I, though."

"Do you? Hate me?"

"What do you think?"

"I think I'm a terrible bitch. It was unforgivable, what I did to you. First Royce, then Paul Johnson, then taking everything I could get my hands on and running off like a thief in the night."

And then Fred Cotler, I thought. But I had no more intention of bringing him up than she did. I wasn't supposed to know about her and Cotler, or that she'd told him all about me, or that she'd been a willing partner in the attempted blackmail. It would be a mistake to let her know that I knew.

"What about the twenty-six thousand?" I said. "All gone now?"

"Yes. The jewelry, too. I don't have anything left."

"How long did it take you to blow it all?"

"I didn't blow it, not the way you mean. I spent it on essentials—food, rent, utilities."

"Johnson didn't keep you long, is that it?"

"He didn't keep me at all." She said it bitterly.

"How about giving you design work with his company? Or an intro into the fashion industry? That is why you ran off with him?"

"Yes, but he didn't keep any of his promises. He used me and then he dumped me."

"What did you do then? Find another sugar daddy?"

"I'm a bitch but not a whore, Richard. Though I don't blame you for thinking I'm both. I tried to find design work on my own. When I couldn't I gave up, finally admitted to myself that my designs really weren't very good and I was never going to make it in the industry."

"Big admission for you. Big letdown."

"Yes, it was."

"What did you do then?"

"Took a job selling lingerie in a department store. The money was running out and I had to pay the rent."

I said, "Sounds like a shitty job," and managed to keep the malice out of my voice.

"It was. But it's the only kind of work I had any experience with. I stuck it out for more than a year."

"What happened then?"

"They laid me off. Three weeks ago. No warning, they just decided to downsize the department. Two weeks' severance pay and out the door."

"You're being very candid about all this, Annalise—the mess you've made of your life the past two years. Why? What're you leading up to?"

"Jobs aren't that easy to come by up there," she said. "The kind that pay you a decent living wage. I just couldn't stay there any longer, I'd had enough. The airline ticket down here used up most of my severance pay."

"Answer my question. Why did you come back to St. Thomas? What do you want from me?"

"Another chance," she said.

I stared at her.

"That's all. Just another chance."

"Jesus Christ," I said, "you expect me to take you back? As if nothing ever happened?"

"No, not as if nothing ever happened. A chance to make amends, to prove how sorry I am and that I'll never do anything like that again. To be there for you the way I was before."

What gall the woman had! And how desperate she had to be to come crawling like this!

"It can be like it was for us in the beginning," she said. "Even better. A new beginning, a new commitment of trust I swear to God I'll never break."

I didn't say anything.

"If you ever feel I'm not living up to that promise, you can tell me to leave and I'll go, I won't argue, I won't even ask why."

I didn't say anything.

"You probably won't believe this," she said, "but I still care for you. I did what I did because I'm selfish, not because I stopped loving you."

"Bullshit, Annalise."

"It's true, I swear it. My feelings got lost in what I thought I wanted more than to be with you. I'm not that person anymore. What was important to me before isn't important to me now."

Sure it was. A free ride, that was what was important to her. Johnson hadn't given it to her and Cotler hadn't given it to her and however many there were after the mailman hadn't given it to her. The fashion industry and the Big Apple were shattered dreams. She'd reverted to what she was that night in Perry's: a half-alive bitch who felt as if she were running around and around like a hamster in a wheel. The difference was that then she'd had other options, and now the only one she had left was me. Her last reach for the brass ring. Her last chance to live on the edge, to feel alive again.

"You still have feelings for me, don't you?" she said. "Deep down? They can't all be gone?"

"Can't they?"

"I don't want to think so. Richard, it *can* be like it was for us in the beginning. It can, it *will*."

Earnest throb in her voice. Pleading eyes. Oh, she had all the words and all the emotional maneuvers down pat.

"You don't have to give me an answer right away," she said. "We can take it slowly. Get to know each other again. I can stay with JoEllen for a while—she said she wouldn't mind. Just think about it, that's all I ask. Will you do that?"

"Suppose I say no right now? Then what?"

". . . I don't understand."

"What will you do? Try to use threats to force me into taking you back?"

"God, no! I wouldn't do something like that."

"Wouldn't you? You've got the perfect hold."

"Not without hurting myself, I don't. I'd never hurt either of us that way."

"Never tell anyone about Jordan Wise?"

182

"Of course not."

"You never let anything slip to anyone while you were in New York?"

"Never." Looking me straight in the eye. "I swear it."

I finished my beer. Put some money on the table and got to my feet.

"Richard?"

"I need to get back to my boat."

I turned and walked out. I knew she'd hurry up and join me; I hadn't given her a satisfactory answer and she wouldn't go away without getting one. When we reached *Windrunner*, I knew she would ask again to come aboard—beg for it this time if she had to—and what she had in mind. I knew her so well. In Perry's that night, she'd said she knew me and I didn't know her at all, and now the reverse was true. In some ways I knew her better than she knew herself.

So I let her come on board. She walked around topside, exclaiming over this and that. Then, as I knew she would, she asked if she could see the cabin. I said all right to that, too. There was something I needed to find out about myself and only one way to do it.

In the main cabin she did a slow pirouette and said, "Why, it's bigger than I remember. Cozy."

"You'd hate living here."

"No, I wouldn't. The studio apartment I had on Long Island wasn't much larger. I don't need a lot of space anymore."

I didn't say anything.

"The bed . . . or is it a bunk?"

"Bunk. Or berth."

"It's almost the same size as the one in our villa, isn't it?"

I didn't say anything.

"But I wouldn't have to sleep here if you didn't want me to. I could sleep in the smaller one up in the front."

"Bow," I said.

She nodded. Then she said, glancing around, "Oh, you still have the pirate's chest we bought on Tortola."

"That I bought. One of the few things you left me when you ran off."

"I'm so sorry, Richard. You'll never know how sorry I am."

I didn't say anything.

"Well, I'm glad you kept it," she said. "The chest, I mean. I like it there on that wall shelf."

"Bulkhead shelf."

"I don't know all those nautical terms, but I'll learn. I want to learn all about your boat, about sailing—"

"Yawl," I said.

"Yawl. I want to be a part of your life again." She moved closer, gazed up into my eyes. Hers glistened with yearning and sorrow, but those emotions had nothing to do with me. "If you'll just give me the chance."

I didn't say anything.

She put her palms flat against my chest, standing so that her breasts almost touched me. "Will you think about it, Richard? Please?"

"I'll think about it," I said.

She said, "Thank you," and kissed me. Quick and hard, as if with impulsive relief. I knew she would. I knew her so goddamn well.

She looked into my eyes. Wet her lips. Kissed me again. Lingeringly this time, fitting herself against me, her arms sliding up and around my neck, her fingers combing through my hair.

I just stood there.

Tongue sliding into my mouth, breath coming faster, loins making slow, sensuous motions against mine—all just as expected. But I'm not made of wood. No man can completely resist the sexual advances of a woman like Annalise, not for long and no matter how much he might want to. I let myself return the kiss. She gave a little cry. It was supposed to be a moan of pleasure, but it came out sounding exactly like what it was—the voice of triumph.

One hand began to tug at the buttons on my shirt, the other dipped inside the waistband of my trousers. She was breathing heavily now.

The wet mouth was feverish on mine a few seconds longer, then she broke the kiss and drew back. The shirt and halter and shorts came off in quick, practiced movements. Like a stripper's. Like a prepaid whore's. I knew she wouldn't be wearing anything under the shorts, and she wasn't.

Long, motionless pose, showing off her nakedness. Her body was the same and not the same. Incipient fat roll at her middle, little pouches of fat forming on her hips, cellulite starting to show in her thighs. Too much liquor, too much bad food, too many wrong men. In ten or fifteen years, she would be fat. Once she stopped caring about her appearance, and I knew she would, she'd let herself go rapidly and utterly.

I let her undress me, not helping. When we were both naked, she pulled me down onto the bunk and twined herself around me, her hand moving expertly between my legs. Into my ear she breathed, "I've missed you, oh God, I've missed you so much, I've missed being with you like this."

Hot, moist, whispered lies.

Her caresses grew more insistent. Always before, the touch of her hands and the sweetness of her mouth and the feel of her bare flesh had fired my blood. No more. I felt nothing for her. Numb below the waist. Dead soldier down there. None of the manipulations of fingers, mouth, tongue produced so much as a twitch.

I'd found out what I wanted to know about myself.

After a while she sighed and gave up. Lay with her head on my belly, still stroking me but in a different way now. Absently, as if she were offering distracted comfort to a sick pet.

"Poor Richard," she said. "Did I do this to you?"

I said, "You broke my heart and my pecker both."

She laughed.

She thought I was making a joke. She thought it was funny.

Funny!

I found out something else then.

I found out just how much I hated her.

A short time later, before she went away, she said, "You can reach me at JoEllen's. I left her address and phone number in the bathroom."

"Head," I said.

"Or I'll come see you again, if that's all right. Tomorrow or the next day, after you've had time to think it over."

I didn't say anything.

"If you let me come back, you'll never regret it. I promise I'll fix what I did to your pecker, too. It'll be just like it was before."

I didn't say anything.

"Think hard, Richard. One more chance."

She sounded so sincere. She *was* sincere, because she was fighting for her free ride. But the sincerity wouldn't last. She didn't love me, she didn't give a damn about me. The only thing she was sorry for was that her life hadn't worked out the way she wanted it to, the only thing she was ashamed of was that she'd had to come begging to me, the only person she cared about was herself.

If I took her back I knew exactly what would happen. For a while she would make an effort to live up to her promises. She'd be attentive, loving, deferential. She wouldn't argue or complain or make demands of any kind. She would curtail her drinking and her pill-popping. She would pretend to like living on a thirty-four-foot yawl, go out on cruises with me and pretend to enjoy herself. But in six months or so, boredom and restlessness would set in and she would regress—gradually at first, then not so gradually—into all her old habits and excesses. The bitch would take over. And the bitch was always hungry.

Oh, I knew her so well.

I knew myself so well, too. Knew that if I turned her away, gave her cause to hate me as much as I hated her, to run away again or, worse, to take up with another Fred Cotler, I would never feel safe again. I'd never *be* safe again. So I didn't have to think about her proposal. I knew all along what my answer would be.

I was going to give Annalise her one last chance. Not for her sake, but for mine.

I kept her squirming on the hook for nearly a week. Didn't call her or go to see her at JoEllen's; forced her to keep coming to me. The next two times she showed up, I put her off. The third time she was tearful and pathetic, ready to get down on her knees—to blow me right there in public, if that was what it took. JoEllen wasn't going to let her freeload much longer, she was almost out of money, the only jobs she could get on the island were shitty ones—clerking and waitressing—and they didn't pay much, so how was she going to live? I pretended to take pity on her. All right, I said, she could move in with me on *Windrunner* on a trial basis. She threw her arms around me, kissed me. Cried a little, too—the second and last time I'd seen her cry. They might even have been real tears.

During that week I saw Bone and told him Annalise was back on the island and most of what she'd said to me. I could see the disapproval in his eyes when I said I was going to let her move in with me. He wasn't a man to butt into another's personal business, but he couldn't quite contain himself in this case. He disliked Annalise not only because of what she'd done to me, but because of her treatment of him in their few brief encounters. I think he knew she was prejudiced before I even suspected it. Blacks are much more sensitive in that regard than whites, with good cause.

"What you want to do that for, Richard?" he asked. "Take her back?"

"Everybody deserves a second chance."

"No, mon. Not everybody."

"You wouldn't give your second wife another chance if she showed up?"

He barked a humorless laugh. "Kick her ass straight into the harbor, she ever come round me again."

"Maybe she hurt you worse than Annalise hurt me," I said.

"Maybe so. But a woman treats a mon bad once, her gonna do it again."

"I have to take the risk, Bone. She's in a bad way. She knows what a mess she made of things and she's sorry and she wants to make amends."

"That what she say now."

"She seems to mean it."

"You still love her?"

"No. Not anymore, not ever again."

"Sex, mon? Plenty of women around for that."

"It's not sex, either. Call it pity. There's all the history between us, too, the good years we had. You know what I mean."

"Only history that matters is what you learn from it," Bone said.

"Meaning don't make the same mistake twice."

"You're my friend, Cap'n. I don't like to see you hurt again."

"I won't be," I said. "I'm going into this with my eyes wide open. If she pulls any of the same shit as before, she's gone for good. I told her that and she knows I'm dead serious."

He shrugged and picked up the length of 5/8-inch nylon line he'd been splicing. "Your business, mon. But from now on, don't make it Bone's."

His meaning was plain. I was welcome to stop by any time, but I'd better not bring Annalise. As long as she was living on *Windrunner,* he wouldn't come calling. If I wanted to go sailing with him, it would be just the two of us, and preferably on *Conch Out.* All of which was fine with me. I had no intention of inflicting Annalise on Bone, or on anyone other than myself.

★　★　★

She came on board with one suitcase and a small cosmetic case. The sum total of her worldly possessions, she said. She made herself right at home, commingling her stuff with mine as if there hadn't been a two-day, much less a two-year, gap in our relationship. Took over the shopping and the cooking, did any other chores I asked her to. Even made an effort to learn nautical terms and how *Windrunner* functioned. When I said I was taking the yawl out on an overnight cruise and asked her to go along, she agreed without argument. And as I'd expected, she pretended to enjoy herself—easy enough for her, since the trades were gentle and the seas calm both days.

For the first three weeks, she spent as much time with me as I would allow. Then one day she said she'd like to go to Magens Bay to work on her tan and would I mind if she took the Mini. I told her to go ahead, I didn't expect her to be my shadow. After that, she went to the beach whenever I didn't need the car. But she was always back by early evening, in time for supper, and she was always sober. The only serious drinking she did was with me in the evenings, matching me glass for glass but not exceeding my limit. During the day she kept herself lightly sedated with Valium; I saw her popping tablets a couple of times when she thought I wasn't looking. She had a fairly large supply in her cosmetic case. I knew that because I checked one day when she was out. Either she'd brought the drug with her from New York, or she'd found an island source through JoEllen Hall.

It was not easy for me to get used to being with her again. Sometimes, when I looked at her, the dark feelings would roil up and I'd have to stifle the urge to reach for her throat. Mostly I was able to ignore her. To think of her as just another piece of equipment, like the chemical toilet or the bilge pump.

Nights were the worst, sleeping next to her, having her persist in trying to cure my impotence. She kept making the effort—for her sake, not for mine; Annalise wasn't capable of going without sexual gratification for long, and I had no desire to do what was necessary to satisfy her in any other than the usual way. She wouldn't take no for an answer; my failure and my indifference presented a personal challenge to her, and frustration and determination resulted in methods straight out of the Kama Sutra. Most of the time, her touch made my skin crawl. But the flesh never totally forgets, and eventually it responded even as my mind cringed. The first time it happened, she uttered a cry that was more triumph than desire and climbed on top and moaned and thrashed around ecstatically, though the coupling couldn't have done much for her because it did nothing for me. I lasted no longer and felt no more pleasure than I had with Pearl.

How do I think she felt about living with me again? I can tell you exactly how she felt. The close quarters and the lack of sex bothered her more than she let on; so did the fact that I refused to alter my usual routine for her in any signifcant way. Now and then I took her out for a meal at Harry's Dockside Café, and twice I let her come along on drives up to Crown Mountain. Otherwise we did nothing together except eat, drink, sleep, and, on the one other occasion she managed to resurrect the dead soldier, have unsatisfying sex. In spite of all that, she was relieved to be back on her free ride. And she viewed the status quo as temporary. Given enough time, she thought she could manipulate me into providing another house for her to live in and more money, more possessions, more freedom. She had no real insight into the man I had become since her dual betrayals, and so she underestimated me completely. Sly and calculating but not very bright, that was Annalise.

The second time we went sailing, the weather conditions weren't quite as favorable. She had no sea legs at all, spent most of the voyage lying sick in the cabin. The next time I went out, she begged me to let her stay ashore with JoEllen. I could have punished her by insisting, but I didn't. I'm not sadistic, and cold hate doesn't need to be fed.

I saw Bone regularly. On *Conch Out,* at Marsten Marine, at the Bar or one of the Frenchtown watering holes. Twice I went sailing with him, once for four days among the islands off the coast of Puerto Rico. With Bone I could relax, be myself. With Annalise I was always on guard, always conscious of waiting for the bitch to appear.

The arrangement with her lasted without incident until after the holidays. She gave me a Christmas present, a small native woodcarving; I gave her nothing at all. Maybe that was what triggered her reversion to type, I don't know. Not that it happened all of a sudden. She'd been losing patience with me and the way we lived for some time before she quit trying to hide it.

It started with little complaints, little prodding suggestions. Why don't we take the ferry to St. John or over to Tortola for the day? Why don't we go to a good downtown restaurant for dinner, or to Bamboushay or one of the other dance clubs? She liked living on the yawl, she really did, but the cabin was so confining, couldn't we maybe think about getting a small apartment? The more I said no, the more frustrated she became and the more the bitch began to show through. She stayed out later and later on her beach days, returning more or less sober but with liquor on her breath. Lay around on *Windrunner* other days, stoned on Valium. Began drinking more than I did in the evenings. Stopped making an effort to cook decent meals, serving cold makeshift lunches and suppers instead. Passed a snide remark about Bone when I came back from a two-day cruise with him. Came in after nine one evening, half in the bag, with the half-hearted excuse that it was JoEllen's birthday and besides, why couldn't she have a little fun once in a while?

The second time she came back late, the night before Bone and I were scheduled for another sail, she had a different excuse. She'd met a couple from Dallas, really interesting people, the man was a doctor and his wife wrote children's books, and they'd invited her to dinner at Blackbeard's Castle, and she didn't see why she shouldn't go, *we* never went out anywhere, she was practically a prisoner on this boat—

I said, "What's that on your neck?"

". . . What?"

"On the left side of your neck there, that mark."

She clapped her hand to the spot. A flush crawled up into her cheeks. She dragged a pocket mirror out of her purse, held it up, and tilted her head so she could see her neck.

"Oh, that," she said. "That's just a scrape. The door to the stall in the ladies' room stuck, and when I jerked it open the edge of it caught me."

"Doesn't look like a scrape to me."

"Well, that's what it is."

"More like a hickey."

"For God's sake, Richard! Would you like it better if I told you I was bitten by a vampire?"

"You've got the look, too," I said.

"What look?"

"The well-screwed look."

Her gaze flicked away from mine, just for an instant. "You think I was with a man, is that it? Some other man?"

"Were you?"

"No! I wish I had been well screwed today, but I wasn't, and haven't been in so long I've forgotten what it's like. Why are you so suspicious? I told you how I got the scrape and that's the truth."

No, it wasn't.

She'd been with a man, all right.

Bone and I went on our sail, a five-day trip up through the Mona Passage between Puerto Rico and the Dominican Republic. When we got back, Annalise pretended to be glad to see me. But it was obvious what she'd been doing while I was gone. No more love bites—she must have read the riot act to her lover about marking her—but she still wore that look of smug sexual satisfaction that few men or women can quite hide. And she didn't come near me in bed that night.

That was the final straw.

My estimate of how long it would take for Annalise to blow her last chance had been six months. I was too generous. It took her exactly five months to reach my breaking point.

You remember what I said earlier about love? That it's an individual experience and you don't really have any idea of what it is or what its effect will be until it happens to you? Well, the same is true of hate. Hate isn't just the flip side of love, or a crossing of that thin line everybody keeps yapping about. It's more, much more.

Hate is dry ice held close to raw nerve ends, so that you never stop feeling its burning cold.

Hate is a succubus that whispers and moans in your sleep.

Hate is a disease that burrows through the dark side, like a slow-moving, flesh-eating bacterium.

Hate is another word for death.

I think I knew all along that Annalise would have to die.

It was never a conscious consideration, yet it must have been there in my subconscious all along. Bone was wrong. You can't run away from a poisonous viper that has bitten you twice before; sooner or later you have to kill it before it sinks its poisonous fangs into you again. If you don't, then you'll be the one to die. As simple, as elemental as that.

What I had to do is murder in the eyes of the law, yes, but not in my eyes. To me it was not even an act of aggression. It was justifiable self-defense, the same as Cotler's death; the only difference is that with Annalise it was necessarily premeditated. There was no real malice involved. The decision, the final act were as cold as the hate. A cold equation, but not a cold-blooded one. The distinction is important.

I am not a murderer.

The blame for Annalise's death was entirely hers. You can see that, can't you? There was no hate in me until she put it there. If she had stayed with me from the beginning, stayed faithful to me, she would still be alive today. If she hadn't betrayed me to Cotler and helped him try to blackmail me, she'd be alive today. If she'd remained on Long Island instead of crawling back to St. Thomas, she'd be alive today. If she'd kept her promises after I gave her her one last chance, it would've amounted to the viper emptying its own poison sac and my hate would have lain dormant and I'd have gone on living with her. And she'd be alive today.

I didn't kill her, when you look at it in that perspective. I didn't kill Cotler, either. I was merely the instrument, like a gun or knife or cut-glass decanter, by which they died.

Fred Cotler killed himself.

And so did Annalise.

It's one thing to devise a boldly audacious scheme to steal a large sum of money and then carry it out with systematic precision. It's another to destroy a person in a moment of irresistible impulse and blind rage, and then to improvise a method of covering up the mess. And it's a third thing entirely, so much more than just problem-solving, to carefully plot someone's death. You can't design a method strictly by using the principles of mathematics, as an intellectual exercise; you can't approach it with emotional detachment, or hurry up and put it into action. There's a hell of a difference between executing an abstract equation and executing a human viper.

The best way to approach the problem, I decided, was as if I were one of Amthor Associates' engineers embarking on a construction proj-ect. The building of a wall, a perfect wall, from scratch. First there were the basics to be worked out, then blueprints to be drawn. That much was pure mathematics. Then the materials had to be gathered, the foun-dation laid, and finally the wall itself could be erected. The actual con-struction required skill, determination, courage, total commitment. No, not courage. Fortitude. I had plenty of that. I was nothing if not tenacious.

Simplicity was the keynote. The more elaborate you tried to make a wall, the greater the chance for a flaw that would cause it to collapse. After deliberation, I decided the first of the concepts I considered was the best. Annalise had disppeared once suddenly and without a trace, she had to disappear again the same way.

I shaped the plan and drew the blueprints off of that. Her death had to be bloodless—I couldn't bear a repeat of the kind of clean-up I'd had to do after Cotler—and it had to be tempered with a quality of mercy. I didn't want her to suffer. Cold equation, start to finish. So I couldn't do the obvious thing of taking her out to sea in *Windrunner* and throwing her overboard. Death by drowning was cruel; letting the sharks have her alive was barbarous. Besides, if anyone knew or suspected she'd gone out with me and then didn't return, there would be an investigation. I didn't dare report an accidental death for the same reason. I discarded several other methods before I settled on one that was bloodless, humane, and relatively easy to accomplish.

But there was a sticking point, the same one I'd had with Cotler: disposal of the remains. I liked the irony of putting her where I'd put him, but I couldn't do it that way. Too risky. I'd been fortunate to get away with a cemetery burial once; trying it twice was a fool's gambit. The safest choice? Burial at sea. That could be done easily enough, but how to manage it without risk? If she disappeared on the same day I happened to go out alone on *Windrunner,* somebody might conceivably put two and two together. Whatever I did, it had to be free of the remotest possibility of an investigation.

At first I rejected the only workable answer. It meant involving a third party, and that third party would have to be Bone. He wouldn't know it—he'd be an unwitting accomplice, an innocent witness—but I didn't like the idea of using him that way. There was the y factor, too; you increase the possibility of hidden dangers when you bring an outsider into an equation like this. I toyed with other solutions. None fit the fundamental plan nearly as well. So then I considered other methods of building the wall, using different types of bricks and mortar. None was as basic, as easy to work with, as certain to guarantee solidity.

Like it or not, using Bone was the only way to do it as it needed to be done.

Preparations.

The first thing I did was to see Bone and have a talk with him. I said he'd been right about Annalise, I'd been having problems with her just as he'd predicted and I felt like six kinds of fool for taking her back. It was typical of him that he didn't give me any I-told-you-so's. All he said was, "You got no exclusive on being a fool, mon."

I laid the groundwork for her disappearance by saying that she'd been acting secretive of late and I thought it was because she'd been having an affair and might be thinking about leaving me again. I said I needed a few days at sea, on *Windrunner* in case she had any notions of leaving while I was gone and taking more of my possessions with her, but that I didn't want to go out alone. It took some coaxing, but he finally agreed to accompany me. I'd already called the Weather Center and the forecast was good for the next several days. We set a sail date for Monday morning, three days hence.

On Friday Annalise asked to use the Mini. Beach trip, she said. I said no, I had a lot of errands to run. Well, would I drop her off downtown? I said, "Why? You have a rendezvous with the man you're screwing?" That set off a fresh rush of indignant denials. She wasn't screwing anybody, she said, why couldn't I stop making these ridiculous accusations? But if she did have an affair, who could blame her since I couldn't do anything for her anymore. Underneath her pique was the emotion I'd intended to stir up: anxiety. She didn't want to push me too hard or too far; she still needed me to pay for her ride. So she lapsed into a pout and the old "Why are you so mean to me?" bit. I dropped the subject. I had what I wanted. If whoever she'd been sleeping with was still on the island, she'd stay clear of him for the next couple of days.

To get her away from the marina, I gave her enough money for the Water Island ferry and a day at Honeymoon Beach. When she was gone, I drove over to Red Hook and picked up a new mizzen at a sailmaker's shop. On the way back, I made two more stops in Charlotte Amalie. The first was a marine hardware store, where I bought two small hasps and padlocks, two extra padlocks, two lengths of anchor chain, and several lead sinkers. The second stop was an air-conditioning and refrigeration dealer, where I bought several packs of Freon refrigerant.

On *Windrunner*, I stored the Freon packs in the big ice chest in the galley, under ice to keep them frozen. Then I installed one hasp-and-padlock on the door to the aft sail locker, emptied the locker of the spare sails stored there, and put the lengths of anchor chain and the extra padlocks inside. I stowed the old spare mizzen and the lead sinkers under the berth in the main cabin. The new mizzen and the other spare sheets went into the forward sail locker, the second hasp-and-padlock onto that door. Annalise wouldn't notice the new locks. I knew Bone would; if he asked me about them I'd say somebody had been seen prowling around the yawl and it had prompted me to take security measures.

In the main cabin I plundered a dozen tablets from Annalise's extra supply of Valium. She wouldn't miss them. She had a half-full bottle in her purse; I'd checked on that the night before while she was in the head. I emptied out an aspirin tin, put the dozen Valium inside and the tin into my pocket.

After lunch, I ran *Windrunner* over to the fuel dock and topped off the gas and water tanks. I knew the Puerto Rican who manned the pumps fairly well. I pulled a long face when I came in and grumbled enough to get him to ask what was the matter. "Problems with my wife," I said. "I think she's fixing to run out on me again." He was sympathetic.

Maybe I ought to show her who was boss, he said. "Slap her around?" I said. "Hell, no. I've never laid a hand on her and I never will."

That finished the preparations. Now I was ready to build the wall.

Saturday morning, I let Annalise have the Mini to go shopping. She was back in time for lunch, and she stayed on board *Windrunner* all afternoon, sunning herself and sipping rum punches on the foredeck, while I made pre-sailing checks and went over the charts. I hadn't told her I was going out, of course, and she didn't know enough about boats to understand what I was doing.

That night she tried to kindle some sexual interest in me. Her hands felt like sea slugs on my bare skin. I said, "Leave me alone, will you? I'm too tired," and rolled away from her.

Sunday, her last day, she slept late and moped around when she finally got up. She suggested we go to Harry's Dockside Café for lunch; I said I didn't feel like it, why didn't she just go by herself. I gave her some money—twice as much as she needed to buy a meal. As I expected, she spent the extra on liquor; she was tight when she came back, and she didn't seem to care whether I noticed or not. I didn't say anything to her about it. She stayed in the cabin for a time—more liquor, Valium, or both—and passed the rest of the afternoon sleeping in the shade on the foredeck.

I thought I might be a little apprehensive as construction time grew near, but I wasn't. My resolve was too strong, the hate as cold as the Freon packs in the chest below. That's not to say I was looking forward to finishing the wall. No one in his right mind looks forward to a job like that.

Annalise woke up about five thirty. She said she could use a drink; she was bleary-eyed from a combination of the ones she'd had at lunch and the afternoon heat. I said I was hungry, we'd eat first and then have drinks. Supper was day-old French bread, some ripe Camembert, and papaya. While she was setting the table, I poured two large glasses from a bottle of red wine. With my back to her, I slipped two tablets from the tin of Valium and stirred them into her glass. She emptied half the wine before she even looked at her food. Neither of us ate much.

When her glass was empty, she asked for a rum punch. I built it strong, stirred in two more Valium tablets with the pineapple juice and Grenadine. She said when I handed it to her, "Let's go topside. It's like an oven down here."

"It's not that bad. There's the fan and a breeze through the porthole."

"Why can't we go up on deck?"

"I feel like sitting here tonight."

"Dammit, Richard, sometimes I think you're trying to torture me. Haven't I done enough penance for my sins?"

"I have no intention of torturing you," I said. "On the contrary. I'm making it as easy for you as I can."

"Then why can't we go up on deck? This damn heat is making me woozy."

"Drink your drink. You'll be all right."

She drank it. And the refill I gave her, that one more slowly. I made the third with three full jiggers of rum and three Valium tablets.

"Whoo, that's strong," she said when she tasted it. "Trying to get me drunk, fella? Take advantage of me?"

"Yes," I said.

"Well. Well, well, well. I better slow down, then, don't want to pass out."

"We have plenty of time." I raised my glass. "Cheers."

"Up your poop chute," she said, and giggled.

She was sweating heavily by the time she finished half that drink. Her eyes had an unfocused glaze. She pushed the glass away.

"Had enough," she said. "Too much. Rum and wine . . . shouldn't mix."

I pushed it back. "Go on, drink up."

"Why?"

"Drink it, Annalise. Can't let good liquor go to waste."

She drank it, gagging on the last swallow. "No more, no more." She sat staring blankly at the empty glass. Then, slurring the words, "Jesus, I feel shitty."

I didn't say anything.

"Can't keep my eyes open. So hot in here . . ."

I didn't say anything.

"Think I'm gonna be sick . . ."

She started to get up, lurched a little and would have fallen if I hadn't caught her. I eased her down onto the double berth. She struggled in my grasp, tried to stand up again.

"No, the bathroom . . ."

"Stay right here."

". . . spinning . . ."

"Close your eyes. Lie still."

I held her down until she stopped struggling, then turned her onto her side and knelt beside the bunk. Her eyes were slits, the lids drooping. Her breathing was already fast and ragged. Sweat plastered strands of her hair against the mottled skin of her forehead. I remember thinking that it was astonishing I could ever have loved this creature. I didn't even hate her very much in that moment. It was like looking into the face of no one I'd ever seen before.

"Annalise, listen to me."

". . . so tired . . ."

"Don't go to sleep yet. Listen. I know about Fred Cotler."

". . . What?"

"I know about Fred Cotler. I know you told him about me; I know you were part of the blackmail."

I had to say it three more times before the meaning penetrated the drug and alcohol haze. Her body twitched; her head came up. She said in a clear, vicious whisper, "You son of a bitch!" and then she sagged back and her eyes closed and she was still.

200

I poured a triple shot of Arundel and went topside. For a long time I sat on the foredeck and watched the harbor lights and listened to the seabirds and the night music. Two hours, three, four—I had no sense of time. When I went down to the cabin again to check on her, I thought she might have stopped breathing. I couldn't find a pulse, but I still wasn't sure. I took the pillow out from under her head, lowered it over her face. And then I was sure.

The difficult part of the wall was finished.

"Good-bye, Annalise," I said.

You keep asking how I felt. How do you think I felt? Relieved? Happy? Sick? Sad? Remorseful?

None of the above.

I felt nothing.

I'd done what I had to do, and it had burned me out and left me empty inside.

I sat on deck again until long after midnight. The marina was quiet by then, everybody asleep on the nearby boats, the scattered nightlights the only breaks in the moonless dark. I stirred myself and went down the companionway again.

I'd draped a sheet over the mound on the berth, so I wouldn't have to look at her anymore. I double-checked the curtains over the port-holes to make sure they were tight-drawn. Then I packed all of Annalise's belongings into the one suitcase and the cosmetic bag. Every single item, every last trace. When I was done, I added the heavy lead sinkers to both bags, locked them, took them to the forward sail locker, and padlocked them inside.

Before I dragged the mizzen out from under the bunk and spread it open on the deck, I put on a pair of gloves. The dead weight was much easier to handle than Cotler's had been; I left the sheet in place as I lifted her down onto the Dacron. I brought the ice chest from the galley, took out half of the Freon packs, laid them down alongside her, and rolled her onto them. The others I arranged on top, then wrapped the sail around her and the refrigerants. Half a roll of duct tape sealed the bundle as airtight as I could make it.

I keyed open the aft sail locker. There was nothing in it now except for the lengths of anchor chain and the extra padlocks. The bundle was heavy, but I hoisted it over my shoulder without too much struggle and carried it to the locker and wedged it inside, in a position that would make getting it out again fairly easy. The entire business took less than five minutes.

I remade the bunk, sprawled out on it, and fell into an exhausted sleep.

Bone was there at eight A.M., prompt as always on sail days. I was in the cockpit, going over charts and slugging coffee. In the mirror in the head earlier, my face had looked puffy, the eyes red-veined and heavily bagged. He noticed the haggard appearance right away.

"You look beat up, Cap'n," he said.

"Didn't sleep much," I said. "Annalise packed up and left yesterday. Sooner than I expected."

He nodded. "Better it happen quick."

"Yeah. I'm relieved she's gone. Reason I didn't sleep much is that I'm still kicking myself for letting her come back in the first place."

We headed out north-by-northwest, on a starboard tack through the Windward Passage. Brisk trades at about twelve knots, light cloud cover—another fine day for sailing. It was cool out there with the trades blowing strong; the Freon packs probably hadn't been necessary. Bone had little to say once we were under way. He was like that sometimes, taciturn, self-contained. His silence was all right with me. I didn't feel much like talking, either.

The course I'd set took us up past Sandy Cay, off Jost Van Dyke

Island, then along the Tortola coast on a broad reach past Guana Island. Familiar territory. And tonight we'd be well away from land, in waters where we weren't likely to encounter many other vessels.

Bone went below to fix the noon meal, came back up again a couple of minutes later. "No beer, Cap'n," he said. "Ice chest's empty."

"Damn, I thought we had some. I guess I forgot to check. We can put in somewhere and load up—"

"No need. Plenty of rum, enough ice in the fridge."

The wind died in the late afternoon and we were down to about two knots, riding close-hauled, as the sun began to sink. I lashed the wheel and went below to pour us a couple of Arundels in preparation for the sunset. It was spectacular that night, the clouds a puffy mix of cirrocumulus and altocumulus, the colors vivid bronze and burnt orange, smoky grays and deep purples. The long day's sail and the sunset had leached the tiredness and most of the tension out of me. Once I was finished with the night's chore, I felt sure the emptiness would be gone—that I'd feel a measure of peace again.

My turn in the galley, and I dawdled over the meal so it would be close to eight o'clock before it was ready. We ate on deck, still without exchanging more than a few words. When we were done, I took the plates and empty glasses down to the galley. The coffee pot was on; Bone liked a mug of sugared coffee laced with rum after his evening meal. I poured another Arundel on ice for myself, fixed his coffee—a generous dollop of rum, plenty of sugar, and two of the remaining Valium tablets. I debated making it three, because Bone was a light sleeper, but I was afraid of doing him some harm. Two ought to be enough.

Six-hour watches in clear weather like this. It was my boat, so I had first option; I told him I'd take the nine-to-three watch. He was still quiet, but he hadn't tasted anything wrong with his drink: he'd drained the mug. He was yawning and rubbing his eyes by nine o'clock. I pointed out the time, said he'd better get himself some sleep. He nodded and took himself below.

I waited two hours before I lashed the wheel and tiptoed below to check on him. He was sprawled face down on the vee bunk in the fore cabin, snoring loudly. I opened the forward sail locker and got the suitcase and cosmetic case and carried them topside. Before I dumped them over the side I made another scan for running lights in the vicinity. Nothing but black, starlit sea.

Belowdecks again I opened the aft locker and dragged the bundle out and propped it against the bulkhead. I put the extra padlocks in my pocket, looped the lengths of anchor chain around my wrists and arms. It was awkward getting the bundle over my shoulder, a strain on my back and legs carrying it up the companionway. Topside, sweating in the cool night air, I lowered the bundle against the starboard rail and held it there while I wrapped the lengths of anchor chain around it, top and bottom, and snugged them tightly in place with the extra padlocks. My grasp slipped a little as I lifted the bundle up onto the rail; before I could set myself, one of the damn chain links scraped a furrow into the smooth mahogany. The bundle made a splash that seemed very loud in the night's stillness. The weight of the chains took it into the depths almost immediately.

I went below again. Bone was still out, still snoring; he hadn't moved.

Now the wall was complete.

I got the flashlight from the cockpit and checked the mark in the starboard rail. It wasn't deep, noticeable only when you were up close and looking. If Bone spotted it, he'd know it hadn't been there when he turned in. I'd think up a story to explain it if he questioned me.

I put the flash away and sat against the deckhouse wall to rest and and watch the night. I couldn't seem to enjoy the starstruck vastness, couldn't find any of the peace I'd hoped for. The burned-out emptiness remained. I shouldn't have expected it to fill up again so soon. After all that I'd been through, the healing was bound to take a little time.

Bone didn't come up at three to take his watch, so I went down to call him. He was still asleep, but thrashing restlessly now. I shook him awake, told him the time. It took him a few seconds to shake off the grogginess. His mouth worked as if it were dry and foul-tasting; the way he heeled his temples told me he had a headache.

I said lightly, "Too much rum last night, Bone?"

He didn't answer. He stood, pulled a T-shirt over his head, and headed up the companionway.

I slept well enough, but only for about four hours. At seven I got up, turned the flame on under the coffee pot, sluiced off under a cool shower before I dressed. The coffee was ready by then. I poured two mugs full, added sugar to one, and carried them topside.

As soon as I saw the position of the sun, I knew that we were heading in the opposite direction from the course I'd set the day before. Bone was standing at the helm, stiff-backed, staring straight ahead. He didn't answer when I said good morning. I extended one of the mugs; he shook his head without looking at me, so I set it down on the chart table.

"You changed our course," I said. "How come?"

"Heading back, Cap'n."

"Back to St. Thomas? Why?"

"Heading back, Cap'n."

"What's the matter? Are you sick?"

"Yeah, mon. A little sick."

I laid a hand on his arm, the way you do. He shrugged it off as if it were an annoying blowfly.

"What the hell, Bone?"

His gaze rounded on me, and there was a look in his eyes I'd never seen before. As if something had caught fire in their depths. As if he were looking at somebody he'd never seen before. He said nothing, just stared at me.

He knows, I thought.

He knows!

Moment of panic. Involuntary reflex because of it. A sudden roll as we plowed through a wave trough. All three of those things caused the mug to slip out of my hand. It tilted in Bone's direction as it fell, splattering him with hot coffee on the way down. More coffee splashed his pantlegs when the mug shattered on the deck.

I don't know, maybe he thought I did it on purpose. Or maybe something just broke loose inside him. Whatever the reason, his reaction was snake-sudden.

He spun toward me and grabbed two handfuls of my shirt. I said something, I don't remember what, and clawed at his wrists. He had a grip like an iron fluke. He crowded in close and swung me around and slammed my back up hard against the mizzenmast. Pain tore a yell out of me; I fought him but I couldn't pull free. He had me pinned tight against the spar.

At some point in the brief struggle one of us must have kicked down on a leeward spoke, causing the wheel to spin counterclockwise. *Windrunner*'s bow fell off to port. Wind hammered into the lee side of the mains'l with a crack like a big limb breaking off a tree. The main boom swung inward as the yawl jibed. Bone and I both saw it an instant before it swept across the cockpit. He was the one in harm's way, his body shielding mine, and there wasn't enough time for him to twist aside. The boom smacked him on the shoulder with enough force to send him staggering into the starboard rail, and the rail catapulted him overboard.

The end of the boom missed me by no more than two inches. I heard the sound of him hitting the water and instinct sent me lurching back to the helm. I spun the wheel hard to bring her up into the wind, then ran forward and ripped the life preserver off the starboard shrouds and flung it back into the wake.

Bone had surfaced a dozen feet from where it landed. He bobbed there for a few seconds, not making any move toward the doughnut.

I thought he might be hurt or too dazed to see it and I yelled above the wind, "Bone! In front of you!"

No answer. But then I saw him start to swim in a strong crawl toward the preserver and I knew he was all right. I scanned the sea around him. No dorsal fins, just white-flecked blue water.

I ran aft to the wheel, steadied *Windrunner* up into the wind until she was right in stays. Then I hurried forward again, dropped the main and staysail, came back aft. Bone had reached the ring, was resting there with one arm looped through it, looking in my direction. I waved at him. He didn't wave back.

I went below to start the auxiliary engine. At the wheel again, I circled the yawl under power until I could see Bone and the doughnut bobbing to windward. I idled down a hundred feet from him, eased the yawl upwind until I was close enough for him to reach up with one hand and catch hold of a rail stanchion. He tossed the preserver on deck, hung there two-handed until the roll was right, and then heaved himself aboard.

He wouldn't take any help from me. Wouldn't look at me until he'd hoisted himself to his feet, streaming water, and then it was only a brief glance followed by a short, sharp nod. There was an angry-looking welt on his shoulder where the boom had clipped him.

"That was close," I said. "Too close."

He didn't say anything.

"You shouldn't have grabbed me like that," I said. "The coffee . . . it was an accident. The jibe, too. One of us must've kicked the wheel . . ."

Silently he tugged at his wet clothes.

"Bone, listen to me—"

"Don't say it, mon. Ain't nothing I want to hear."

He made eye contact for three or four seconds and then moved past me and went belowdecks. But that look stayed with me, left me feeling chilled and empty. The burn in his eyes had been extinguished; there was nothing in them for me any more, no feeling at all. Cold, blank, like the unseeing eyes of a dead man—

What? Did I think of what?

Not rescuing him? Leaving him out there to drown?

My God, no! Not for a second. The thought never entered my head. I could no more have killed Bone than I could have chopped off my right arm, to save my ass or for any other reason. He was my mentor, my friend—my only friend. I loved him like a brother.

What do you think I am, some kind of monster?

All the rest of that day Bone stood on deck with his back to me, working when necessary, the rest of the time just smoking his pipe and staring out over the water. Wouldn't talk to me. Wouldn't make any more eye contact. There was no way to guess what he was thinking; his face was like a stone mask.

How did he know about Annalise? The question kept nagging at me. It couldn't be from any mistake in my calculations. A combination of little things, probably. My telling him she'd left me. The empty ice chest. His abnormally long sleep and the hangover effects of the Valium mixed with rum. The new padlocks on the sail lockers and the fresh scrape in the starboard rail. Bone noticed every detail on a boat. He may have been sensitive to anything abnormal on one, too, in the same way he was sensitive to atmospheric conditions. He was an intelligent man; give him enough components and he could fit them together into the correct equation.

What would he do about his suspicions? Turn me in? I didn't think so. Didn't want to believe he would. His code of noninvolvement was why he hadn't confronted me; it would also keep him from going to the law. Our friendship weighed in my favor, too. And the fact that I'd saved his life had to count for something.

Still, you can't be absolutely certain how anyone will react to a given situation. You can't even be certain how you yourself will react. He could never condone the taking of a human life, no matter what the reason. He couldn't even sanction the killing of sharks. If his moral code was stronger than all the factors in my favor, there wasn't anything I could do about it. You could talk until you were blue in the face to a man like Bone, and the only voice he'd be listening to was his own.

Time would tell. All I could do was to keep as silent as he was and sweat it out.

Nothing happened after we returned to St. Thomas. Bone had his gear packed and ready before we entered the Sub Base harbor, and he walked away without a word as soon as we docked.

Two long days passed. No one came around asking about Annalise. By the end of the second day I began to relax again. I'd been right, I thought, to do nothing, keep my distance. Bone had had plenty of time to think things over; if he was going to the law, he'd have done it by then.

That night I had a bad nightmare. Awake, I didn't think about the Annalise crime; my conscience bothered me not at all. But asleep, my subconscious dredged it up. I awoke suddenly, or thought I did, and Annalise was sitting naked on the foot of the bunk, dripping wet, her body draped in seaweed and rusted chains, her hair hanging in sodden strings, part of her face eaten away by sea creatures. I screamed once and really woke up, shaking and pouring sweat. For a time afterward I worried that I'd have the nightmare again, but I never did. Just that once, as if it were a purge.

On the third day, I debated the advisability of a visit to JoEllen Hall. She hadn't contacted me when Annalise disappeared the first time, so it wasn't likely she'd be concerned enough to do it this time. But if Annalise had confided in anyone about me or her new lover or her future plans, it was JoEllen. Safer for me if I knew what she might have said.

I drove over to Red Hook and hunted up the woman at her rundown beach cottage. I asked first whether Annalise was there, then whether JoEllen had heard from her in the past several days. No, she said, why was I asking? "I might as well tell you," I said. "We had an argument over her drinking, among other things, and she packed her suitcase and walked out. Took some money with her that I had stashed away. That was three days ago, so she must have left the island."

"Well, I don't know where she went and I wouldn't tell you if I did. The shitty way you treated her, I don't blame her for leaving."

"The shitty way *I* treated *her*? Is that what she told you?"

"She never should've come back, that's what she told me. She practically crawled to you, but you never let her forget the mistake she made two years ago. Always giving her orders, forcing her to live like a dog on that damn boat of yours. Poor kid was miserable."

"That's all lies, JoEllen."

"So you say, when she's not here to defend herself."

"Did she tell you she was planning to leave me again?"

"Not the first time and not this time. Why should she? Her business where she goes and what she does, not mine. And not yours anymore."

"You're right about that," I said. "Tell me something, will you? The answer doesn't make any difference now, but I'd like to know. Was she having an affair the past month or so?"

JoEllen had never cared for me, and Annalise's lies had cemented her dislike. Her smile had an edge of malicious satisfaction. "Damn right she was. With the same man as before—Royce Verriker. She said he was the best fuck she'd ever had."

That night, I went to talk to Bone. I had a story all worked out, a way to convince him that Annalise was still alive, an explanation for the padlocked sail lockers and the chain scrape and even for his drug hangover. But I don't remember what it was, because I didn't get to use it.

His slip at the marina was empty. He and *Conch Out* were gone.

He'd left the previous morning, I found out. Hadn't told anybody where he was bound. One of his periodic solo cruises, prompted by his suspicions of me—a long one, maybe. He'd be back in a week or two, three at the outside. He always came back eventually.

But not this time.

I never saw Bone again.

THE VIRGIN ISLANDS

1984–2005

THERE ISN'T MUCH MORE to tell.

Oh, sure, I know—twenty-one years is a long time, a lifetime. But they were mostly uneventful years. Only a handful of high spots—and low spots—worth mentioning.

I got away with the Annalise crime. It was as perfect as the Amthor crime and the Cotler crime. Perfect.

That is what's important.

Life goes on.

How many times have you heard that, and all its variations? Life is for the living. Take each day as it comes. Live for the moment and don't look back. It's the state of mind people slip into when they've suffered irreparable losses. A refuge for the grief-stricken, the depressed, the unhappy, the emotionally wasted. And the unrefillably empty.

My refuge, after a while.

I should have been content again. Annalise and the threat of exposure were gone for good. I was safe. The tight, structured little world

I'd established for myself on St. Thomas was secure. I could continue to indulge my simple tastes for the rest of my life. I could be at peace.

Only I wasn't. The barrenness remained, like a seared landscape on which nothing that had been there before could be rebuilt and nothing new would grow. The reason for it, most of the reason anyway, was a deep sense of loss and privation that I couldn't shake. It had nothing to do with Annalise. It was Bone, of course, the wrenching away of his friendship, his companionship, his knowledge, his wisdom. And it was something else I'd lost that I cherished as much as Bone.

Windrunner, and all the yawl meant to me.

I don't mean physical loss; I continued to live on her, to take her out now and then. Psychic loss. Spiritual, maybe. The symbiotic connection of boat and man to the sea had been severed somehow and I could not seem to splice it back together. It was as if I'd tainted both *Windrunner* and my love of sailing beyond repair or redemption, as I'd tainted my relationship with Bone, by using them as instruments in Annalise's destruction.

Over and over I berated myself for not devising a different equation that didn't involve either Bone or the yawl, for rushing ahead with a deficient plan. I could have designed a better one, if I'd invested more time. Instead I'd opted for the quick and easy answer, and for that miscalculation I paid a damn high price.

Nothing was ever the same for me again.

The magic of singlehanding was gone. I still derived some pleasure from the wind, the sea, the night sky, the fast-running tacks and the dead-calm afternoons, but it was never again as intense or as lasting. Even the magic of Laidlaw Cay was gone—something else I lost. The first time I went back there, the terns and frigate birds had abandoned their nesting ground; without them the cay was just another barren sandspit. The second and last time, I discovered that heavy storm seas had diminished it to less than half its original size and all that remained were the reefs and a slender hump of sand strewn with sea wreckage. A dead place.

After a few months, I was sailing infrequently. Not working on *Windrunner* as much, either; the day-to-day tasks required to maintain upkeep on a yawl her size seemed to have grown tedious. Snorkeling also seemed to require too much effort, so I gave it up. Gave up driving around the island, too, except for shopping trips and an occasional visit to Marsten Marine. The closest I had to a friend now was Dick Marsten, but he was a workaholic and had a family and I saw him only for short periods at the boatyard.

I took up walking. Long walks in the morning and sometimes in the evening, along the winding streets of Frenchtown and the edge of Crown Bay, once all the way down Veterans Drive to Emancipation Garden and back. It was good exercise, it passed the time, and I learned to occupy my mind by concentrating on details of the surroundings.

I lost interest in sitting alone and communing with the night; I craved companionship, the kind I'd had with Bone. So I took to frequenting Harry's Dockside Café and some of the other local hangouts. But there was no substitute for Bone, not at the marina or in Frenchtown or anywhere else on the island. I had to settle for the brief, boozy company of natives and of tourists hunting local color, and for meaningless conversations about women, politics, all sorts of topics I pretended to be interested in but wasn't.

I thought about Bone quite a bit that first year. Had he gone back to Nassau to be with his daughter? Down to St. Lucia or Carriacou or one of the other as yet unspoiled islands in the Windwards or Grenadines? The Turks and Caicos? There were any number of possibilities. I might be able to find out if I tried hard enough, but then what? It was better if I didn't know.

I wondered how much longer he would have stayed on St. Thomas if it hadn't been for what I did. Not long, probably. The commercialism and the overcrowding would have driven him away. Would he have let me tag along with him? Two men, two boats, seeking fresh horizons and a brave new world? Maybe. Maybe not. Better if I didn't know that, either.

Wherever he was, whatever he was doing, I hoped he was happy and that his daughter would become a marine biologist as planned and make him even happier. He deserved it. He was a good man, he'd never harmed anyone, he'd never committed any crimes or thrown away any of the things that were central to his life. He deserved happiness a hell of a lot more than I did.

Dick Marsten contacted me in May of '86, to ask if I would consider selling *Windrunner*. I'd confided to him that I wasn't as keen on keeping her as I'd once been, and he had a buyer who was interested in a secondhand yawl or ketch of her size. I wasn't as keen on Sub Base harbor, either—too many memories, too many changes in the waterfront. I'd been thinking about moving over to Red Hook, maybe trading *Windrunner* for another, smaller boat. It was possible a different environment and a different craft would rekindle my interest in sailing and the sea.

So Marsten brought the buyer, a chubby, middle-aged Florida transplant, over for a look. The man liked what he saw, made me a generous offer, and I accepted, contingent on Dick finding me an acceptable replacement.

It didn't take long. Within a week, Marsten located a twenty-eight-foot schooner for sale at a reasonable price on St. Croix. I took an interisland flight to Christiansted to check out the schooner, *Joyleg*. She was clean and well maintained, with a new mainmast. The owner and I went out for a half day's sail so I could see how well she handled, and that sold me on her. I told him he had a deal, then notified Dick Marsten to go ahead with the sale of *Windrunner*.

I returned to St. Thomas to sign the papers and rent slip space at the Red Hook marina, then flew back to Christiansted and sailed *Joyleg* across. That singlehand voyage was the best I'd been on in the two years since Bone went away. And the ambiance at Red Hook was more like what it had been at Sub Base harbor when I first went there. The change seemed to be what I'd needed, all right. New boat, new environment—new beginning.

The new beginning lasted about a year.

I sanded and painted and varnished until *Joyleg* was in tiptop shape. Took her out more or less regularly, once on a long sail to Puerto Rico. Adapted well enough to living on her and to Red Hook. I even became the nominal drinking buddy of the ex-navy, ex–charter fisherman who'd once given me sailing lessons; it amused me that he didn't remember me from Adam's off ox and treated me as if I'd never been anything but his equal. I told myself the scars were starting to heal a little, that I'd found a measure of peace again, but of course it wasn't true. The pleasure and the illusion of peace faded along with the newness; I began to lose interest, the way I had with *Windrunner* and Sub Base harbor.

Thirteen months after I bought *Joyleg* and moved to Red Hook, I was again spending more time in waterfront bars than I was on the schooner in port or at sea.

In September of '89 the Virgins and Puerto Rico suffered one of the most devastating hurricanes ever to slam through the region. Maybe you remember reading about it. Hurricane Hugo. A howling, snarling, Category 4 monster—torrential rain, 130-mile-an-hour winds, widespread devastation everywhere it ripped across land. More than twenty people died, and tens of thousands were left homeless. The worst carnage was on St. Croix, but St. Thomas took a heavy hit as well. The blow knocked out electrical power and phone service, and caused severe road and marine damage. There was major flooding in low-lying areas; countless trees and plants were uprooted, some beaches badly eroded, some coral reefs ruined.

There was enough advance warning for frightened residents and tourists to flee in droves before the storm battered the island. That left rooms available at high-ground hotels like the Inn at Blackbeard's Castle. I booked one there, and rode out Hugo in flickering candlelight and relative safety behind the inn's storm-shuttered stone walls. At the height of the hurricane, the noise was deafening—thunderous bellows, banshee shrieks, savage wailing gusts that literally shook the building. Annalise would have freaked out before it was over. I considered it something of an adventure—until I went down to the Red Hook marina afterward.

Some boats survived relatively unscathed; others were battered beyond recognition. It didn't matter how well they'd been secured by their owners—the effects were a matter of pure random luck either way, good or bad. *Joyleg* was one of the casualties. Her spars were gone, one side of the deckhouse had been caved in, holes had been torn in her hull in two places above the waterline. She was salvageable, but just barely.

I could have filed an insurance claim, as so many other owners did—insurance is mandatory when you buy and register a boat in the Virgins—but it would have taken months for payment to come through and I was afraid that a claim might trigger a background check on Richard Laidlaw. I could have paid for the repairs out of my own pocket, but it would've cost thousands and I didn't have enough emotional attachment to the schooner to make it worthwhile. Boat living had pretty much lost its appeal for me by then, anyway.

I sold what was left of *Joyleg* to Dick Marsten, cheap, and moved back onto dry land for good.

The island wasn't the same after Hurricane Hugo. It had been changing before the Big Blow, as Bone and I had lamented often enough; the massive damage, the millions it cost for cleanup and rebuilding, hastened the process and turned St. Thomas from an island paradise into a large-scale commercial enterprise. Fancy mega-resorts to lure more and more tourists. Expensive new villas and condominiums, and new and expanded marinas, to lure more wealthy full-time and part-time residents and yacht owners. Gentrification of districts like Red Hook, Frenchtown, Sub Base harbor. Out with the old, in with the new—the glitzy, gaudy, expensive, hypermodern, bullshit new.

But all this took time, and while it was going on I lived in Frenchtown and avoided the commercialization as much as possible. I rented an old-fashioned three-room cottage down a lane off Rue de Grégoire. It was quiet, it had everything I needed, and it was within easy walking distance of everything else I needed. The Bar had been condemned and torn down before the hurricane, but there were other watering holes and cafés, and the waterfront wasn't far away. I was known in some of the places, and accepted, because of my association with Bone.

Not a week went by my first six months in Frenchtown that somebody didn't ask me about him. What happened to Bone, why did he leave St. Thomas, where did he go, would he ever come back? I don't know where he went, I said, I don't know why he left. Maybe he'll come back, I said, maybe he won't. You know Bone, I said, he's his own man, he goes where he likes and does what he pleases. Good old Bone, I said, he was my best friend. And then we lifted our glasses and we drank to good old Bone.

One night, in one of the watering holes, a slumming Frenchwoman fresh from Martinique decided I would make a worthwhile conquest. My blue eyes, maybe. I'd given up wearing the brown-tinted contacts; enough time had passed, and the aging Richard Laidlaw looked nothing at all like Jordan Wise, so that the risk was negligible. Enough time had passed since Annalise, too, to make me boozily curious if what she'd broken had healed of its own volition. Until that night, I just hadn't cared enough to find out.

So I let the Frenchwoman pick me up, and took her back to my cottage. And the answer to the broken question was no. Nothing the woman did—and she was as much a sexual animal as Annalise had been—produced so much as a quiver. She said something that sounded like "Bah!" and got out of bed and threw her clothes on. Before she went away into the night, she reached down and picked up my cock between her thumb and forefinger and shook it as if it had been a bad little boy.

"*Quéquette mort,*" she said disgustedly.

Little dead weenie.

I haven't been to bed with a woman since.

Royce Verriker died of a sudden massive coronary in the spring of '91. I read about it in the *Virgin Islands Daily News.* He'd been playing racquetball at the Royal Bay Club, he'd just made a winning shot and turned to shake hands with his partner, and he fell over dead.

I thought about going to the funeral home where he was laid out for viewing. Not to pay my respects: to spit in his dead face. But of course I didn't do it. I settled for the knowledge that the bastard wouldn't be giving any more men's wives the best fuck they'd ever had.

The new St. Thomas palled on me enough by the early nineties to force me off the island. Frenchtown was turning into a "historic" district filled with trendy restaurants designed to attract the snowbirds and cruise ship passengers. Many of the Cha-Chas had assimilated or moved away, and mainlanders were buying up the old frame buildings and renovating them in what they considered to be quaint Caribbean styles. It was all sham and window dressing, and I couldn't stand to be a part of it.

I thought I might like living on Tortola, so I packed up my meager belongings and moved over there. It wasn't as tourist-ridden; I liked what I'd seen of Kingstown and Cane Garden Bay, and there was the lure of the Arundel distillery. But I didn't feel comfortable there, didn't fit in with the British residents and the island lifestyle. I stayed only about a year.

From there I went to St. Croix—the west end, Frederiksted, a town that had the look and feel of an old-fashioned Caribbean outpost on the five days a week it wasn't being invaded by the cruise ship armada. I rented a cottage near LaGrange Beach, one of a series of beaches perfect for long morning and evening walks. I might still be there if I hadn't come home late one night and walked in on two strangers ransacking the cottage. They beat me up, left me in a bloody heap, and ran off. As far as I know, the local law never caught them. I wouldn't have pressed charges if they had. I considered myself lucky, as it was, that the police didn't think of me as anything more than an unfortunate victim.

The thieves took $200 I had stashed in the cottage, and another $60 out of my wallet. They didn't get my passport and bank books because I keep them in my shoes, but in addition to the cash they stole the brassbound pirate's chest—the last of my possessions that I cared anything about.

When I got out of the hospital, I said to hell with St. Croix, and that was when I moved to St. John.

I've been here seven years now, living in the same south-end saltbox and spending most of my days in Jocko's.

I bought an old VW when I first arrived, drove it up to Coral Bay to shop a couple of times a month and a few times over to Cruz Bay. Once during the first year, on a whim, I rode the ferry from Cruz Bay to Charlotte Amalie, but I didn't go any farther onto St. Thomas than the King's Wharf dock. There were seven or eight cruise ships in the harbor, and the downtown streets were so thick with tourists there might have been a parade going on. I took the next ferry back to St. John and I haven't been over there since. Or to Cruz Bay, for that matter.

The VW died a couple of years ago. I sold it cheap to one of the local natives and he hauled it away. I wasn't driving it much, anyway, by then. The saltbox is only a mile and a half from here, easy walking distance, and Jocko supplies everything I need in the way of food and drink. I don't go anywhere else. I don't have anywhere else to go.

End of the line.

ST. JOHN

THE PRESENT

I STOP TALKING and lean back in my chair. Talley has kept my glass filled and I'm very drunk, but I know it doesn't show. The one thing, the only thing, I haven't lost is my control while under the influence.

Talley is looking at me in a new way now. Part of his revised opinion of me is a grudging awe. The rest . . . I don't care about the rest.

"That's one hell of a story," he says.

"Meaning you don't believe it?"

"Oh, I believe it all right. The essential facts are too easy to check."

"Could be I don't care about that," I say. "Could be I made it all up to cadge free drinks from gullible tourists."

"Not with the amount of emotion you put into it. Or all the gory details about Cotler and Annalise. I've written fact and fiction both—I know one from the other."

"Details make for a better story. And emotion can be faked."

"Are you trying to unconvince me?"

"Hell, no. On the contrary. I don't want you to have any doubts."

It is late afternoon now. Brassy hot outside, sticky hot in here under Jocko's lazy fan. Sweat rolls down my cheeks, drips off my chin onto the sodden front of my shirt, but I don't bother to wipe it away. Heat and sweat have no effect on me. Nothing has much effect on me anymore.

"All right," Talley says, "so the story's true. Every word of it?"

"Every word."

"And you want to publish it."

"That's right. Is it publishable?"

"You know it is. But you don't need me to write it up for you. It can pretty much stand as you told it, in your own words, with some minor editing."

"I wouldn't know how to go about getting a book published. You do. Do whatever it takes, and you can have all the money."

"Entire advance, full royalties?"

"Every penny. I don't care about money. I have more money than I'll ever need."

He's hooked. But he says, "Before I do anything, I want the answers to a couple of questions. The first one is, Why me?"

"Why not you? You're the only writer I've ever met. I knew that's what you were before you approached me. Jocko told me the last time you came in. If you hadn't sat down with me today, I'd've gone to you."

"So spilling your guts wasn't spur-of-the-moment."

"Not hardly. Been on my mind for a while now."

"Okay. Second question: Why do you want your story published? Now, after all these years?"

I roll some Arundel around on my tongue, savoring the taste. Outside, the sun is coming low and the bay is starting to darken. Later tonight, after moonrise, the water will be as black as cold tar and moonlight and starlight and nightlights on the anchored boats will paint it in shiny gold and shimmering quicksilver.

Talley says, "It can't be published anonymously—you'd have to use your real name. As soon as the book comes out, you'll be arrested and tried, and there's not much doubt you'll be convicted. There're no statutes of limitations on federal crimes or on murder. And murder could be proved if the authorities care enough to go digging in the old French cemetery. You must know all this."

"I know it."

"Then why confess?"

"Is that what you think this is, a confession?"

"Isn't it? A way to bring yourself more punishment?"

"*More* punishment?"

"Come on, Wise. Those three crimes of yours weren't so damn perfect. You may not have been caught and prosecuted for any of them, but that doesn't mean you got off scot free. The woman you committed the first one for betrayed you not once but three times. You lost your only friend, your boat, your love of the sea, your sexual ability, and your zest for life. You've got the deaths of two people on your conscience. And all the stolen money hasn't kept you from spending the past twenty years on a drunken downhill spiral. What's all of that, if not punishment?"

"Bad luck?" I say.

"Bullshit," Talley says.

I smile a little. "So you think I'm tired of living with guilt and I just don't care any more what happens to me. You think I want to purge myself, cleanse my soul before I die."

"Well?"

"You're dead wrong," I say. "I don't feel any guilt and I never have. I doubt I've got much of a soul left to cleanse, if I ever had one in the first place. I'm not sorry for any of it, except for driving Bone away and losing my passion for the sea. Punishment? Confession? No way."

"Then what the devil is this all about?"

"I'm sixty-two years old and I drink a liter of rum a day. They say a sick animal knows when its time is short. Well, humans can intuit, too. I don't have much life left in me, a couple of years at the outside. I've come to terms with that—I'm not afraid of dying. All I want is to live long enough to see my story published."

Talley frowns. He's getting it now.

"The only things that lift my life above the mediocrity of millions of other lives," I say, "are my three crimes. Not one, not two, but three technically perfect crimes. They make me special, they give my time on this earth some meaning and importance. If I took them to the grave with me, nobody would ever know the full scope of what I've done. Jordan Wise would be nothing more than a 'Whatever happened to that embezzler?' footnote in some true-crime book. This way, Jordan Wise is Somebody with a capital 'S.' This way, he'll be remembered."

"Your little piece of immortality."

"That's it. Exactly."

"You know something, Wise?" Talley says. "Annalise's last words to you were right on. You are a son of a bitch."

"Damn right," I say. "But I'm a special son of a bitch. One of a kind. That's the whole point, isn't it?"

He shakes his head, gathers up his pocket recorder, gets to his feet. "I'll need to check a few things and then contact my agent," he says. "Then we'll have another talk."

"Any time. You know where to find me."

Talley goes away, and after a while Jocko brings me a fresh glass of rum. He says, "What you staring at out there, mon?"

"The sunset," I say. "Look at those colors. Scarlet, burgundy, old rose. And the way the light comes through that bank of clouds."

"Pretty much the same like always."

"No, you're wrong. This is a special sunset, Jocko. A special sunset for a special son of a bitch."

He laughs. I laugh, too.

I say what I'm thinking as the colors and the light shift and coalesce: "It was worth it."

"What was, mon?"

"Everything. For the sunsets and the Arundel. And the time I had with Bone. It was worth it and I'd do it all again if I had the chance."

Jocko laughs.

This time I don't laugh with him.

A NOTE ON THE AUTHOR

Bill Pronzini is the author of sixty-five mysteries, thrillers, and westerns, including the Nameless Detective series and stand-alone novels such as *Blue Lonesome, A Wasteland of Strangers,* and *Nothing but the Night.* He lives in northern California.